LUNA STATION
QUARTERLY

Issue 051 | September 2022

Editor-in-Chief
Jennifer Lyn Parsons

Editors
Angelica Fyfe • Anna Catalano • Bridget Siniakov
Cait Ryan • Carly Racklin • Cathrin Hagey • Izzy Varju
Katrina Brown • Katrina Schroeder • Sara Doan
Sarah Pauling • Shana Ross • Gô Shoemake

LUNA STATION PRESS
NEW JERSEY

Luna Station Quarterly publishes short fiction on March 1st, June 1st,
September 1st, and December 1st. For more information and submission
guidelines, please visit our website at lunastationquarterly.com

For Luna Station Press

Creative Director - Tara Quinn Lindsey
Editor-in-Chief & Founder - Jennifer Lyn Parsons

LUNA STATION PRESS
www.lunastationpress.com

CONTENTS

EDITORIAL...8
Jennifer Lyn Parsons

PEANUT BUTTER ELEGY......................................14
Jenna Glover

FELT..28
Denise Khng

THERE IS A COTTAGE BY THE WOODS........................70
Rebecca Burton

FISHBONE..96
CL Glanzing

EXTERNAL PROCESSORS 118
Sherry Yuan

FOX RIVER..142
Dana Foley

THE WITCH AND THE WATER...........................162
Ashley Libey

85 DAYS IN FLIGHT..178
Madeehah Reza

THE HALL OF BEING..194
T. K. Rex

2122, BARREL-AGED AND BIDING 216
Jordan Hirsch

ANWEN'S SONG, EFA'S SHOES,
AND THE HALLS IN THE HILLS............................222
Rebecca Harrison

REDBEAN...234
Dixon March

MYSTIC MAMA 252
Megha Nayar

MISRULE..262
Fiona Moore

THE LAST WAKE 286
Kathryn Keane

THANK YOU TO OUR SUPPORTERS................................303
ABOUT THE COVER ARTIST 305

Editorial

Jennifer Lyn Parsons

Jennifer Lyn Parsons is a writer and senior software engineer. Currently, she enjoys writing fantasy stories about middle-aged people who aren't into the whole "going on a quest" thing but do it anyway. When not writing code or prose, she is also the editor-in-chief of the venerable Luna Station Quarterly. She finds joy in baseball, tea, discovering music new and old, and making analog things.

Mushrooms are on my mind as I write this. They're glowing on the cover of this issue and in a few weeks they'll be everywhere in my yard. I feel very lucky to live in a place where I get to see such a variety of them, though we do not have any of those amazing spring Morels in the yard, unfortunately.

When I think of mushrooms, I think of cycles as the plants around me begin to decay, the trees already showing hints that they're preparing to sleep. As the plant matter dies and decomposes, mushrooms are there to make it happen, and thanks to them there is rich soil for the plants and trees to use for their rebirth in the spring.

As we move into Autumn here in the Northern Hemisphere, I start to look forward to going inward, embracing the harvest and then the quiet that comes after. I start looking at where mushrooms emerge in my life and my work. Where is the decomposition happening that I can use as fuel and energy for the future? As I get older, do I keep changing and growing? What is possible for my second half?

Recently, My Chemical Romance put out a new song after almost a decade of hiatus. It's called "The Foundations of Decay" and when I was thinking about what to write for this editorial, the song came to mind. The lyrics have lots of metaphor in them that people are trying to parse out, but for myself it feels reflective of coming into middle age and deciding whether it's time to lay in the foundations of our own decay and settle into decline or to, as the lyrics say, "get up, coward" and keep going, keep growing, keep changing.

I choose the later, but I also recognize that those foundations of decay should not be rejected out of hand. They are the old versions of myself and that is where I should look for mushrooms that tell me where there is good, rich soil from which to build that new version of myself.

Many of the stories in this issue follow a similar theme. I wrote in our March editorial about how the pandemic has, unsurprisingly, started to produce stories of loss and loneliness. This issue, we found many of our submissions were centered on the aftermath of climate change and how it will effect our future generations, if not ourselves. With our the effect on the environment producing changes that are becoming more obvious by the day, it does not surprise me that our authors are turning to their work to process their thoughts and feelings, and perhaps even imagining a better future when it's all done.

In the stories within these pages, some hopeful, some more bleak, characters find ways to carry on. They have found ways of surviving, even thriving, in a more literal type of decay. I hope they enrich your day as the soil is enriched by the life that has come before. If you keep your eyes open, you may find there are even a few mushrooms scattered through these lines.

L S Q | 051

Peanut Butter Elegy

Jenna Glover

Jenna Glover is a speculative fiction writer from California. Her work has appeared or is forthcoming in Tree and Stone Magazine, Flash Point SF, Daily Science Fiction, After Dinner Conversation, the Santa Clara Review, and multiple cycles of F(r)iction's Dually Noted. Alongside writing (and reading— so much reading!), Jenna enjoys being a mediocre knitter and an excellent cook. You can read her work and learn more about her at www.jennaglover.com or follow her on Twitter and Instagram @ JennaCGlover.

When my husband died, I told our five-year-old daughter Abigail he had been turned into a dog and run away. That was the thing about living in a magically integrated community: anything was possible. And when anything was possible, nothing bad had to happen. So instead of telling my daughter that her father had been killed in a stupid hit and run while on his way home from the grocery store, I told her that somewhere out there was a man turned dog running free and happy.

She believed me, of course she did. On our block alone there were three witches, one elf, and the twin boys next door were changelings. Abigail suspected every single one of them of committing the foul curse on her father, and for three tense days she refused to go outside lest she be the next victim of mammalian transformation. In a desperate bid to save my sanity, I impressed upon my daughter that, though we still didn't know who or what had cast the spell on Daddy, the police were doing a thorough investigation and already found our neighborhood and neighbors to be completely safe (except for Mr. Jenkins during full moons). All that was left to do was wait for the spell to wear off, and then Daddy would find his own way home, and everything would be all right.

Abigail believed me about this as well.

I knew it was wrong to lie to her. She was old enough to handle the concept of death, and it wasn't even that I thought the truth would destroy her. It was just...my husband died buying *peanut butter* in a *car crash*. If he had died from a spell gone wrong or a vampire attack or something, I wouldn't've had any problem telling Abigail about it because that made sense. We didn't move halfway across the country to a community with potion masters in the hospitals and safety spells on the school campuses just so mortal problems like car crashes could destroy our daughter's world. Magic was supposed to protect us, so why was my husband dead?

I didn't have an answer, for myself and certainly not for Abigail. So, like a good mom, I lied to my daughter and never bought peanut butter again.

***

Several weeks after his death, Abigail came home from kindergarten with a note from her teacher. I frowned when she handed it to me but didn't have time to read it because Abigail demanded a snack.

Snack time was a chore now. My husband had always been in charge of the food. Unfortunately, that meant Abigail shared his love of peanut butter. Peanut butter sandwiches, cookies, crackers, peanut butter on fruit, on vegetables, a dollop on a spoon. For days Abigail threw colossal tantrums whenever her snack didn't include peanut butter. It wasn't until a PTA dad shared the secret of magically altered vegetables that Abigail started eating her snacks again in sullen silence. Magic foods cost a little bit extra, but my daughter never threw a fit when presented with neon purple celery that sparkled when bit, and I could have some peace and quiet when she came home from school.

I wondered if the note was something from the PTA. Perhaps another call for me to speak at the Magic and Mortals community night. What they thought I had to contribute to such an event was beyond me. There was no trick to living a mortal life, I'd say. We all just do our best not to die so quickly. And look, my husband failed at even that.

I slit open the envelope and found two sheets inside, one a handwritten letter from my daughter's teacher and the other a form titled 'Submission of Magical Accidents, Grievances, and Complaints.'

Dear Ms. Sousa,

I was sorry to hear of the loss of your husband a few weeks back. I hope you and your family are doing well. I wanted to keep you abreast of Abigail's time at school since the loss of her father. She has been doing surprisingly well, has not missed a single assignment, and seems in good spirits. However, she said something that concerns me, and I felt it best to bring it to your attention. Abigail has told the other children that her father is not dead. Instead, she insists that he has been transfigured into a dog by the work of an unknown magical being and has therefore run away.

I do not presume to know the details involving the death of your husband, and I apologize profusely if I am overstepping my boundaries, but given Abigail's assertions, I felt I should speak up.

In an integrated community such as our own, there are strict rules for the use of magic around, for, and on mortals, as I am sure you are aware. I know many mortals feel intimidated to come forward with any issues regarding their magical neighbors. However, these rules were put in place for your protection, and I have included the attached form as a first step to report any such magical grievances you may have. I myself am willing to aid you in navigating the process, and I can assure you everything will be kept in the strictest of confidences here at the school.

Please do let me know if there is anything I can possibly do to aid you and Abigail during this trying time.

Most Sincerely,

The Lady Gwyn, Professor

Well...when trained childcare professionals started questioning the mental and physical wellbeing of your daughter, that was when you knew it was time to give up.

After a Mommy Minute in the bathroom, I returned to the kitchen ready to confess my utter failure as a parent.

"Hey Abby," I said. My daughter turned around to look at me, mouth stained a dark plum.

"Can I have some peanut butter?" she asked.

I swallowed, a phantom taste of peanuts on my tongue.

"No," I replied smoothly, like her favorite peanut butter.

Abigail pouted immediately. "Why *not?*" We were five seconds away from a tantrum. It was now or never.

"The stores are sold out of peanut butter, baby. I'm sorry."

***

So Doggy Daddy remained the story in our household, but only our household. I sat Abigail down and told her that it was for the best that she keep Daddy's predicament to herself when with others. She asked me a million questions that I couldn't answer, but eventually she was satisfied. It was, after all, a special secret, and there was nothing greater a girl her age could ask for. Except maybe a unicorn.

And if I searched for where to buy unicorns on Google that night, sue me.

But that was, unfortunately, not the end of the matter. At home, Abigail continued to bring up her father at every possible turn. She speculated on what kind of dog he had been turned into, where he had run off to, was he a dog or a werewolf, and if he was a werewolf did I think he might be staying with Mr. Jenkins?

And always the peanut butter. Did the store get more peanut butter in stock? How come Nanae had peanut butter in her lunch at school but Abby didn't? If we got some peanut butter, would Daddy come back?

I started avoiding Abigail just to get a break from the chatter. I signed her up for an afterschool class, left her at friends' houses for playdates, and paid almost $200 for a child-approved potion that allowed her to hover two feet off the ground, outside and away from me, for three hours.

I did everything a good mom does. But I didn't talk to Abigail. I couldn't tell my daughter that the thought of peanut butter made me want to cry, that the smell of peanuts turned my stomach, that if I ever had to see that sticky brown mess of a condiment I couldn't be held responsible for what I did next. And I couldn't tell her that all this was because Daddy was not a dog, but dead, and I was so sorry because if I had just died instead she could have all the peanut butter she wanted.

I couldn't tell Abigail about any of that, so I didn't tell her anything at all.

* * *

What a dreadful night, I thought as I trudged up the walkway home, lethargic from having drunk a little too much.

In the mortal world, grieving widows would most likely attend several therapy sessions to help them get over their loss. In magical communities, we had séances.

Lucille was a fellow mom and presumably had the gift of speaking to the dead. I had never had any desire to see her before, and I really didn't then either, but she had offered me a free reading when my husband first died, and I had been dodging her attempts to cash it in for me ever since. Finally, she cornered me during pickup, promised wine and chocolate to go with the reading, and I couldn't say no.

I stopped at the steps to the front door and tried to compose myself. I didn't know what I had expected from Lucille. As far as I knew, the magical community was split on the efficacy of spirit communication as a magic, and I wasn't sure what I believed. In the end, I spent over an hour answering questions my supposed dead husband was asking me, all about the state of the household, Abigail's schooling, plans for the summer break—all vague enough to be sourced from anyone. In the end, the only peace I came away with was the kind found at the bottom of a bottle.

I dug out my keys and was about to open the front door when I smelled roasted nuts and oil. I looked down. Beside the door, there was a plate of crackers smeared with peanut butter and a card that said 'For Daddy.'

My vision turned to static and my stomach felt hot. *Don't throw up, don't throw up, don't throw up.*

It took all of my willpower and the prying eyes of my night-vision neighbor across the way not to kick the plate into the bushes. Instead, holding my breath, I picked it up and carried it with me inside.

"Abigail! I'm home!" I called, voice shriller than I intended. I hastened to the kitchen to dump the crackers into the trash. There was an open jar of peanut butter on the table. I was staring at it when Abigail came skipping into the kitchen followed by Kiera, a teenage witch and Abigail's babysitter. I gave Abigail a quick hug and then dug out my wallet for some cash.

Be normal. Don't throw up. Be normal. Don't throw up.

"Everything go all right?" I asked Kiera, but Abigail answered.

"We played Sunset Demons, and ate snacks, and learned about trans-o-fig-ma-tation, and Kiera helped me with my homework!"

"Not in that order," Kiera assured me, trying to look like she wasn't counting the bills as I pulled them from my wallet.

"Trans-o what?" I asked, giving up on counting and just handing over the entire stack. Babysitting rates were ridiculous, and the magical beings charged double because they could offer emergency spells, and what teenager would seriously protest getting paid extra. *Be normal.*

Kiera slid the wad of bills into her back pocket with a smile before answering, "Transfiguration. She saw my textbook from school. But no worries. I didn't go into the nitty gritty."

"Right." I leaned against the counter and tried to look like I wasn't about to have a nervous breakdown. "I noticed the crackers on the front step."

Kiera gave an apologetic grimace. "Oh, yeah. Abby was going on about peanut butter, but I noticed you didn't have any, so I grabbed some from my house. She wanted to leave those outside, but wouldn't tell me why. Sorry. I meant to grab it before you came back."

"It's fine." I gestured to the jar on the table. "Have a nice night."

"Oh, you can keep it. I got a two for one deal at the market."

"No, you don't have to do that."

"It's no biggie."

"Oh, no, I couldn't possibly."

"Really, it's whatever."

"Just take it!"

Kiera paused, eyeing the crazy old lady that cared way too much about condiment ownership, but she dutifully scooped up the jar.

"...Okay. See you."

"Good night."

***

The next day, two and a half months into the disaster I called motherhood, it finally happened.

Except, I thought 'it' would mean a conversation, not an old, grimy sheepdog drooling on my living room carpet. But really, at that point, I shouldn't've been surprised.

The dog must have come by sometime in the night, lured by the peanut butter treats left in the garbage bins. I didn't hear Abigail get up, didn't hear her open the door, and I didn't hear a peep from the dog. That was concerning. I should probably ask after some more security charms for the house. Or never drink wine again.

But Saturday morning, when I passed the living room on my way to the kitchen, there was Abigail clutching that disgusting dog and watching cartoons.

"What is *that?*" I demanded, abandoning my quest for coffee and coming around the couch. The dog squirmed in her arms, wiggling away to hop down and sniff at my slippers. I resisted the urge to kick it away.

"It's Daddy!" Abigail crowed, jumping off the couch to resume snuggling the dog. "He came back!"

I opened my mouth to say *No, that isn't Daddy. This is just a normal dumb dog.* Then I followed that conversation to its natural conclusion: *Hm? How do I know? Oh, sweetie, because Daddy is dead, and I know because I identified his corpse at the morgue weeks ago. Mommy's a liar, and you will probably never trust me again. Now, who wants Coco Puffs?*

"Are you sure this is Daddy, honey?" I asked, kneeling down beside her. "This dog looks a lot older than Daddy."

Abigail tilted her head thoughtfully. "He probably got changed into dog years," she said solemnly. "Poor Daddy."

"Mm-hm." The dog nosed forward, pressing its wet snout into

my crotch. I pushed it off roughly. "Well, tell you what, I'll go and take the dog—Daddy—to the shelter today. That's the best place for him to be now."

Abigail frowned. "They'll change him back?"

"...I'm sure they'll try."

"But what if they can't?"

"Well, then, they'll take him somewhere where he can live happily as a dog."

Abigail gasped and hugged the dog tight enough to threaten suffocation. "Daddy belongs with us!" she cried. And now there were tears in her eyes, and I was halfway to a sobbing mess myself because what was I supposed to say to that?

Daddy did belong with us.

***

Five days later, Abigail was still calling the dog Daddy, a secret appointment was made with the shelter for an afternoon surrendering, and I was on the back porch holding a jar of peanut butter and a spoon.

After the crash, the tow truck company had collected everything that was in the car and given it to me. One bag held miscellaneous car junk like a grungy sweater, a broken flashlight, and some tissues so old they disintegrated at a touch. But the other bag was from the local grocery store. It had been filled with the bits and bobs my husband was getting for dinner that night. Rice. Artichokes. Some spices we were out of.

And peanut butter.

I rolled the jar in my hands. It was the store brand, my husband's favorite. Mine too, but I honestly didn't know if it was my favorite because I actually liked it or because my husband refused to eat any other brand, so I just told myself I liked it. That was what marriage did to you: blurred the lines between two people and made them into one, greater person.

Except I wasn't a greater person anymore. I was a middle-aged widow who hadn't showered in three days and was about to spoon peanut butter into her mouth and call it lunch.

The dog was laying in the grass in front of me, having given up on convincing me to play fetch, and it now judged my poor nutritional choices. Or hoped I'd share. But this peanut butter wasn't for dogs. It was for dead husbands.

Abigail had wanted to go to school and tell all her friends about Daddy's miraculous return, but I convinced her not to. We didn't want to embarrass Daddy by telling everyone he was still a dog. We could wait until he was a human again. It would be another of our special secrets.

I wondered how many special secrets I could feasibly demand her to keep.

I twisted the lid off the jar, dug in the spoon, and lifted out a giant glob. The dog's nose twitched at the nutty scent. He half rose, tongue lolling out, drool dripping down the sides of his jowls.

I hated that dog. How dare he come to my house? How dare he jeopardize my daughter's peace of mind? I told those lies to protect her, and this stupid dog was ruining that. He would hurt her because he was a dog and not a human and eventually, inevitably, that fact would be revealed to Abigail and crush her world.

I was her mother. It was my job to crush her world, and I was supposed to do so months ago when her father had actually died.

Now, with Doggy Daddy scheduled to disappear, I didn't know what I was supposed to do. Honestly, it would've been better if the dog had just died, preferably in front of Abigail since I now knew I was incapable of breaking bad news to my daughter. If the dog had just gotten hit by a car, right in front of Abigail and died, then Daddy would've been dead for both of us, I could've had a peaceful afternoon, and we both could've just moved on.

That was what you were supposed to do when someone you loved died. Somewhere there was this healing path forward that I was supposed to follow. Except instead of finding it, I lied to my daughter and got myself into a mess that led to me spooning peanut butter out of a jar on the back porch with someone else's lost dog and planning a clandestine trip to the pound, with no idea what to tell Abigail once Doggy Daddy was gone for good, and no idea how to get an idea because I'd never had to do any of this life stuff by myself because that was what my husband was for. He was supposed to be here to help me with Abigail and magical lies and all the rest of it. So really this was his fault, and I hated him too.

The spoon bounced in my grip, and I looked down to see the dog licking the end of it. I set the spoon down and the dog followed it, tongue a blur, completely forgetting about me in its delight. I reached out and rested a hand on its shaggy head and closed my eyes. I smelled dirt and grass and dog, but also roasted nuts and oil. I breathed deep.

"I miss you," I whispered.

The dog said nothing because it was just a dog.

Felt

Denise Khng

Denise is a writer and director from Singapore. Her writing can also be found in Entropy Magazine and Coldnoon: Travel Poetics. Her short film, Late Night Talk Show, screened as an Official Selection at the Portland Film Festival. Her next short, Motherland, is upcoming.

I always knew the time would come for me to lose you. I don't mean death, like how everyone's supposed to die eventually. I mean I knew our friendship would end early. I never told you this but after graduation, I went to a shaman and asked her what your future looked like. What I really wanted to know was whether I'd be included in yours. I gave her your name and birth date, and she told me you were going to be powerful, that your rise would effect a monumental change on the world. She didn't say what kind of change, but I knew what she meant because I felt it too with you. You had a gold star to your name, marking your ascent even before you entered this world. You'd probably say it's bullshit, she was a charlatan enjoying her moment, because if anyone truly knows the future, they'd know too that the knowledge isn't theirs to share, without permission. To even things out, I gave her my name and birth date, and she told me to let you go.

There was a conversation we had a long time ago, on your twenty-fifth birthday, when you'd just moved to a continent with three extra seasons, and you blew out your wish over video call. You were holed up in your spartan room, encircled by the light pouring through a window just out of frame. The cake from your housemates sat incongruously on your table, a cream triangle haphazardly mounted on a paper moon. Outside the window of your little shelter, stencilled through the dusty gold flush of the afternoon, was a skyline woven from the grandeur of bygone power, its spires watching over you, breathing cold love over the outlines of your hair, the slant of your cheek, the cloud of white sheets spilling over the edge of your bed at the bottom right corner of the screen. For a moment, I wondered if you'd spent the night with someone. But you mentioned you hadn't slept the night before—you'd been working in the lab.

Even on your birthday, you'd proudly chosen to maintain a level of austerity to your day-to-day existence. Work to you was meditative, a reflection of who you were becoming even more: the serious thinker, sustained only by necessity, leagues above the frivolity of material excess. There was an air of dread and excitement that year brewing through the summer gold; a continent was to be remapped, and the ground was swelling with the arrival of a new social order, a stage that kindled the combustion of progression and resistance, where all players risked capitulating to the adult forces of their childhood insecurities.

I figured your wish was something noble, like the mass eradication of ignorance. After all, it bothered you greatly that most people don't think very deeply, if they do any thinking at all.

"It's endemic," you said, wrapping your arms around yourself against a chill I couldn't feel. "You'd think people would be more careful."

"Overthinking screws up your instincts," I retorted, for the sake of it. "I mean, the point of life is spontaneity. Look at what's happening around you. You're in the second act of a revolution. Take it in."

There was your gaze, studying me closely.

"I'll take in the carnage of the third," you said, smiling to curb your dissent.

"Alright, I was kidding," I said. "Just a little."

"I wish everyone had more time."

"Neal, if all goes well, you have a good fifty years left."

"No, I mean enough time to actually understand ourselves, and then live it over, with all the right decisions. So the second time round, we don't hurt anyone as much, while living out our fullest potential."

"So a life that's careful."

"And risky. Being careful allows you to take the biggest risks. Deliberate ones, of course."

"Who knew you were into reincarnation?"

"I meant the same life, not a different one," you smiled patiently. "It's just a wish."

"Why?"

You sat still at your screen, head bowed in prayerful thought. You did this whenever you were in serious thought. I took a silent screenshot of you, as if it would have captured your mind.

"I think the future opens up to those who risk being ignited by it," you said finally.

I was conscious of the clutter on my desk: the surplus stationery haphazardly scattered around my laptop, my old cardigan tossed over the back of my chair. In contrast, your taste was minimalist and refined, compositions distilled down to their purest essentials: a desk, a super single bed on a frame without a headboard, a ceiling fan with a lightbulb at its centre. It was your code for living, for seeing things at their core, returning to base, starting over, starting clean, on surfaces so smooth and seamless and timeless that the influence of any one person or thing or event would slide off. Perhaps you'd hoped the past would be washed away, leaving only what binds all of life through the ages—time, or some semblance of it.

"And what do you think happens after people make these really ignited decisions and everything falls into place, as I assume it peacefully would?" I asked in jest.

You crossed your elbows on the table and tucked your chin into your arms. "First, peace like you've said," you grinned. "As for the rest that comes after, I wildly reckon it'd be an elevated sort of living."

"Trusting entirely in the goodness of human nature, I see."

You laughed off my derision. But your eyes had veiled themselves, and you shut yourself away behind another door in your heart.

"Sorry, I really should think before I speak," I said. "That would teach me, when you finally win your Nobel and I'm still having to clock my nine-to-six."

"A Nobel's a long way off," you chuckled. "But thanks for your vote of confidence."

We were silent for a while, and you hugged your arms around yourself tighter so I could see who you were as a little boy. Shy, awkward. Unsure of why he'd been born at all. This was you the night your mother left; when you'd sat waiting for her through the night even though you knew she wouldn't return because she'd taken the suitcase with her. She wouldn't return at all, because the taxi she'd gotten into would an hour later swerve into the path of an oncoming truck. It was quite impressive she'd even tried, you'd said dryly.

The sight of your vulnerability unlocked an honesty within me, and I found myself telling you, "On occasion you meet someone, and you know that they're going to be somebody important to the world. They're going to move on to do great things—they're going to move on to greatness. It's a rare quality—you only see it in one or two people in a lifetime. But you can feel it in your blood when you talk to them, when you witness the way they work. And everyone else who meets them can sense it too: that this person is set to be the point at which history diverges from what it's been barrelling blindly towards. They will seize the future and sear it with greatness while the rest of us won't ever make it to the footnotes of history, even if we try."

From the window, the brilliant afternoon light cast a halo over the crown of your head, shielding your features from sight so they seemed to be continually dissolving in gold. I sketched in your expression. At the turn of an invisible hand, the light receded, and as a gentle affection traced the corners of your mouth, I saw that you were moved, your lips parting lightly, ready to break your code of distance, surrender the sovereignty of discretion to sentimentality. You were beautiful and spectacular—perfectly made for loss. In the bated silence, I longed to step into that golden light with you, to keep history waiting forever behind a window. Everything would stay the same in that light. Everything precious and yet to be fulfilled. But as you wavered in your deliberation, the call of the world came rushing back, shutting your mouth to keep your heart a secret, so only the world would know it.

**

Tropical heat softens people. Back home, the humidity made them languid, forced them to take cover in cavernous air-conditioned shopping malls which made them comfortable enough to forget human endeavour. They could continue to talk about food, shopping, insurance, kitchen renovations—tangible, concrete details that didn't matter after dark, but which distracted enough from the vacuum of non-ambition, the pre-made future for the well-behaved. This softness made citizens obstinate, made them not leave even if they fantasised about doing so. At night, they didn't look up at the stars. They didn't see the point of it.

I felt the grip of fixed-ness whenever I took the train to work. I felt it most when people pressed in beside me, listless and unseeing, plugged into their phones to hide themselves. They and I travelled at an automated pace, in a hive-like swarm, passing industrial estates and high-rise flats where laundry hung along corridor rails and windows were little stamps of ceiling fans and television glow. It was no wonder people tended not to look out at the view. I thought those who loved the heartlands were desensitised. I thought their desensitisation happened gradually and unwittingly—perhaps mid-way through secondary school, or while they were still children—when they surrendered imagination to the Lego-block landscape, to the geometry of concrete pathways, to punishment or humiliation whenever they failed to follow a rule. In order to thrive here, they had to find something to love about the place: the food, the twenty-four-seven convenience, the hard resistance to tenderness that passed for love. I stayed because, perversely, I was fascinated by the willingness of people to embrace something that was, clearly to me, killing them inside. I thought I could hold up a lens to their travesty of settled existence; expose it, shame it into changing.

After graduation, I joined the national paper, with the crusading hope of breaking a story that would reset culture—or everything

I hated about it. Instead of the foreign desk, I was posted to the lifestyle section. I reported to Warren, my supervising editor, who had a penchant for camel blazers and penny loafers. For gravitas, he sported a five o'clock shadow and a genteel finish to his speaking style. He spoke with passion about how most people lacked the discipline to see through their ideas. If they only pushed themselves more, he wagered, they'd actually finish things. Warren's maxim was that talented people weren't the ones who would succeed because early attention made them complacent—but the hardworking ones, they would rise in the end. He followed briefs from the Editor-in-Chief to the letter, and preferred trends such as listicles or historical soundbites that were government-friendly enough to be mildly fictitious—articles that came without implications. Here, potential wasn't meant to be fulfilled, it was meant to go unseen, shelved as some vestigial offshoot of the Un-Adult, as inconvenient as a tantrum devolved from a child's attempt at make-belief. It was transgressive to aim for anything higher than what had already been established as acceptably competent, a standard several paces removed from the seismic threat of novelty, so everyone could reach it, this communal level that was fair to all. *When you write, think of the Common Man. Think of the masses.* It was difficult to fault Warren for thinking within orderly lines of obedience; slowly but surely, he'd built the foundations of his world according to state-approved self-actualisation. He had a weekly column, *Dinner With The Editor*, in which he interviewed a rising profile over dinner at a restaurant of their choice, and asked questions about their favourite childhood memory or the food they missed most when they were abroad. Because he loved the country just the way it was, none of the content he oversaw should have been life-changing. Instead, it would shed light on the literal things that mattered for a good life here—an espousal of the status quo in preservation of the build-by-numbers pathway he and many others had trodden, to be inherited by his children and his children's children to come, and if people were disgruntled in a city as easy to live in as ours was, it was because they hadn't suffered enough early on in life to appreciate what they had today.

Editorial meetings were where he could hold court competitively. He had a habit of perching on the table while leading discussions such that whenever a suggestion floored him, he had enough legroom to give his ankle a good wiggle, a tic I suspected he'd never shaken off since boyhood. "Come on, what's the buzzword?" he'd say, snapping his fingers for pizzazz. The point would then circle back to a trending article he saw online or a viral something his wife had watched. It was moments like this that made me miss your unintentional sweetness, your proclivity for quiet understanding. And it was during these moments that I'd feel the urge to tell Warren what a poseur he was, that his work was a pastiche of ideas stolen from the weak or unsuspecting.

Your wife will leave you eventually, I thought cruelly whenever I caught him frowning in concentration at his screen. *She'll leave you when she realises you're a sham of who you try to be.*

Over time, I ceded my convictions to the uniformity of working life. I wrote mindlessly about whatever was assigned to me: red carpet fashion, home interiors of local celebrities, *Ten new cafés for that Valentine's date!* After work, I spent more than I deserved to on things I didn't need. It was as if my absorption into frivolity had set off a voracious need to self-preserve by consumption. I bought dresses and shoes I didn't wear. I went to dinner at the restaurants that were chronicled in the listicles. I rented a room in an apartment close to the centre of the city. It had a pool and a gym. It wasn't lost on me that the softness I'd detested had billowed into the chamber of my most malleable beliefs and altered without resistance the way I'd existed in the world. The suffocation happened slowly, and by the end of my second year at the press, I no longer had the motivation to leave. My submission to the system surprised me, and I wondered if the heat death of my initial drive to report on something ground-breaking—to be a part of something bigger and purposeful and worthy of sacrifice—was ultimately due to the shapelessness of my own potential. It wasn't specific enough, like yours was.

Initially, I found it funny to rant about how banal my assignments were—how corny, how derivative—but I stopped sharing details about work with you once the chances of any grand escape from its ordinariness steadily dimmed. I couldn't shake off the uneasiness that I'd failed to fulfil an implicit obligation merited by our bond; I was afraid if I articulated fully the foreseeable permanence of my regime, you would see me for who I had become. Then I'd lose you the way I was losing myself—as a stranger.

But to you, things were constantly in the making, even if they didn't seem to visibly progress. Most events were improbable in the first place. Wars began and ended. Empires rose and fell. A decade ago, no one could have predicted the detours they would undertake today.

When I was posted to the London bureau to cover the peace summit for two weeks, you smiled and said it was what I should have already expected.

***

Nothing could pull you away from the enormity of time and space.

I knew you'd been troubled by work, though you never disclosed details. You were enamoured still by the sprawling dream-singed capital you'd landed in. You'd watched in awe as the sun sunk low over bridge towers, navigated with pride the underground maze we'd willed to a playground of parks and theatres and museums, whispered in my ear an incantation of faith. But in moments of quiet, you often drifted into that immense place beneath the tide. You'd taken to shutting yourself in your apartment whenever you weren't in the lab.

Beyond the walls of your mind, a procession of zeal had taken hold of the city as it awaited a truce between nations or a deadlock among men. A reclamation of power was taking place, to be witnessed and recorded and summoned again for posterity. The crowd lit their flares, white as starlight, and crossed the gridlines of ordinary restraint into Westminster. Their messages merged as they rallied in a chorus of shouts and pleas, each voice echoing the one before it, each person a canvas for the passions of others. I tried to memorise everything: The woman standing on the podium, a pilgrim, a magician in disguise, her garland of pearl-grey tendrils blowing in the wind as she chanted her song of restoration. Daffodils that had been distributed as tokens of peace, fallen by the wayside and trampled into cinder. Every face I photographed, unmasking only solidarity or hostility. But an event can never fully be captured, only re-imagined—and in its first retelling, the story would always be as extraordinary as the instant life first began.

As soon as the summit was over, I raced over to your place, breathless from the wilderness, the great feast of life I'd partaken in simply by observing, and firmly convinced that the outcome in the room had been transformed by everything outside it. To sustain the fullness of the extraordinary, to share it with you before it could perish into understanding, I had to reach you at the speed of light.

I found you at rest.

Your bedroom door was open, blown against the wall like a sail. You lay upside-down at the foot of your bed, staring at the ceiling, blinded light from the window splayed all around you like wings.

"Neal? Hey."

You stayed still, waiting—for intervention, for truth.

I sat down beside you. "You missed the whole thing. Do you want to see the pictures?"

A decision turned in your mind like a pebble.

"Renee." Your voice was audible, but only just, so it was closer to thought than speech. "Why haven't you walked away?"

"From what?"

You sat up, and your hair fell over your eyes. It was difficult to read your face in the semi-light. Through the blinds, a blue dusk was deepening across the aether, high above the snow-painted branches of a tree. The whisper of an answer hovered just beyond reach—around you, within you.

Far out into the streets where frost was melting into new grass, the throng of marchers were reassembling themselves, galvanised by the same call to devotion. The quest to assume a higher nature, to fall into our rightful, honoured places in time, until everything falls to darkness, until the point at which we reach equilibrium. *Did you know it then? How things would end?*

"Do you want me to?" I asked.

"No, it's just a question," you mumbled. Your gaze fell past the edge of the bed towards the shadows on the wall.

Elsewhere, the distant sound of sirens. The speeding towards something dramatic, towards the climax of an ending or the beginning of some unwanted descent into truth.

I lit a cigarette.

"You shouldn't smoke," you said.

"Then you shouldn't ask questions that necessitate smoking."

"It'll set off the alarm," you murmured, taking the tab from my fingers. You took a brisk drag, then opened the window to stub out its smouldering glow on a bed of frost that had bloomed along the sill. Winter screamed into the room, constellating with sparks of ash and ember, little runes of time blown back to their source with vengeance. Wasn't it Leibniz who proposed that every individual substance contains the entire history of the universe including its ending? The marks and traces of the world's story, gleaming beads of drama and spectacle, each one unspooling with calculated precision, each one its own remarkable contribution to humanity, each one descending from the previous—*Would it be different this time? The next time?*

With every breath, the world grows less coherent, undoing itself atom by atom, in a slow dissipation of potential. But our lives provide an energetic substance so rich and dense and complex that by the time the universe contracts, it would implode into new galaxies, new variations of us.

Elsewhere, a Molotov arced its way through the air. Glass-cut skin pressed up against riot shields. The story was already drifting across the airwaves, eddying through the minds of those who would repeat it, until it congealed into something fictive enough for belief. I should be there, send my version of it to the holographic fragment of my life back home, where Warren and the rest were awaiting my expected, fail-safe return, this foreseeable arc of destiny I was bound to and behind which my part in your story would end.

But life with you felt the most real—it was the only life that mattered.

I would have to leave eventually, but not now. Not when the air was sweet with cigarettes and winter, and the dusk was deepening steadily, approvingly, as you stood by the window wrapped in the dusk-glow. I stood with you, so we were both now wearing the light, to look into the mirror of the world. Your face was close enough to mine I could feel your breath on my cheek. Smoke ghosted its vanishing voyage between us. The draught bore through our clothes. Neither of us made to close the window.

"I should go," I said.

But I reached for your face instead. You remained stock-still under the winter light. I slid my hand under your shirt, over your heart. Your entire body tensed, then surrendered. Your heartbeat pulsed through the warmth of your skin, every beat in proof of time. The opening of a valve. The rush of blood, unconstricted by expectation. Life opens, briefly, and closes as quickly as it begins. You didn't own this force, not physically. It derived its continuation from a prior covenant through which it had welded its authority with yours, so you were now powerless to its honouring. *How much time did you agree to? How much time remained?* You were made aware of it, absently, through your dedication to truth, to the answers you'd demanded about why you'd chosen to live. Caged under your ribs, the life within you coursed freely, on its own time, immune to any change of mind. It wasn't meant to be outrun.

Elsewhere, the chanting began again. Amidst the roaring invocation of change, the woman on the podium knelt down to pray. *I should be there.* The reel would hurry on without me, and I would lose my place in the world; perhaps the next opportunity would be something less vital and defining, divine punishment for my resistance to providence, for my stubborn collusion in the rearrangement of my own destiny.

But as your hand closed over my wrist, you looked at me and dissolved all other wars.

***

Hours later, I awoke through a fog of sleep to a presentiment of empty rooms. Around me, frissons of darkness had settled in thick, grainy layers. The blinds were drawn and the blue had all but disappeared, as if the earth had withdrawn its love to compensate for an overextension of generosity earlier that evening, and drawn you along with it, along with the echoes of the crowd. Stretched across the other half of the bed was an aching absence that rested in your place.

What time was it?

Perhaps you'd gone off to the lab, for a walk, for a visit to a different realm in search of an answer to whatever kept you up at night. I should have expected it of you. I should have known better. A formless dream clawed through my mind, and the only conscious thought that remained was a passing realisation that I needed to live more years before... *Before what, exactly? An understanding of my own life?*

It was too late for questions and far too early for answers.

The next morning, as if to indicate that the scale had been balanced by whatever had been taken in the night, light threw the room into stark relief, and I found you in the kitchen making coffee.

***

In a science trivia interview, you said your favourite experiment of all time was the twin-photon experiment in Geneva: When a stimulus was applied to one of two photons of light that were separated by several miles, both photons simultaneously moved along the same pathway, even though there were equally possible alternative paths to choose from at random. No matter the distance between them, they remained connected, identical in movement.

You said it functioned like a prayer.

***

You first found Clauser in a storm drain, on your way to work. But you were in a hurry, you didn't stop to act. When you headed home that evening, she was still there. Collarless, motherless. Fur matted with mud and dirt. You took her presence as a sign. You wrapped her in your jacket, carried her back to your apartment. You let her sleep at the foot of your bed. You joked that she was your wolf pup, said she was frightened of her own shadow so she followed yours.

When you disappeared, it didn't take her long to go missing too.

***

Every year, you got closer and closer to the centre. A television interview. A press conference. Your permanent move to London. Your visits home. My visits there. Then one day, you reached it: an innocuous pivot into what had once seemed impossibly possible, and suddenly, predictably earned, a secret of the world was yours. The weight of it crashed through your apartment, seeped into the tiny breaks in your routine, pulling and twisting around the grids of tables, burrowing through the neat airy fissures separating coffee mugs and paper folders, before curling up on each of our shoulders, anchoring us to opposite sides of your living room. I had broken the comfort of ambiguity between us, spoken what was supposed to be sacred, unutterable. I thought it would have unlocked you.

"Why now, Renee?"

"Then when? The next life?"

You looked away. "Not now."

"Why?"

You turned back to me. "You have to be careful with time, Renee. It's only enough for the greatest thing you're meant to do with your life."

"Not everything's about accomplishment."

"It is when it means the difference between life and death."

"Well, not everyone's like you. Not everyone ends up changing the world."

"You will if you try!" you thundered. Almost immediately, you drew back. "Sorry, 1 didn't mean it like that—" You took a few steps forward, reached for me. "Renee, I'm sorry—"

I backed away from your touch. "Why are you so afraid of intimacy? Because it's the one risk you can't take?"

Your flinch was barely perceptible, but it was there, otherwise you remained perfectly still, your features curtained by shadow. Suddenly, I was afraid that I'd gone too far, pushed you further into yourself. But it was impossible to hold back now.

"You shut the warmth out. You're contemptuous of it."

"I'm not contemptuous of it."

"Then why can't you tell me what you feel?"

The air grew still. Everything waited. We stayed like this in interminable silence, unable to look at each other. The distance between us was now insurmountable, spanning the countries we'd each travelled to, calls that were never dialled, texts that were never sent, thoughts that were conveniently, cowardly pushed aside for a false sense of self-respect. It was the knowledge buried behind your gestures that hurt most; the buttoning of coats, the wrapping of scarves, the way you reached into a warm wool pocket for your phone as it rang, as your thoughts hurtled towards the obligations of your destiny that awaited you after you made your exit.

It was your ride. You answered the call haltingly, told the driver you were sorry, you were on your way down. Quietly, simply, you gathered your things and left the room. I watched your shadow halt briefly before it disappeared altogether past the slit of crystal light under the door.

***

I met Ben at a company reception. He'd walked up with two glasses of champagne, said he hated the pretend-fun of corporate shindigs, but hey, that's life, so why not humour it? I liked how unguarded he was, how he carried himself without any hint of self-consciousness. His view of the world was unadorned and direct, just like his reporting. He was unfazed by global anxieties—too much worrying, not enough doing—and had dedicated himself to spotlighting positive entrepreneurial advice for the local business beat. The bombings and sanctions, the demonstrations, the violence—these were far-flung events that hung loosely on the periphery of the everyman's priorities, and they would surely occur again, whether or not anyone was watching.

After I'd lost touch with you, settling for contentment seemed essential, even radical. As if the next steps had been preset, he moved into my rental within a year and we put in a ballot for a new flat. Gradually, unabashedly, his possessions took over the spaces that had once been wholly mine, and the practicalities of our lives melded and fitted together like ready-made parts of a dollhouse—accessories included. His books on game theory and pluralism closed out the gaps along my bookshelves. The wardrobe displayed a new row of immaculately pressed linen shirts, arranged according to hue and marked with the breezy arctic scent of his aftershave. Jointly taken photographs were framed along the mantelpiece in the living room and gladly replenished with ever more recent ones. I was intrigued by the way things fell into place, as antipodal points on an unfinished map.

With Ben, the world was regular and dependable. I didn't have to second-guess. We cooked dinner together, saved each other's schedules on our calendars, made plans to travel to Hokkaido for the ski season. He made it a daily habit to tell me he loved me. To complete the ritual, to keep all of it, I said it back to him. His confidence, his sureness that we had everything to be grateful for, seemed enough to keep us both safely moored to a well-marked shore.

Just once, while lying in his arms, I asked if he was afraid this was all our lives were ever meant to be.

"It doesn't get better than this for most people," he reassured. "We're the lucky ones."

But I knew I had mistaken a different set of expectations for simplicity.

When I told Ben I was leaving him, he was in the living room working on an article. He looked up at me, confused. "We'll lose the deposit," he mused plainly.

Then he stood up and asked if there was someone else.

The fear of freedom—it was in everyone who stayed. It wasn't the chaos or anarchy they'd imagined would someday come, but the illumination of what they'd forsaken for a proximation of fulfilment. The pain of it lay dormant, feeding quietly in the recesses of domestic squalor. It was there, every day on the news. The phantom reach of childhood, appearing as a turntable of recycled incidents, one household at a time. The threats. The arrests. The recriminations. Progress, delayed once more, on the road to peace. The rage was waiting to be set free, whether or not we were paying attention.

He didn't see it coming either. It happened in a flash—so sudden and stunning it seemed not to have come from him but the hand of God.

I froze, the ache in my jaw reverberating the knowledge that this was true, this was the preset event, the shattering of the illusion he and I had built around ourselves. He was frozen too, in horror. The angst, the propensity to hurt—it was in him, as much as it was in me. It freed us into being human again.

When I walked out the door, he was seated on the couch, hugging his knees tightly to his chest as he rocked himself back to a stolen point in time.

***

If I asked you, perhaps you would have said I should have been a better person, that I should have been more careful with my thoughts. Or maybe you would have thought it silly. But I happened to be writing at a café in town when I spotted Warren's wife entering, dressed in the striped wool dress she wore in the picture on his desk. She seemed smaller in person, and for all her posed girlishness, was strikingly womanly. For a moment, I thought about leaving in case Warren walked in. But then her lover entered, and slid into the booth beside her. They erupted in raucous banter like old friends, his arm around her shoulder, her heel sliding up against his shin. As she traced his fingers with hers, a new burden was released into the world.

***

When you won the Nobel, people started seeing the future differently. You'd quantified the existence of life after death. You'd proven the existence of a continuing consciousness in each of us, separate from the brain. Many were comforted, uplifted by the validation of what they'd already believed at a primordial level to be true. But your calculations also deduced that our souls were not eternal—that consciousness would end once the universe reached maximum entropy. You found that the same equations governed every living system, even the most sublime. Everything would cease to exist. Until then, we had a hundred trillion years more to make meaning out of existence, to understand the purpose of its finiteness.

Perhaps it unsettled you that the equations were within us, controlling the decisions we made but eluding observation by slipping under the many guises of conscious reasoning, so by the time our truest intentions emerged later, our destinies would have already been fulfilled. Date of birth, date of death, every thought, event, action—these were all predetermined, if what you'd discovered were to be believed. You insisted in interviews that we still had free will—even if its operations were confined to the outer folds of a churning fate machine—because no one could remember all the details of their contracts, and so couldn't see through the end of their lives. If people remembered anything, they caught only glimpses in dreams or in rare waking moments when the future collided with the present. Elsewise, choice was created through the forgetting.

Back home, people took risks more frequently. They quit their jobs, started their own businesses. They stood up to their bosses. They loved more openly and spoke more tenderly. They broke away from old relationships. They made amends. They reconciled themselves to the prospect of faraway death—not just of themselves, but of all thought and feeling and belief. It was a shift so subtle it would have gone mostly unnoticed if not for how your name fed into conversational justifications for these decisions. Every school you grew up in claimed you as their poster boy. Parliamentary speakers often quoted you when they brought untested policies to the table, because your words imbued their arguments with the glamour of free-thinking morality, regardless of your approval. Your existence made people hopeful. It freed them into dreaming. Even if you hadn't asked for it, the rigid mores of the previously dreamless softened enough to cloak you in something close to motherly affection: national pride.

***

I saw your father for the first time, at the press conference the night your car was found. It wasn't my assignment, but I'd asked to go. In the lobby of the hotel, local reporters jostled for space with those who had flown in from elsewhere in the Asia Pacific.

49

There were representatives from AP and Reuters. A photographer from SCMP.

A hush fell over the press pack as two officers sympathetically ushered him to the centre of a long table which was covered by a white tablecloth and upon which rested three microphones. He sat in the middle seat, flanked by the two officers, as the cameras devoured micro-traces of grief in his countenance. He wasn't how I'd expected him to be. He was tall and rail-thin, and wore a grey polo tee dampened by rain. He spoke haltingly in Mandarin, in short, inadequate statements. He referred to you by your Chinese name, which was the first time I'd heard it spoken. Someone asked him to speak up because the rain was beating down on the windows. But everyone was so quiet. Whenever lightning flashed through the glass, faces illuminated softly.

He said you were a good boy. You studied hard. You did well in school. You were always careful, so he thinks it must have been an accident not through any fault of your own—you could have been distracted by the high beams from a passing vehicle. Those things could be blinding. Maybe your car had malfunctioned. He said hadn't known how to reach you, he hadn't known you had returned. But it was a good thing you had come home. It was what fate had ordered. It brought everything to rest.

When I got back to the office shortly after midnight, only the intern, Carolyn, had remained. She offered to transcribe the recording. I told her not to come in the next day, and sent her home.

I broke your story.

I chose the most visceral photograph of the crash: A deformed sculpture of crushed metal, silvery and river-soaked, hanging off the crane that had been sent to retrieve it. A fringe of torn leather hanging off the seats. An etching of stones and minerals along the grooves of the bonnet. Spidery cracks in the crumpled windshield like the replica of a dragonfly's wing.

I wrote about the certain impossibility of your survival. I backed it up with the officers' report blaming the shitty weather that made the roads too slick. I translated your father's statements. He said you were careful. You were always too careful. I included too the undocumented fact that you could never bring yourself to speak in Mandarin.

After it went to print, I tendered my resignation.

***

I started smoking again. Initially, I tried to keep it to a pack a day, but you know how it goes. I read somewhere that in Greenland, tobacco leaves were used by the Inuit as a medicine for the heart. They're supposed to help release pain and gratitude. In the aftermath, I tried doing that whenever I was on a smoke break—release expectations of you back into the world. Be grateful for everything I had. The peace usually lasted for about fifteen minutes. Then the thoughts would come flooding back again.

Sometimes, I'd look up forum discussions online to see if I'd missed out on any new updates. Most theories had already been dissected repeatedly. Commenters uploaded stills of the crash site, tribute videos that edited these montage-style with an analogue filter—the same pictures that had been frozen in newsprint: Your car hanging off the bridge, the driver's door open in mid-swing over the glistening, roiling river that surged out to sea. Theorists argued over discrepancies in weather conditions, the timestamp on surveillance footage, the blank pages of your boyhood on the foreign equatorial island where twelve-year-olds were cultivated to rank globally in test scores for math and science. There's always a motive, they reasoned, for someone so exacting. It was poetic that you'd returned to the place of your birth without telling anyone—*A homing instinct*, wrote one—and driven to the heart of the city in the middle of the night to enact upon it the death of possibility.

They were all in consensus that the crash was unsurvivable—it was an accident, suicide, or an assassination by deep state actors. I resisted the theatricality of their conclusions. But no matter how the discussions threaded themselves, they led only to the kernel of myth that seeded the lure of its mystery: the belief that illustrious lives did not—*could not*—produce ordinarily simple ends.

***

Friendship to you was a sustenance of your different social needs; those you let in you'd selected carefully over the course of at least a year, so they each fulfilled one emotional or physical aspect of your being. To contact another from this circle would be tantamount to something worse than an intrusion, a gross violation of the sacred spheres created between you and each person. No one spoke of what you meant to them. To say anything would be to unravel a mystery that was true only in imagination. To speak would be to question the mutuality of their feelings for you—and what then was the basis of an insecurity so unbecoming? What you felt for one friend couldn't be broadly applied to another—that was the unspoken lie we'd blissfully sheltered behind, away from the reality that you had taken care to treat all relationships that mattered with a fixed standard of consideration.

Everyone in your circle was replaceable as long as you treated them the same. If one was gone, you'd just have to find another who could be initiated into a friendship within the same amount of time it had taken you to get close to us. Not that you certainly made such calculations deliberately, but I suppose if each person was a variable instead of a constant, curiosity of all parties except you would be inevitably reduced. In the event of an accident, or a disappearance, or the confidence of a secret, you could leave without a trace. You could fall away any time you wished and the equation would dissolve on its own, taking your secrets with it. This was your form of social encryption.

But Lydia's different. She was in the grey zone between acquaintance and friend, someone from our undergraduate years, the only other person I was acquainted with whom you'd allowed into your life. Lydia, whom I'd been in classes with, who'd greeted me with a friendly embrace whenever our twenty-year-old selves passed each other on the walkway to our classes. She was a woman beyond her years even then—certain of the way she thought, in possession of the way she moved. When she spoke, her sentences were devoid of qualifiers. Even the way she dressed spoke nothing of indecision; a leather jacket or red lipstick was brought out not on special occasions but on a random, otherwise inconsequential day so that one couldn't help but wonder if this was the girl, the one with the spontaneous, celebratory existence. Lydia, whose presence itself commanded a celebration.

I'd been afraid to ask what your friendship with her had been like, whether she'd provided a crucial outlet for your thoughts that I couldn't, whether you'd felt understood by her in ways I could not reach, if she needed you less than I did and thus your friendship with her had been freer, her companionship more warranted. I saw how you were comforted by the motherly touches she gave to you and those around her, her nurturing words, her reassuring calmness. She did everything right, didn't cave to ambiguity. She wasn't as assailable to intemperate compulsions as me. It was why I never kept in touch with her after graduation; I'd feared I'd fall short in her eyes—and the fall would have been inevitable, contained in a moment of lapsed propriety like an off-colour joke or showing up late for an appointment—so I kept my distance.

Until I got a call from her about your memorial service—the one she'd been organising.

We met up in town. When I arrived, she was already seated by the window, draped in a blush sheath dress and buffered from the glass by a black Birkin tote.

"I ordered you a coffee, hope you don't mind," she said, rising for a quick hug.

"Thanks."

I'd forgotten that the light here was white and harsh in the mid-afternoon. It reflected sharply off the tiny silver studs in her ears, the delicate crucifix hanging from a thin chain set against the tanned skin of her clavicle. As she reached for her mug to take a sip, my eyes followed the glint of her gold wedding band. Against the sun, her face revealed only practical, angular stories: A young child her schedule orbited around. A husband making his steady climb up the civil service. The down payment on their new flat. An eventual upgrade to a condominium. Then ideally, a transplant to the States, or Western Europe, or Shanghai. Their current life in the city was temporary, a stepping stone arranged on a manicured hill. Lydia had worked for the right to that mobility. For all the approved frills with a touch of substance. Her daughter would be raised as a global citizen—she would see to it. Lydia's life would renew itself, flourish through the lifeblood of her descendants in the order of increasing elegance.

"I hope this wasn't too out of the way for you," she said.

Fine creases appeared at the corners of her eyes whenever she blinked, fleeting reminders of years of information we weren't privy to about each other. It's a funny thing; when you don't see someone for over a decade, they just don't look as real. Seeing Lydia, it was hard to remember exactly what we had been like as students. It was as if she and I were in costume, playing ourselves as who we'd thought we would be at our current age. A double-exposed assemblage of the person in imagination and the person in their present physical reality, one layered self over the other. We were only half-present, half-real. The other halves of ourselves belonged to the kids along the walkway to class, who were embracing lightly, who trusted in the future, trusted that they would always do the right thing, who believed they would permanently remain on the right side of history. They were still out there, standing on the threshold of adulthood, living out the moment of goodwill over and over.

"It's been, what? A decade?" I asked.

"More. It's been thirteen years. You and I. I've always wondered about you," she said warmly. "Are you still with the paper?"

"No, I left. Decided to take a break. And what about you? How's your family?"

"He's met my daughter, Sophie," she said, looking down at her hands. The beginnings of a smile tugged at the corners of her lips as she recollected a memory I didn't want to know.

"That's really lovely."

"She turned four in August."

"Wow."

Beyond the spread of families, the lotus petals of the ArtScience Museum rose in perpetual mid-bloom. Somewhere in the children's section, her husband and child were playing with light projections in a darkened gallery. Thirty-two dollars for an adult, sixteen for those twelve-and-under. Later, Lydia would join them for dinner in a nearby restaurant overlooking the river, overlooking the lights of the commercial buildings and the lit bridges and the tourists who crawl all over the bank like ants. They'd drive home later in their car, with their child securely fastened in the child seat. In private moments with her daughter, she'd speak of you, a mythic figure, her mythic friend.

"She'll be there on Saturday, so you'll finally get to meet her. The programme starts at ten. At the Good Shepherd." As if it were the thoughtful thing to do, she added, "It's walking distance from City Hall."

"He's not religious."

"It's just a venue. The logistics were easier," she said lightly. "I'm giving the eulogy. But if you have something you'd like to say, let me know, and I'll include you in the line-up."

"It's alright, I don't have anything prepared," I said. It was hard to look her in the eye. "But thanks for asking."

Outside, the children's voices rose feverishly, small footsteps pummelling frenzied blows onto concrete. Their grandparents sat close by, staring, but not watching. Age had vaporised any kind of distinguishing feature that made them part of the recognisable. If they went missing, would they go unnoticed by members of the public?

"Renee."

I turned back to Lydia.

"You're attending, aren't you?" she asked.

"I'll try to make it."

Back in school, it was always easy to spot someone who had been raised solidly by the ease and assurance of their interactions with others. Theirs was an etiquette that was calmer, steadier. They graced social spaces with poise and skill that seemed to flow from a vast emotional resource. They could assert themselves without hesitation, effortlessly fall within behavioural margins that connoted being on the right side of social order: Show up on time for class. Knock coolly on a door and wait to be called in. Greet professors with deferential admiration. Infuse emails with an adequate supply of Ps and Qs. Volunteer with the most desirable social causes, endeavours both virtuous and profile-enhancing, their Rumspringa into communes of harder-won survival, exotic terrain upon which benevolent life purpose could ascend. But these sojourns into disorder were part of the ecosystem of securely cultivated upbringing—they were orderly in essence and lacked the stickiness of desperation that grows from neglect. The most successful recipients of the parental lottery turned out confident and enterprising, privileged but self-aware. They could witness abjection, participate in its alleviation, but never plummet into the hot centre of toxicity that unleashed its primal scream.

Lack of nurture shows up desperate and ugly. It grows up wild. The goals of the maladjusted were the same, the stakes different. The jagged edges of hypervigilance, the commitment to a different set of rules, to instinctual rebellion against control, against structure not their own. I saw it in you, too—a similar shame, which you disguised as coolness. You were careful to avoid anything that would inadvertently lead to the disclosure of who you really were—too tightly bound by self-repulsion. In light of your discovery, you could convince yourself, for the duration of its relevance, that you existed on the cusp of newness. Discovery kept you newborn, allowed you to move further away from yourself, become the version that was closer to some bright, numinous divinity, so you could arrive at a new point of origin.

Lydia wasn't acquainted with the impulse to make up for what had been lacking—the need to mess up, to be irresponsible, to welcome an invasion of immaturity at unpredictable intervals in adulthood. Lydia wouldn't understand. She's never known neglect first-hand, never had her life even mildly affected by it, even though she heads the manpower ministry's poverty reduction campaign. She sees the first signs of irresponsibility as an uncorrected aberration, an inexcusable weakness of character. She wouldn't understand that a decade after graduation, lack shows up as the difference between ordering a coffee for a latecomer and flaking out on a corpse-less funeral.

"I understand it's difficult," she said. "But I know it would mean a lot to him. It's a proper goodbye." She reached into her purse, and took out a sealed brown envelope the size of a postcard. "He wanted you to have this."

The envelope was pristine, carefully taken care of. It was padded inside with bubble wrap, and carried a small solid object.

"He made me the executor of his will," I heard her say.

I felt my throat constricting.

"I felt seen by him too. He had that gift," Lydia continued, gazing out the window at the light that haloed the children playing outside. "Gosh, I used to think—" She stopped, then looked down at her mug, unable to shrug off the thought. "I used to think I was in love with him. But I realised later on, after I met my husband, that I was mistaken. With Neal, I felt privileged—Just so special, you know?—that he'd let me in. I never wanted to let go of that feeling."

"Do you think he loved you, at some point? Neal."

She took a sip of her coffee. Took her time. Searched for what to disclose, what to keep. "Renee, he means a lot to a lot of people," she said finally. "I know it's not an easy thing to accept." She reached for my hand. Her palm was soft and warm. Was that why you kept in touch with her all these years? Because her presence pulled you closer to the soothing hearth of normality?

"And you've accepted it?"

"You know what I've learnt as a parent? A person can power through anything. Anything, Renee. As long as they have a sense of self. If they don't, and they lose a sense of purpose, they're either forced to become a different person or they break apart like a porcelain doll. He was a boy in need of guidance. Instead of that, he found enablement. People who saw only his brilliance and what it represented, and they found it difficult to say no to him. But there's a limit to every kind of momentum, no matter how blazing it begins. When he discovered he couldn't bend the universe to his will, he decided his greatest act of revolt would be to leave by choice. Now, I know you're afraid to know this, but truth doesn't hide—it grows. It invades every corner of your life. It makes sure you acknowledge it. When you don't, it destroys you."

"You didn't stop him."

Lydia froze. A flash of pain swept across her face—only for a second—but she composed herself with the poise of a dancer in a duel. "Could I? Could *you*? He was trying to *disprove* his calculations, Renee—He wanted to prove the existence of eternity—" She covered her mouth to suppress her sob, and dropped her voice. "I've gone over this in my head every day for too long and I'm not here to apportion blame. When it comes down to it, we're all equally accountable."

"Lydia—"

She gathered her bag, and stood up gracefully, becoming fully the woman she was always meant to become. "I'll see you on Saturday. Please don't be late." Wiping her eyes hurriedly, she put on her sunglasses, then strode briskly out into the blinding sunlight where the children were still playing, their laughter tearing through the air in joyous, life-filled shrieks.

I blinked back the blur of my reflection.

I unsealed the envelope.

Nestled at the bottom was a key. Attached to it was a note in your handwriting, spelling out the address of your old apartment.

***

After your disappearance, I dreamt frequently of a murmuration of starlings, a black spell across a coast I've never been to. The flock freewheeled, dipped, swerved, billowed in a smoky shape-shifting orbit to the sky, higher and higher, in a synchronised beating of wings, until a sudden decision came to roost upon them, and the shadowy swell disappeared back into the marshes, sucked to the ground as breath.

I understood this to be a part of you—a seasonal pattern, an inborn instinct towards flight, towards visibility of the highest order and sudden oblivion. It kept you out of reach of anyone.

In the still hours of night, I'd imagine being you, wherever you were. Sometimes you were back home in the city, standing in the evening train, incongruent in a trench coat, tall and serene amongst the proletariat who were herded and washed-out and desperately focused on the nearness and sureness of tangible, concrete pleasures. Sometimes you were in that dream marsh, alone and at peace with yourself. These inventions of my anxieties barricaded me against the prospect that you had been wrong: maybe consciousness ended with physical death so you were now permanently nothing.

It was oddly comforting then, that whenever I lay submerged in anything close to panic or fear or rage, I felt I could single-handedly tilt the direction of the future a fraction away from any kind of prediction, wrestle it from the minds of others, by an assertion of thought. I could fracture the power of the collective just by wanting something else. I believed if I desired your return enough, a trail would be set outside in the world which would lead me to the sacred place that held your presence.

Equally so, you could follow it and come back.

***

On the cab ride from Heathrow, your voice played from the radio. The station was doing a revival of your podcast in recognition of World Science Day. I took it as a signal that the distance between us was closing. Through the mouth of a tunnel, cars were swallowed whole and spotlit, their bodies shimmering like iridescent beetles as they slid along the rain-washed tongue of asphalt with limitless haste.

As the cab glided further into the turn of the decade, your voice spoke about compassion and restitution in an age where it was fashionable, appropriate, to be cynical. I almost remembered how you'd sounded when you were young and familiar, in a moment locked in the past, when you were still seated by the window that light-filled afternoon, permanently and unalterably hopeful.

But there was an edge to your voice now, coarsened by years, vacillating between resolution and regret, the steady cadence of your words dissembling a tide of anger, the pauses between your sentences drawn out by the weight of your disillusionment. In my mind's eye, you were in a room, large and hollow, isolated from the outside world, speaking in the darkness, hunched over by the weight of your mortality.

There's hardly enough time, your voice was saying. *But we make do with it.*

A profound grief for the past lodged itself in my chest and soldered its way through my throat. I was alone. I was alone in the world because I'd become separated from myself. Yet here I was, halfway across the globe, bent on retrieving your presence—the success of which was predicated on how much I trusted in your previous self-belief. What could I have told Lydia? That your existence hadn't been diminished, but in fact had become amplified by the circumstantial probability of your death—and why the fuck so? That to listen to her eulogy for you would somehow send you across the threshold, make Heaven and Hell real places, beatify you and absolve you of all your choices so you would no longer be fallible, reachable. You would cease to exist, completely.

After this, I resolved, I won't be tethered to anyone else. You would be the last.

The cab emerged from the tunnel. Up ahead, lights polluted the sky.

I watched the meter cross the sixty-pound mark in glowing red numerals and mildly regretted not taking the rail. The heat from the vent cut a warm channel through the centre of the cab, but spread unevenly out towards the sides. I put on my earphones.

"Here for holiday?" asked my driver.

I pretended I couldn't hear him.

He turned off the radio and concentrated on the road. Around us, traffic had slowed to a glacial crawl. In the car next to us—a red Vauxhall pulling slightly ahead—the angelic face of a child peeked out above a row of miniature teddy bears lining the rear window. She placed a palm against the glass. She looked at me, then breathed into her reflection. An exhalation of life, her whole future ahead. The Vauxhall accelerated and the child disappeared from view.

My driver made a left and our cab parted ways with the commuting ensemble as we entered a quick-flowing turn lane. A traffic officer in a neon green vest stood at the axis of the junction, waving us on.

"There was a protest a few hours earlier," said my driver. "You missed the excitement. Group of yobs with Swiss Army knives— the whole lot of 'em arrested. I saw it from out here. Roads jammed all the way to the park."

We slowed down at another turn, and his eyes met mine through the rear-view mirror again. I averted my gaze.

"You speak English?" he asked.

"No."

My driver shook his head and smiled. He hummed a ditty to himself as we stopped at a red light, and drummed his fingers on the outer curve of the steering wheel.

We rounded a corner into a private cul-de-sac where several of the window fronts were pigmented with festive lights in the colours of birthday cake sprinkles. I heard the tires crunch through the frost that glazed the road. I sensed we had circled into a dark snow globe, one which had stood still for too long, waiting to be shaken by the right confluence of person and circumstance and will.

The cab pulled up along a row of white terrace houses, all harshly lit by LED streetlamps that burned with cloudy mist. All the windows were dark, revealing only the mirrored version of the street: lines of white and black, speckled with streetlight. Yours was the third door from the end of the street. Snow covered the steps to the front door. I could hear my own breathing. I could feel my pulse throbbing through my neck. My own mortality figured as a separate presence beside me.

"Home sweet home," my driver announced.

I stepped out into your world. On the ground, shards of gold and silver smeared across black tar like glitter spray on a child's wet hair. My driver helped carry my luggage to the steps outside the door. He searched his pockets, then presented me his name card; dark gold serif engraved on waxy card stock. "When you need a ride to the airport, you call me," he said kindly. He gave a little bow, said goodnight, and with a last affable smile, turned and got back into the cab with a lilt in his step. I heard him pull away only after I'd turned the key in the lock.

As the cab vanished round the bend, an active quiet hung over the street, starless and milk-grey, and I was made aware of my singular existence in the landscape of your mind. I had slipped into your reality and broken the links to all others. It was as though the top layer of the world, deadened and reflexive, had been pried open to reveal what had always been there: a river of aliveness that coursed through the centre of a great being. Everything was as it was, materially the same, but meaningful, purposeful; an elevation so slight it was only noticeable with the sudden intentionality of every innocuous action, such as the unlocking of a door. There was no going back. I was to be here for an indeterminable amount of time, setting in motion the course of your will.

I pushed open the door and felt for the light switch. There were footsteps, quick and light—an animal's.

Clauser.

***

Temperate weather is highly textured. It's a cold that's dry, that moves in currents across your cheeks, nose, forehead. When you inhale, it scrapes against your lungs, shocks you into conscious breathing. It makes you think you want to survive. You walk out, you need a jacket or you'd feel a stronger sense of your own mortality, for even though it's not cold enough to freeze to death, it's cold enough to remind you that you're on your own. So you get familiar with the presence of this alien weather as it terraforms a home around you, a displaced adult, unlovable and grotesque in your constantly mutating pangs of abjection and loneliness and neediness, caught in incremental stages of a half-baked self-care routine: buying the same groceries, throwing out the trash, reheating last night's dinner, replying last week's text from a friend. These are the bare necessities of a functional life, enough to hoist you over the parapet of passive annihilation. It's movement that almost always saves you, sweeps you up in its hurry towards finality—*Of what?*

It keeps you curious enough to live.

***

It was snowing today, a continent away from home. Here was

where the stairs leading up the underground were lined with dirt-caked gold, where lines of poetry were plastered intermittently between carriage ads, and the air got cold enough for people to notice the brevity of being alive.

Every evening, Clauser and I would head to the park before it got dark. She slept by the front door every night. She was brave like a wolf now—no longer your scared wolf pup. But she missed you, and I didn't make up for it.

Outside your apartment, time flowed unreservedly.

I stopped at a kiosk to buy a pack of Marlboro Silvers and peanut butter M&M's, and walked into the dry cold with Clauser tugging ahead. The crowd—mostly tourists and families—was headed the same way, towards Green Park. A shaft of light cut through the foliage. Bathed in its luminosity, the crowd slowed—time morphing into a freeform spectre, pulling away from the dictates of consistency in rebellion of its own purpose, time enacting its own death. The light shifted again, tracing a path straight through the crossing ahead.

I thought of you.

You tended to surface in my thoughts at odd moments. At a street junction. In a crowd. In traffic. Traffic always sounds like the wings of a plane taking off. I sometimes pretended I could hear the traffic in someone else's mind, most of the time yours. It was nothing more than a game, not unlike the feeling that comes when you're standing still in a moving crowd, the feeling that one could be in a vast many places at once. First, the drumbeats, pounding in my ears as I crossed the road just before the light turned red. I blinked back a snapshot of you, barely past the quarter turn of your life, a figment of potential, closing years and distance by smiling, running, embracing. Every movement, every breath, falling in photographs around me. You with your hood pulled over your head to block out the wind where your hair didn't fall over your ears, the lapels of your coat folding over your mouth like wings so your thoughts, with their startling blinding clarity, fell through the air like powdered glass. *We can change the future.* The insatiable wish, more potent than the sum of eight billion inarticulate desires, cutting through everything except the truth. I watched you smiling. So happy, so golden. I knew if we both stayed at rest just a little longer, I would still eventually believe those words. But you didn't choose to linger, because once the lights changed and the crowd dispersed, you disappeared into the stream of people with places to go.

The park was awash with a forlorn prettiness, a lace of bare trees and autumnal shrubs wrapped around a partially frozen lake. It had started to snow lightly, and ice shavings fell and disappeared into the furred hood of my parka. I took Clauser off her leash, and she bounded happily towards the edge of the lawn. Up ahead on the lake, a flock of swans had gathered where the ice allowed for rest. As I moved towards them, I tripped over a branch. I put my hand out to break the fall and braced for a hard hit. But when I made contact with the ground, the earth crumbled softly between my fingers. I stooped down at the edge of the embankment to wash the soil off my hands. The water was a bottomless grey sky where the ice had shaved off. My fingers plunged in, and the cold bit at my skin. All at once, a strange fear of drowning flooded me. My face stared back at me, features rippling and distorting as if to accommodate the shadows of my thoughts, but never to a point beyond recognition, so I was always the open reflection of what I hid.

I pulled myself up and glanced over at the ice patch. There was an ugly scratch along the surface leading up to the flock. The mark tore along the ice, razoring through the violent stillness of an immobilised current, its tributaries fanning out in opaque threads of smoke—the aftermath of a crash. Was this part of the thread you had weaved with your thoughts?

I lit a cigarette, and inhaled deeply.

The light was fading. The last rays touched the surface of the lake, tingeing the rippling edges with a deep fiery glow. This was how life would end—consumed by a magnificence that was continually burning itself out.

In the distance, Clauser barked. I exhaled, and called out to her.

We needed to keep moving, keep up with the future until its radiance ate into the present.

***

Once you were officially presumed dead, people back home reverted to their old ways of living. Mourning took place stoically, as an acknowledgement of your humanness after all. Your absence created room for the sudden awareness of futility, as everyone else edged closer towards distant extinction. It confirmed their earlier fears that big dreams came with a price tag; you'd died young because your triumphs were incompatible with the smallness of your station. To wish for more than realism was greed. Those who lived pragmatic existences lived longer, were given the chance to leave things neatly in place, to leave nothing unsaid—wasn't that what mattered in the end?

They did this in preparation for the death of the universe, though they did not consciously know it. They did this to guard against losses they thought too great to bear, even if they themselves would become the losses of others. Before they decided to meet, fall in love, say the rites that would seal a union, build a home, have children, leave a legacy in the minds of those who would remember them, become a memory in order to prolong existence—they had a knowing that was still within them, that made them feel: The will to live and the will to die both indicate the existence of something eternal, even if it's nothingness. You know this.

***

Back in your apartment, I sat in your living room where time stood still. Where all risks had already been taken, and all that was left to ignite was my belief in the possibility that your greatest discovery was yet to come—and that your future, and mine, were still unfolding.

So I waited. I lit a cigarette.

A wintry breeze swept inside the room and crested along my cheek.

I noticed the window, bordered by a white casement frame, a landscape of glass where faint light poured gently in, to be refracted in a rainbow beam visible only if one stood at the right spot, viewed it from the right angle. And through the cloud of light, the bare branches of a tree in its final chapter, patterning the multitudinous courses of life, ready for renewal.

I felt the smoke clear, felt the vanquishing of thoughts. An intimation of your arrival.

I watched the light shift under the door gap—the shadow of footsteps, weightless and unhurried. As silence cast its spell over the fading evening light, Clauser ran towards the door.

I stayed still, and felt.

There Is a Cottage by the Woods

Rebecca Burton

Rebecca Harrison sneezes like Donald
Duck and her best friend is a dog who
can count. She was chosen for the
WoMentoring Project by Kirsty Logan,
and long listed for Wigleaf's top fifty.

There is a cottage by the woods, right on the edge of town. They say a witch lives there. They say her cauldron stirs itself. They say... a lot of things. They said Santa was real. And the Easter Bunny. If you want to know the truth, you have to go see for yourself.

Seven-year-old Helen wants to know. She leaves her friends behind at the rickety kissing-gate at the end of their cul-de-sac and walks up the grassy hill to the cottage and the woods.

As she walks, the sounds of town vanish. No more cars, no more shrieks from her friends playing tag. Just birdsong and the rustling of leaves in the trees.

She reaches up and knocks on the door.

A woman answers it. She's old—but in the way that all adults are old, not in the way that Helen's Great-Grandma is old. She invites Helen in and offers her a glass of milk.

Helen isn't sure whether you should accept drinks from a witch. Or maybe that's fairies. But the woman seems nice, so she says yes. The kitchen has wooden beams and a big table in the centre, with bowls and bundles of herbs scattered across it.

The woman asks her why she came.

"To find out if you are a witch like they said. And if your cauldron stirs itself. But I don't believe that. It's just silly."

"Take a look for yourself. What do you think?"

Helen has a good look around. There is an open fire, with a small cauldron hanging over it—or at least she assumes that the metal bucket thing is a cauldron. She's never seen one before. And the spoon is going round and round on its own.

"It does stir itself!"

"Look again."

Helen crinkles her brow. What does the woman mean? But she looks, tilting her head and squinting and there... She can just make out a faint, blurred human-ish shape.

"What is that?"

"I think you mean who, dear. That's Albert. He helps me out around the cottage. He likes to be useful."

The gauzy almost-there shape waves and Helen waves back. It's only polite after all.

"Why can't I see him properly?"

"I'm afraid he's dead, dear. That's his ghost you're seeing."

"Oh. You are a witch then, if you have a ghost working for you."

"If that's the criteria, then I guess I am." The woman laughs.

Helen drinks her milk and the woman goes back to chopping herbs, reciting the names as she selects them.

When Helen finishes the glass, she leaves. But she's not quite the *same. She is inclined, more than ever, to believe her own eyes over what "they say."*

And it's not the last time she visits the witch.

***

Helen stood at the old kissing-gate, a letter clutched in one hand. Over ten years, since she last stood here and looked up the hill to the cottage by the woods. It hadn't changed a bit.

Funny that, when everything else had changed so much. Especially her.

She'd almost forgotten the cottage existed, and the witch, until the letter from the solicitor arrived on her doormat.

She'd nearly thrown it away as some poor phishing attempt. Who would have left her any kind of bequest—much less a cottage? And she'd never heard of Mrs. Maybury in her life.

But the law firm was reputable so she'd called them, to let them know someone was using their name, and it had turned out to be real. The cottage by the woods on the edge of Horsham was hers, on the condition that she live there for one full year.

It had been a phone call from her mum that made her decide to accept.

"Hello, dear," her mum trilled. "Just calling to check the details of your graduation ceremony. First master's degree in the family!" A squeal had reached down the phone and Helen winced as she pushed the receiver away from her ear. "And how are the job applications going?"

Helen sighed. "Not great, Mum. I've had another two rejections."

"Not even an interview?" her mum asked. "Oh, Helen."

"But I've applied for a post-grad position," Helen said quickly, trying to push away her mother's disappointment. "With a full scholarship! You know I didn't get on too well in my gap year job. Maybe academia is a better fit."

"Maybe, dear. But where are you going to live? Doesn't your lease end in a few weeks? You'd better move home with me and Paul until you get on your feet."

Helen grimaced. The thought of moving back in with her mother and step-father made her stomach twist. She couldn't do it. Not after five years living on her own. Her mother would suffocate her.

"There is another option, mum," she said. "There's a cottage, just outside Horsham—where we lived when you and dad... when I was younger. I can move there for a bit, until I get the post-grad place."

"All right, dear. If you think that's best." And then her mum had segued into the latest gossip from her Women's Institute group.

But that had been the moment when Helen had decided to accept the bequest. Even if the one-year condition was odd, it was still better than moving back home.

A brief meeting with the lawyers a week later and she had the keys, and an address.

The sat-nav got her safely to Horsham, which had grown swollen with new build houses and a massive supermarket since she'd last visited. Even the town-centre was unrecognisable when she drove through—all shiny new shopfronts and new pedestrianised zone.

As she got closer though, the sat-nav failed her, and she spent half an hour driving around half-familiar streets until she finally found the cul-de-sac she'd grown up in and the gate, and the field, and the wood. She parked her car by the curb and climbed out, breathing in the fresh country air.

As unlikely as it seemed, having grown like some sort of urban tumour, Horsham had never spread in this direction. The meadow and the wood were as large and unspoiled as ever, with the cottage nestled under the welcoming arms of the trees and bathed in the orange glow of the setting sun.

With one last glance at the letter, Helen pushed through the gate and made her way slowly up the hill to the cottage door.

The kitchen door was exactly as she remembered: sky-blue paint peeling around the edges and slightly warped so that she had to lift as well as push to open it.

"Hello," she called, feeling foolish, and yet she couldn't imagine the kitchen without the witch in it.

Only silence answered her, and Helen stepped inside.

The kitchen was clean and bright, floor recently mopped and surfaces gleaming. Someone—presumably the witch herself, as the lawyers said they had never visited the cottage—had cleaned every inch and laid out the full inventory on the long wooden kitchen table that took up most of the room. Pots and pans and spoons, a teapot, bundles of herbs—everything that belonged to the kitchen laid out for Helen's inspection and, at one end, two folders with peeling labels and one white envelope.

Helen chewed her lip as her eyes roamed the neat piles. A sturdy pot with a handle to hang it over an open fire caught her eye. A cauldron, she'd called it once. A long wooden spoon rested in the empty pot, waiting for someone to stir its contents.

"Albert?" she called. "Are you there, Albert?"

But there was no reply.

Helen squared her jaw. It seemed she was on her own. Nothing for it, but a nice cup of tea. Then, she could relax and settle in properly.

She dug out the electric kettle and a mug from the pile of crockery, and set the water to boil. A further search found a half-full caddy of tea bags; although there was no milk. She'd need to go into town tomorrow for supplies.

At last, with a cup of tea in hand, Helen sat down to look at the folders and the letter.

The folders were old, cracked ring-binders, handwritten labels curling up at the edges. On one, someone had carefully written 'recipes,' and on the other 'garden.' The letter was addressed to Helen.

She stared at the envelope for a while as it lay on the table.

Helen couldn't quite say how, but something was telling her, some ancient instinct residing in her gut, that once she opened the letter, there would be no going back.

But she couldn't resist it forever. Half-empty mug of tea cooling beside her, Helen reached out and tore open the envelope, tipping the letter out into one hand and unfolding it.

Dearest Helen, it said.

If you are reading this, you have accepted my conditions

and you have come to live in the cottage. I hope you will be as happy here as I was.

Everything you need is here. And if something is missing, you only have to ask. The cottage will provide.

People will come to you for help. They will come with desires and wishes and dreams. But what we do is not about dreams. Learn to see through what they want to what they need. *That is where the magic lies. Not in what we do, but how we see.*

Remember, need not want.

The Witch

P.S. start with the garden. Soil never lies.

Helen sank back into her chair, the letter dropping onto the table before her. *Need, not want.* She had heard those words before, many years ago.

***

Fourteen-year-old Helen sits in the witch's kitchen, a glass of lemonade clasped in her hands, legs swinging under her—not yet tall enough to reach the ground from the high stool on which she perches.

"I don't want to leave," she says, voice nearing a whine. "It's not fair."

The witch smiles at her, but it's a sad smile, not reaching her eyes. "Life's not fair, darling. You know that."

Helen pouts. "But you're a witch! Can't you make my parents fall back in love again, or just forget about getting divorced. They don't have to like each other. I just want us all to stay living here, together."

"No, you don't want that." The witch shakes her head. "You don't know what you're asking for."

"I know that I don't want to move away and live with my mum and her stupid new boyfriend!" Helen slams the base of her lemonade glass on the table.

"I'll miss you too. And so will Albert. But you must go." The witch stands and picks up a cloth to wipe the spilt lemonade from the table.

Helen flushes. It's worse somehow to have the witch clean up after her calmly than it would have been to be rebuked for her display of temper.

"I'm sorry," she says. "I didn't mean to get mad."

The witch just smiles.

"Are you sure you can't make it so we can stay?" Helen pleads.

"I can," the witch admits. "The question is whether I should."

"Of course, you should." Helen frowns. She can't understand why the witch wouldn't use her powers to do what they both want. She doesn't want to move away, not when there's so much still to learn.

The witch hums, a tuneless sound. Her gaze flicks to the corner where Albert stands or sits perhaps—Helen can't tell.

"You're right, my love. As always." The witch nods once, a decisive movement, and turns back to Helen. "There is one key thing you must know, if you wish to be a witch yourself one day. People *will come to you because they want something. You must look through their wants, and discover what it is that they need."*

Helen's brow furrows again as she thinks. "You mean, they're different?"

"Yes, very often, they are."

"But I need to stay here, so I can see you." A tear gathers in Helen's eye. "I don't want to say goodbye."

"I know, my darling, but it is what it must be. I can give you one last gift–the gift of forgetting. You will not miss me, because you will not remember me. Not until it is time." The sad smile is back on the witch's face and tears gather in her eyes, too.

Helen knows that there will be no forgetting for the witch, and that is perhaps the harder fate. She holds still as the witch presses a kiss to her forehead.

"Remember, my darling," the witch whispers in her ear, "need, not want."

And Helen remembers nothing more.

***

The next morning, Helen rose early, feeling restless despite the dreams and memories that had chased themselves through her head all night. The clearest had been of a kitten, grey as smoke, that had washed its paws in a patch of sunlight, its amber eyes locked with Helen's and full of cunning.

But even that faded as she made her way downstairs to the kitchen and put the kettle on. Grateful for her own foresight of putting everything away the night before, and of bringing a loaf of bread with her the previous day, Helen sat at the kitchen table with a cup of tea, a slice of bread, and some bramble jam she had found.

Remembering the witch's letter, she also placed the 'garden' folder on the table and started to flick through it as she ate.

Along with instructions for taking care of the plants already established, Helen found a schedule of activities and harvest times for the vegetable patch and a long bibliography of further reading. She raised her eyebrows at the handwritten note at the bottom of the page that suggested she visit the local library.

"I'm certainly not buying all those," she muttered to herself. "Not with my overdraft."

She flicked back to the timetable and list of daily tasks. "I guess I'd better do my chores before I go into town." She snorted. Less than twenty-four hours and she was already talking to herself.

The sky looked grey through the kitchen window as she washed up, specks of rain on the glass, but by the time she made it outside, the sun was peeking through the clouds.

Helen took the folder with her, matching the growing plants to the diagrams the witch had left her, then settled down to weed between the rows of vegetables that grew in raised beds running from the kitchen window down to the low hedge surrounding the cottage.

On the other side of the path, surrounding the living room with colour, was the flower garden, but she didn't dare touch that yet, not sure what was meant to be there, and what was not. At least with the vegetables, if something was growing in between the rows, it *probably* wasn't meant to be there.

"Definitely need to get those books," she said, wiping sweat from her forehead with the back of one hand.

An odd chirruping noise brought her head around. *What was that?*

It repeated, and Helen followed it on hands and knees into the shade of some tall early rhubarb—well, she thought it was probably rhubarb. Might be leeks. Something tall, anyway.

Something moved and she froze.

"*Prrp?*" A small grey kitten tilted its head as it stared at her, one paw hanging in the air where it had been washing itself and stopped to inspect Helen.

A relieved laugh pulled itself out of her chest. "Hello, little one," she whispered. "You startled me!"

The kitten stood and trotted over to her, rubbing its cheek against hers.

Helen sat back on her heels, picking up the small bundle of grey fluff and cradling it to her chest. The kitten immediately started to purr.

"How did you get in here?" she asked it. "Have you run away from home?"

The kitten had no collar and seemed quite content to stay in her arms.

Helen stood and carried it back into the kitchen. "Let's find you something to drink and somewhere safe to sleep," she said. "I'm afraid there's no food in the house, but I'm going out in a bit. You can stay here with me until your owner comes looking for you."

She settled the drowsing kitten in a box with an old blanket, and set out a saucer of water and some newspaper for it.

The kitten blinked at her and its amber eyes caught the light coming through the kitchen window.

Helen gasped. "I dreamt about you," she murmured. "I'm sure I did." She shook her head. "Never mind, I should get going."

Leaving the sleeping kitten behind, Helen left the cottage and headed down the hill. As she walked, the sun slid behind a cloud and she shivered, grateful for the shelter of her car as the first drops of rain hit the windshield.

Horsham Library was almost exactly as she remembered it. New posters on the wall, and perhaps a new coat of paint somewhere along the way, but otherwise nothing had changed. It even smelt the same—dust and old books, and that institutional smell of cheap floor polish you only got in council buildings and board-ing schools.

She walked up to the front desk, the list of gardening books and the lawyer's letter clutched in one hand, wondering how she was going to register with no proof of address.

The librarian smiled warmly at her. She was an older woman, twinset and pearls and a helmet of immaculately blow-dried hair, but her face was open and friendly. "Hello, dear. How can I help you?"

"Hi," Helen said, chewing one lip. "Er, I want to register to use the library but I only just moved here. I don't have proof of address, but I do have this." She proffered the lawyer's letter.

The librarian took it, scanning the contents with a swift eye. "Ah, you must be Helen," she said, her smile widening further, eyes crinkling at the edges. "I've been expecting you. No need to register, you're already set up. Here's your card." She fished around under the desk and brought out a blue barcoded card with Helen's full name on the front.

"How?" Helen asked, but her question was waved away.

"Mrs. Maybury has told me all about you, and I expect you're here for some books." The librarian's eyes twinkled. "I helped her put the lists together. Which have you brought today?"

"I thought I'd start with the garden," Helen replied, unable to avoid the question, but struggling to follow what was going on.

"Excellent choice. Come with me." The librarian click-clacked her way across the scuffed parquet floor on heeled court shoes. "We'll start you off with just a couple of them." She pulled book after book from the shelves, until Helen had five large hardbacks clutched in her arms.

She followed the librarian back to the desk where they were rapidly scanned and issued.

"There you are, dear. Enjoy! And we'll see you again next week." The librarian offered her another smile and then turned away to greet a different customer.

"Er, yes, next week," Helen muttered, still confused. But as she took the books and turned to go, a thought struck her and she paused.

"Excuse me," she asked when the librarian was free again. "Do you know where I can buy some kitten food?"

"Of course, dear," the librarian replied, and gave her directions to the pet store.

An hour or so later, Helen stumbled up the hill, a big pile of books under one arm, and several bags of groceries, kitten food, toys, and cat litter clutched in her other hand.

"Can I help you with that?"

The voice startled her, and she dropped one of the bags, swearing.

"Sorry." The owner of the voice stepped into view from behind her. "I didn't mean to make you jump. Here, let me." They picked up the dropped items, put them back in the bag, and then deftly liberated Helen of her stack of books.

She sighed with relief. "Thank you. I was going to drop something eventually. This hill seems much bigger on the way back up!"

Her Good Samaritan laughed, throwing his head back.

Helen took the opportunity to get a good look at him. He was about her age. A little taller than her, with thick black hair and dark eyes. Laugh lines formed easily as he chuckled and, when he stopped, she noticed a dimple in his right cheek.

"I'm Jake," he said, falling into step beside her up the hill.

"Helen," she replied.

"I thought as much. Mrs. Maybury told me all about you. Your hair's darker than she remembered though."

Helen lifted her free hand self-consciously to brush her hair out of her face. "She seems to have told everyone about me."

"All good, I promise," Jake said, with another grin.

Helen put her bags down on the kitchen table and waved Jake in to take a seat. "Thank you for the help. Can I get you a cup of tea?"

"That would be lovely." He sat down, putting the books in a neat pile in the centre of the table, and reached out to stroke the kitten, who yawned at him. "Er, I should probably say, I didn't just come to rescue you. I..." He paused and ran a hand through his hair. "Mrs. Maybury used to make up a drink for me, to help my hands. She said she'd leave you the recipe."

"Oh, right." Helen put the teapot down on the table and reached for the red binder. "It'll be in here somewhere." She flicked through the pages until she saw his name at the top. "Helping Hands Healing Hope?" she asked with a laugh.

Jake chuckled. "Yeah. Mrs. Maybury had a bit of a thing for alliteration."

Helen scanned the recipe. "I should have everything I need, I think. It won't take long. Why don't you pour the tea?" She gathered the herbs she needed and a saucepan. The witch had probably made this in a cauldron over the fire, but Helen hadn't lit one this morning. The weather had been too warm for a daytime blaze. A saucepan would have to do.

When the ingredients were simmering, filling the kitchen with a deep herbal scent, she sat down and picked up the tea Jake had poured for her. She took a sip and sighed with pleasure. "Nothing like a good cup of tea."

Jake smiled, but his gaze was fixed on the bubbling pot and his eyes were sad.

"Do..." Helen paused. "Do you mind if I ask what it's for? The recipe didn't say."

"Nah, it's okay. I have this medical condition." Jake looked at his hands, which he clasped and unclasped in his lap. "My body keeps trying to lay down extra bone–like it never got the message to stop when I stopped growing. It takes over my joints. One day, they'll fuse, and I won't be able to move them again."

"Shit," Helen whispered.

"Yeah."

"And this drink reverses that?"

"Sorta. It keeps my hands and wrists clear, so I can use them." Jake offered her a wry grin.

Helen frowned. "If she could do that, couldn't she cure you?"

Jake shrugged. "Perhaps. It's not important though. As long as I can paint, that's all I need."

"You're an artist?"

"Yes, in fact..." Jake picked up the messenger bag he'd dumped on the floor and fished around in it. "I also came to give you a moving in gift. Here." He passed her a small square parcel wrapped in brown paper.

"I don't know what to say." Helen peeled back the Sellotape holding the parcel closed, folded back the paper, and gasped. "It's the kitten! Did you know it was here?"

Jake shook his head. "Not at all. But now I know why I chose that one for you. Every painting has a purpose, we just don't always know what they are."

The egg-timer Helen had set buzzed, jolting her out of her focus on the painting. It was so very lifelike, and a perfect representation of the kitten, and of her dream.

As she took the pan off the hob and strained the liquid, she couldn't stop herself from glancing at the kitten and the painting again and again.

"Here." She handed a glass jar full of the still-warm herbal tincture to Jake. "Careful, it's hot."

Jake offered her another of his smiles. "Thank you. It's been a pleasure to meet you. Perhaps I could come again, for another cup of tea? Just a social visit, next time."

Helen returned his smile with her own. "I'd like that."

After he left, she hung the painting on the wall and sat staring at it, the kitten curled up on her lap. "It must be a coincidence," she muttered, but she didn't quite believe her own words.

***

"There's no such thing as coincidence," the witch says.

Thirteen-year-old Helen is perched on a stool beside her, helping to chop herbs for the witch's latest potion. Or possibly for dinner, Helen isn't quite sure. But the aroma of the herbs rising around her is soothing.

"What do you mean?" she asks.

"How often do you think two things happen that could be said to be linked and we never even notice?" the witch replies, as she lifts a double handful of herbs and dumps them into the cauldron over the fire. As usual, Albert is there, barely visible, stirring away.

Helen's brow furrows. "I don't know. Quite often, I guess."

The witch smiles at her. "Correct. So, if we notice, there must be a reason for it, don't you think? Because there is some important meaning for us which our subconscious minds have noticed.

They prod us to become aware of it as well, helping us see the 'coincidence' and, hopefully, ask more questions."

Helen thinks about it for a few seconds. "Yes... I think I see what you mean."

A rap on the door interrupts her next thought. It creaks open and a dark-haired boy appears, backlit by the sunlight.

"Ah, Jake," the witch greets him. "Right on time." She turns to Helen. "Now then, if you could strain our potion into a jar for young Jake here, I'll pour us all some more lemonade."

Helen rises, shy in front of the stranger, and does as the witch asks. All too soon, she's sat back down next to Jake, both of them staring at their glasses of lemonade rather than looking at each other.

The witch laughs at them as she takes her place at the end of the table. "Now, children, no need to be bashful. You'll be best of friends one day, mark my words."

But it's too much to ask of them, and they don't speak and, before long, the boy had left and it's time for Helen to go home. She won't see him again before her parents' divorce and she has to move away, forever.

***

After a few days together in the cottage, Helen and Sky, as she'd named the kitten, settled into a routine; breakfast for both of them, some gardening, and perhaps a walk in the morning, lunch, and then studying the folders the witch had left and her library books until it was time to light the fire for the evening.

The more time Helen spent in the cottage, the more she realised that it wasn't quite... normal, somehow. The fridge and the lights worked, the boiler fired and there was gas to cook on, but there was no electric meter or gas meter that she could find. There was no septic tank either, or manhole covers for drains. And no utility bills arrived.

Helen had lived in enough student houses to know that bills "To the Occupier" would arrive almost instantly when a gas or electric account was closed. It was odd that none had turned up by now.

She'd tried to call the Council too—to sort out council tax payments and make sure she was on the electoral roll—but the council tax department had never heard of her address. After an hour on hold and being passed from pillar to post, she was cut off and hadn't bothered to call back. If they wanted her to pay, they could figure it out.

The electoral roll team had heard of the cottage and confirmed that she was already registered. More of the witch's future-proofing, Helen assumed.

What was even weirder was the wi-fi. It hadn't been there when she arrived, Helen was sure of it. But, one night, she'd gone to bed wishing she could log on and watch a bit of TV and, the next morning, there had been a router sat on top of the fridge, humming away. She could connect instantly, faster than any broadband she'd had before, but where had it come from?

The weather was odd too. It never rained; not when she wanted to go out. The rain fell, softly and gently, enough to keep the plants happy, but only early morning or late evening when she was indoors.

And it was just around the cottage. She'd popped into town for milk and as she'd walked through the meadow, the sky had got darker and darker until she reached the kissing gate and the pouring rain beyond. Running back to the cottage for an umbrella, Helen had been shocked by the sunshine and almost not taken the umbrella with her after all–thinking it must have been a squall that had blown over. But when she walked back down again, the rain was still there, splattering against the tarmac and bouncing up to soak her legs.

Curled up in her favourite armchair that night, Sky purring on her lap and logs rackling on the fire, Helen found that she didn't mind the oddness of the cottage, even if she thought, perhaps, she should mind. But it was safe and it was hers and it was home. More homely than anywhere she'd lived for a long time.

She smiled and scratched Sky behind the ears and returned her attention to her books. She had never realised that growing her own veggies could be so absorbing. Perhaps she should think about getting some chickens next.

The next morning, Helen was puttering about the garden, looking up the ornamental plants in her folder as she tried to work out what was meant to be there, when the crunch of footsteps on the path alerted her to a visitor. She turned toward the garden gate and her brows raised in surprise as she recognised her mother, puffing up the hill.

"Helen, dearest," her mother called, pausing at the gate to catch her breath. "Some post came for you at home. I thought I'd bring it over and see this cottage you were so excited about."

"Hi, Mum..." Helen tucked her folder under one arm and went to open the gate. "I, er, wasn't expecting you."

Her mother waved away her words. "I was in the area... Now, are you going to show me around?"

With a sigh, Helen shoved the kitchen door open and let her mother precede her inside. She should have known Mum would turn up sooner rather than later, although she was pretty sure she hadn't given her the address.

Helen stepped inside to find her mother inspecting the kitchen cupboards.

"You really should do a proper clean, dear. The inside of some of these drawers are filthy."

Helen sighed again. "Yes, Mum. Do you want tea?"

"Oh, that would be lovely. I'll just use your bathroom first though. Where is it?"

"Top of the stairs, first door on the left." Helen turned to put the kettle on and listened to her mother's footsteps patter overhead. That squeaking floorboard was her room, and that creak was the door to the spare room, and, finally, that was the bathroom door locking.

A few minutes later, she was sat at the table cradling a mug of tea and wishing for something stronger when her mother reappeared.

"Such a cute little cottage," she trilled. "And you said a friend was letting you live here for free?"

"Something like that," Helen muttered. "You said there was a letter for me?"

"Oh, yes." Her mother sat and pulled her massive handbag into her lap. "It looked important, so I thought I'd better bring it over." She extracted a thick A4 envelope from the bag and pushed it across the table. "University of Surrey, it says there. Looks like you got that postgrad place, at last."

Helen ignored her mother and concentrated on opening the envelope. A thick wad of paper and brochures slipped out into her waiting hand, and she scanned the opening lines of the letter.

She'd got in.

A few weeks ago, she would have been thrilled, but now a heavy weight seemed to settle in her stomach, weighing her down. Was this still what she wanted?

No, that was the wrong question. Remember what the witch said–was this what she needed?

"Well?" her mum asked.

Helen cleared her throat, stalling for time to find the words for what she needed to say, but she was interrupted by a rap at the door.

Jake's head appeared in the open doorway. "Hi, I popped back for that cup of tea. Is this a bad time?"

"No, of course not," Helen said, shaking her head. "Come in. This is my mum. Mum, this is Jake."

Her mother simpered. "Hello, young man. Please, call me Pam."

"Pleasure to meet you, Pam," Jake said as he slid into the chair next to Helen and poured himself a cup of tea from the teapot in the middle of the table. His gaze flicked to the papers lying in front of Helen. "What have you got there? Looks exciting."

"Our Helen has got a postgrad place at Surrey," Pam chipped in. "The first master's in the family, and soon the first doctorate. We're so proud."

"That's... that's awesome. Well done, Helen." Jake's words were happy, but his voice didn't match them.

Helen opened her mouth to reply, but her mother talked over her again. "She's always wanted to be an academic. She tried working a real job for a while, but it didn't quite stick." Her mum's laugh was dagger sharp.

"It was what I wanted, yeah," Helen said softly, "but, that was before."

"What was that, dear? Speak up." Pam leaned forward, frowning.

"What do you want now?" Jake asked.

Helen found that his gaze caught hers and she couldn't look away. "I'm not sure, anymore," she said. "But I think it's more important to figure out what I need."

There was a chirrup as Sky leapt onto the table. Helen had to catch the teapot that threatened to slide off with the tablecloth that Sky had dug her claws into.

"What's that?" Pam shrieked.

Helen laughed. "It's just Sky. She doesn't like being ignored." She put the teapot safely back in the middle of the table and picked up the kitten. "Come here and stop causing trouble, little one."

Her mum snorted. "Can't stand cats. Dirty creatures."

Helen looked at her mother. "I'm not going."

"What?"

"I'm not taking up the postgrad offer. I want to stay here, with my *dirty* kitten and my garden. I'm happy here. For the first time in years. So I'm staying."

Pam stuttered and Helen chewed her bottom lip as she waited for her mother's anger to boil over.

"But this is what you wanted. This is important. I mean, I'd rather you'd taken a job in the city like your brother, but no, you're too good for that. At least being an academic is respectable. What are you going to do here, in this tiny grubby cottage with that horrible creature? How are you going to earn a living? You'll never find a decent husband hidden away here either."

Helen waited until her mother finally grew silent, Jake sitting tense beside her. She reached out and squeezed his hand and was reassured by the tiny smile he gave her in return.

"It doesn't matter, Mum," Helen said when silence finally fell. "I'm happy here, and I'll figure things out. It's my life, not yours."

Pam tried to keep arguing, but Helen wouldn't have any of it. Jake stayed quiet by her side, but steadfast in his support, and, at last, Helen was able to get rid of her mum. She closed the door and sank back into her chair with a groan.

"I'm so sorry, Jake. You didn't need to see all of that."

Jake laughed. "No worries. I mean it wasn't the most fun way to spend a morning, but at least I wasn't the target!"

Helen managed a tired grin.

"Up you get," Jake said. "Let's get some fresh air. You head outside and I'll rustle us up some lemonade. You look like you could use the sugar."

"Thank you." Helen levered herself to her feet and padded outside.

Sat in the late afternoon sunshine with Jake, glasses of icy lemonade beside them, a memory rose to hover in Helen's mind. "I met you before," she said.

"Yes, about three days ago," Jake replied, laughing.

"No, before then. Years ago. I only remembered after you left. You look just the same as you did as a kid."

Jake frowned, then a smile spread across his face. "I remember. Your hair has gotten darker."

Helen pulled a lock of it forward to stare at. "I guess you're right." She paused. "The witch was right too. Good thing we got our shyness out of the way when we were younger. I guess we will be seeing a lot more of each other."

Jake turned to face her. "I certainly hope so," he said as he leaned toward her.

Just when Helen thought he was about to kiss her, he jerked back as Sky launched herself from the kitchen windowsill into his lap.

"I think she's feeling left out," Jake said as he caught the kitten and disentangled her claws from his shirt. "I'll see more of you too," he whispered to Sky as he nuzzled her head.

Helen reached out to scratch the kitten behind the ears. "Daft cat," she said, laughing.

The moment had passed, but Helen didn't mind. She had every-thing she needed—sun on her face, a friend beside her, a kitten to love, and meaningful work to be done. But not until tomorrow. Today, everything else could wait.

Fishbone

CL Glanzing

CL Glanzing is multi-national nomad, never really feeling like they are "from" anywhere, or a citizen of any country. They currently live in London, and work in the field of healthcare research. They have a PhD in Health Policy. In their spare time, they lead a LGBTQ+ bookclub, go cycling, and write short stories. This is their first publication.

The dogs had dug up Mammy's bones again last night. A tangled mess of grey angles protruding from the frozen ground. A few missing now. The frost clinging to what remains, unearthed like sallow mushrooms. Perhaps they were Simon's dogs. Hard to say.

Hannah lifts a rib to her cheek. Slick with dog slobber and mud. She rubs the rough notches made by hungry teeth with her thumb. It's difficult to think of herself and Jeremy once squashed beneath this bone together, as small as apples. The idea comforts her a little.

She dusts Mammy's skull with her sleeve. The jaw is absent. As mad as she is at the dogs, it's sometimes nice to see Mammy again. She thinks about boiling them clean and keeping them inside the boxcar. But Jeremy wouldn't like that.

She plucks one of the tiny, narrow bones from a tangled mass of wizened skin and tendons. It could have been a finger. Or a toe. It comes away easy, like grasping a berry from its vine. It's no longer than Hannah's thumb. There is spongy darkness in its center, and a barbed crack running to the base. She puts it in the pocket of her jacket.

She takes out her tin cup from the sack in the shopping cart and presses the lip against the ground, scooping the mealy earth into it. She empties and refills it until she has made a hole a foot deep and wide. She wants to bury the bones deeper this time, but she does not have the strength. Maybe she will place a rock over them. She unwinds the blue rag scarf from her neck, the one she found drowning in Bad Lake, and wraps it gently around the bones, nestling them within its folds. She ties it in a careful knot and tips the bundle into the hole.

Beneath the sky of opalescent scum.

Hannah thinks about the time Mammy brought them all to the top of the Hill to watch the last airplane leave. No one really wanted to see it, but they also did not want to miss it. Some said it was better to have their wanes witness it once than never at all.

She does not remember seeing any of them in the sky when she was wee. But she knew what they did—lift people into the clouds and take them far away. And never come back.

Never again to the poisoned island.

It was a small group. Tight hands holding threadbare jackets closed. Feet stomping against the solidified ground to keep warm. A few toddlers on shoulders, some crying for having to be out in the cold. Jeremy and Hannah flanking Mammy. Simon fussing in her arms.

From the top of the Hill, you could see where the shanties ended and the swamps began. Back when there were more shacks, more discoloured tarps encrusting the pinnacles of latticed sticks. This was their home, the makeshift camp that lasted longer than many of the folks fleeing from the valley. Mammy said their family always came from Highland stock. They had as much right to the clean air on the mountain peak as any.

Hannah watched the long, grey speck launch itself from the ground, the growl of its belly pulsing through the air into her throat. The last time she would ever hear an engine. The smell of petrol. The lights on its wings blinking confidently against the gloaming of winter. Hannah covered her ears with her discoloured mittens. The plane's body grew smaller, a slim bird determined to pierce those leaden clouds. And just like that, it was gone. Silence in its wake.

'Rich cunts,' she heard someone say.

'This is it then,' someone else added.

This is it then.

Hannah pushes her metal shopping cart against the wind. Jeremy replaced the wheels with sled runners. But it still snags in the solidified grooves of mud with every other step. Her joints grind, her neck burdened by the weight of her tired, sagging head. Her shoulder has not sat right in its socket for many weeks now.

She has two buckets for good water. And a few carrier bags in case any of their traps are full.

She needs to gut and skin the beasts where she finds them. Can't let the smell lure the dogs to follow her heels. Meat must always be sealed tight.

She stumbles down the brambled path to Good Lake. The sky is marbled grey—a green hue adumbrating the sun. Skeletal trees obtruding from the mud in a reluctant manner. The pit of water stretching before her, as the ground dips down a steep slope.

No coots on the water. No minnows rippling below.

She leaves the cart and approaches the water with her two little buckets. The water is cloudier than usual. And simultaneously brighter. Pearlescent. Streaked with a luscious hue, like a pungent oil spill.

A moon-shaped mound is rising from the surface.

At first she think it's a dog, but the snout is too long. The leg closest to the surface ends in a small, brown hoof.

A wee deer. Its mouth is open, braying. The flat teeth peeling from black lips. A bloated stomach breaching the water for the flies to find. White flecked shoulders. A pearl of an eye gaping skywards, full of reverence and resignation. Good Lake is not deep enough for it to have stumbled in and drowned.

Her gloved hand clenches the handle of the buckets. *This is it then.*

She blinks. Then the significance glances off her mind. It has to.

The remainder of her routine pulls her along like a marionette on a string. She checks the traps tucked away in the brush that hems the water's edge. The north side is empty, the traps untouched. Her leg-hold snare rests pristine—the twisted barbed wire still looped above the trap door of metal disguised with dead leaves. A hole crowded with sharp skewers of steel beneath, for good measure.

Hope is a strange bedfellow in the North. Hannah hopes for something larger than a cat in her traps, even though she has not seen anything larger than a stoat before today in many seasons. She hopes for rain even though the resplendent clouds rarely bleed. Nonetheless, you set the traps and lay your buckets. You place your tracks and pray the train will inch forward.

She leaves her buckets on the north side of the lake, tucked behind bushes but still under the open sky. Protected from the wind and any thirsty creatures. No sense having more water spoilt by the shedding flesh of the drowned. Or pushing a hollow weight back up the slope.

Never open your mouth to the rain here. Boil it.

Only one rat dangles from Hannah's snare on the south side. Lucky. More seem to be fleeing the valley. But they don't look like they used to. Bloated heads. Malignant bellies. Sweaty, poultry masses. They might not be safe to eat. At least it's meat.

At least it's meat.

She dissects the rodent on a rag in her lap and bags the skinned pieces. She licks the metallic sap off her fingers, even though she knows she's not supposed to.

Hannah looks over the rot of the world. Stagnant water. The claws of dead wood in the shadow of a mountain peak. Yellow brush compacted beneath her cart. And still, the tell-tale signs of human waste. Black bin bags bursting with decay. The upturned shopping trolleys, beside the plastic triangles of sandwich wrappers. The Fisher Price telephone. Its smile drowning in mud. An oddly familiar grin.

I will kill Simon, she thinks. One day, I will slit his throat.

Mammy gave Simon everything. She remembers how weak she became giving him her breast. He sucked her dry.

A few older folk had decided to attempt travelling down the mountains into the valley and skirt around to the coast. The winds were carrying the South's fallout. Its spill of mephitic particles were inching closer every day. The village could feel it in the itch of their skin, the looseness of their teeth and hair. The mountain's altitude would only protect them for so long. It was potentially the last opportunity to see if any fishing villages had any boats left, and if they would be willing to trade for much-needed supplies.

Mammy volunteered, brave as she was. There were only a dozen families left. She left with six others.

The moon shrivelled and then swelled in their absence. Everyone worried. They lit fires every night for them. Only three staggered home. Including Mammy.

One night, she stumbled into their shanty. A dozen neighbouring voices cried out, seeing her coming up the Hill. She shoved apart the rags dividing their home from the extremities, and collapsed on her knees, planting her face to the ground. Hannah peeled back the matted hair from Mammy's face and kissed her cheek over and over again. Until she could believe she was real.

Mammy carried nothing. Her pack was missing. The cart with supplies they had sent with the older folks had vanished.

Her lips were dried and shrivelled. Her skin was mottled, and began to slough. Maceration pasted her flesh to the thin fabric inside her jacket. Her eyes rolled to the sky. She was trembling, murmuring nonsense. She had soiled herself.

Hannah rolled her onto the best cot, and dabbed her forehead and neck with water from the Good Lake. Jeremy ground some squirrel tripe and tried to spoon it into her mouth. Mammy retched and spat it out. Hannah held her tight, and let her hack the bile down the back of her left shoulder.

''S gone,' Mammy said, her voice a thin, taut wire. 'Fisher villages gone. 'S all...'

Hannah could not make out the last words. But Simon could.

She saw the look of recognition pass over his face before he turned to leave their shack.

Hannah saw Mammy's veins pumping beneath translucent, blue skin. Her cheeks sunk, her teeth were grinding them into bloody apertures. Eventually, Mammy thrashed into unconsciousness. Hannah thought, in the morning I will boil water for a bath. She will like that. Seethe the bad bits from her skin. Let the abscesses weep.

Hannah fell asleep beside Mammy, her hand over hers.

In the dawn's light, Hannah awoke to a muffled scream. And Simon sitting on their mother's chest. His hand clamped over her mouth and squeezing her nostrils shut.

Hannah beat his face, his shoulders, his back, with all of her might. But it was too late. Mammy had gurgled, and deflated like crushed moss.

'Ready Nation,' he said, afterwards. 'It's all Ready Nation.'

He took the respirator mask with the good filter before he left. And most of shantytown was burning by morning.

She hears a leaf rolling and scratching the ground. She ducks behind a boulder, her lower spine grating against the rock. That sore spot where the skin is so thin that she rubs it raw in her sleep. Simon and his pack could be scratching around.

Moving in daylight is usually safe. The unspoken covenant. But if they don't already know about the water, they soon will.

She holds her breath and counts to seven. As high as she knows.

Nothing follows. It must have been the wind.

She retrieves her cart from the mud and pushes it back across the dead heather, up the winding mountain path, cutting through bleached grasses. Around the Hill and where she had re-buried Mammy's bones this morning.

She threads her cart between the felled stumps speckling the back of the knoll. And all around her, the colourful waste of decades past catches her eye, against the russet leaves and brush. Cigarette cartons. Crisp bags. The round balls of carefully trussed nappies. The waste that would never leave the mountains even with the strongest winds.

It makes her sad to see. It reminds her of the older folk and the shanty community they used to share. Back when single-use commodities could still be found in their caches.

Before Simon started spouting that shit about destiny. Taking the youths into the woods each night. And when they return, withdrawn and furtive. Secret symbols cut into the backs of their hands. Fires burning late until morning in the woods around Bad Lake.

Most of the town scattered after shantytown burned. Stumbling down the mountain, or trying their luck towards the coast, never to be seen again.

The few that remained began to believe in the Cleansing and the power of Ready Nation that Simon preached. The chosen ones, ready to accept the chemical baptism. Open mouths, devouring a communion of noxious isotopes.

She'd heard it all. Ever since they were teens. 'We're chosen,' Simon would say. 'We're to become new beasts. T' unserving decayin' from our flesh. 'T new implantin' in our marrow.'

She grips tightly and locks her swollen knees against the sliding current of pebbles as large as foxes' skulls.

The mountain path flattens suddenly into a plateau. She turns east into the wind, her face stripped of warmth, the cold peeling moisture from her eyes.

Soon the spooned feet of the cart ring against hard steel. They find the rail tracks emerging from the bowels of the earth. Hannah follows them until the rusted roof comes into sight, snug against the back of an old, deserted freight station. The discoloured walls of the boxcar draining downwards. The lonely metal box.

Hannah whistles twice, and then knocks against the boxcar door. She hears Jeremy release the latch within, letting her slide the door open.

Her eyes take a minute to adjust to the gloom. She sees Jeremy shuffling back to his corner, and the small lantern flickering against the wall.

'Nae more good water,' she says.

She places the carrier bag with the skinned rat gently on top of the stove. They had punctured a small hole in the ceiling of the boxcar and installed a funnel for the smoke to escape. It's hard to get anything to burn here. Flames refuse to lick damp rot.

'Ye hear me?' she asks Jeremy.

'Need more pine for tar,' he mumbles. He covers a phlegmy cough with the sleeve of his coat. The bulbous mass on his jaw shivers with every exhale. He rubs it absent-mindedly.

His response makes Hannah feels despondent. Even though

she knows there is nothing to be done about the water. She still hoped he may care.

'Pine died last year,' Hannah sighs. At least she thinks it has been a year. It's difficult to tell when there are no leaves to discolour and fall. And no spring to warm your memory.

Jeremy frowns. His single, square lens creasing the socket of one eye.

In the dim light, he sits before the inverted boat hull, its metal spine thrusting into the dark air. An emaciated behemoth inhaling its first fruitless breaths.

Her brother, her twin, playing shipwright. Attempting to build something they have only seen in picture books. And bleary childhood memories of seaside holidays. Two hundred miles away from their lonely mountain now.

Jeremy's movements are slow and furtive. She asks him when it will be ready. Not out of impatience, but the last dregs of congeniality. His voice soothes the dark, softens its rough edges.

'Soon,' he says, as always.

The thirst begins before night falls. Jeremy tells her to suck on a stone. An old wives' trick, he says.

She takes Mammy's bone from her pocket and places it in her mouth. It seems more benign than an old stone from the forest. The texture is spongy and porous. She winces as it touches the abscess at the back of her jaw. The weeping hole that used to hold her molars. Not uncommon in the North.

They eat the rat. Roasted. Their soft teeth peeling the meager meat off the tiny bones. No water for broth. Hannah gives herself the slightly larger pieces. She did catch it, after all.

They lock the boxcar doors tight with chains and bolts. Their fingers catch on the rust. Tiny splinters of festering metal. No water to wash.

Hannah huddles in her corner, piling the limp rags and soot-singed blankets over her legs. Her breath rattles with damp. A sharp wind whips against the boxcar walls. It drums the metal box, the vibrations burrowing deep into the ground. She shivers and pulls the holey, mildewed rug up to her chin.

'Boat may be finished in fortnight,' Jeremy says from his corner. He sounds pleased.

Hannah nods slightly, politely. A fortnight without water.

'Push it 'round Good Lake, down t' southern slope.' He lifts his head, his bulbous profile casting a shadow across the oxidized floor. ''Haps we can lay rollin' logs on t' ground. Make a slipway.'

Jeremy has not set foot in Good Lake's direction in at least a decade. He has no conception of the thistles and brambles and thorns. The kind that shred the shins and moisten the ankles with dew and blood.

'At least ten days te t' coast,' she says, flatly.

'So?'

'Mammy dinae make it.'

'Mammy was stupid.'

Mammy could have been queen. Flowers in her hair. Like in the picture books. Hannah sticks her bottom lip out and pulls the blanket over her shoulder. The soft bone still in her mouth.

She closes her eyes, imagines the taste of cow milk. Colder and sweeter than water. She squeezes Mammy's bone in the pocket of her cheek. Sing me a song, she says to it, thinking of it filling her mouth and throat with loving melodies.

A dog howls. A low, throaty bawl. Hungry and ornery. Loud enough to be in the vicinity of the abandoned freight station and refracting between the abandoned boxcars. The hollow, rusted beasts, dying scattered across oxidized tracks.

Hannah blows out the lantern and lies still, holding her breath. She can feel Jeremy sitting a little straighter, their ears straining against the dark.

Footsteps carry against the frozen ground. Then voices. More feet. The panting and growling of dogs.

A knock thuds against the boxcar, three times.

'Come oot,' a voice says. 'Surrender yer blades 'n crawl before t' Prophet.'

When I kill Simon, Hannah thinks, I can free the dogs. I know what he does to the pups.

At least it's meat.

Jeremy looks towards Hannah. He shakes his head twice. She knows he would rather burn in this metal cavern, frightened and silent.

The fist knocks again.

'We've a man on yer roof,' a voice calls. 'If ye no come out, we'll send fire doon yer chimney.' Even with the years maturing his voice, she knows it's Simon. Hannah shudders. The sound lacerating her heart and lungs.

'Jeremy?' she whispers. His head trembles against the gloom. His nose and mouth buried beneath cloth and rag.

Hannah steels herself. Rises. And unbolts the chains. The rust grinds. Jeremy whimpers.

She grunts as she throws open the sliding door.

She comes face to face with a skeletal man, thin and wiry. His eyes puckered into sockets above sharp, porcelain cheekbones. A hairless scalp gleaming in the light of a dozen torches. His features are pinched, exaggerated, Hannah thinks. Not like the rest of our family.

'Hullo, sibling,' Simon smiles.

Hannah raises her fist to his face, wanting to knock his eyeball into the back of his skull. Before she can, a hand thrusts into her neck and pinches her throat with dirty fingernails. A grinning, shirking demon.

He throws her into the dust. Into the center of a luminous halo of torches. Smirking faces. Shrouded bodies, entombed in discoloured, grey wool. Their parents' wool. Anything left behind.

She bites mud. The impact of the ground forces her to swallow Mammy's bone. She whimpers, feeling the ossein slide down her esophagus into her stomach. Lost.

Hannah raises her hand to her head into the dim light. She watches Simon round on her. A rusted crowbar in his hand. He drums the end against the hollow box of metal that was their house. Now it is bare. A half, spoilt cocoon.

It's been so long since she last cried from fear.

'Gies your water,' Simon says, threading the crowbar over his shoulders and resting his forearms atop.

'We no have any,' replies Hannah, spitting into the dirt.

Simon laughs to himself. 'Ye must think am more stupid than I's look.'

'Ah would've thought youse liked a little fallout in your water. Make youse big and strong.'

'Ye will hold yer tongue aboot tings you dinnae understand,' Simon says. He extends his hands, bares his chest to the sky. As if welcoming the night into his lungs. 'The poison in the South tests us. Steels us. Cleanses us. In a hundred years, all that remains will be tempered. But we no have to die tonight on account o' some foul water. We are the chosen few. We must be smarter, stronger.'

A few 'ayes' ring out around the circle of light. She sees the muddy-faced youths. Younger than she. Clinging to the barbs of fiery torches and the collars of wayward mongrels. They bark and snarl her way.

Simon digs his boot into Hannah's ribs, rotating the toe. As if to cement his conviction. She cries.

Jeremy launches himself from the boxcar, into the mud beside Hannah. 'Leave her alone,' he screams, placing his arm over her torso.

A lackey winds him with a stick an inch thick. Casts him into the clay.

Two men armoured with metal plates lashed to their bodies and limbs enter the boxcar. The sound of crates overturning.

Glass spilling onto the floor. A metal hull being kicked, prodded, and winded.

'Big sister n' brother,' Jeremy mutters, rounding on them. 'Ah know youse no fools.'

'Ah only saw Good Lake was bad this morning,' Hannah pleads. 'We was too sick the days before.'

Simon picks the scabs beside his mouth. The ones that thread to the corner of his ears. Peeling away the matter that binds his face together. 'Am tired of these lies,' he says. 'Burn the box.'

His droogs toss their torches into the bowels of the boxcar. It catches on Hannah's bedding, her crates, her straw dollies, sending the insides into a brilliant inferno. Jeremy howls. 'T' boat,' he cries.

Simon kicks Jeremy's back to the ground. 'More'll burn if ye no tell me where ye keep yer water.'

'T' boat,' Jeremy whimpers again quietly to himself, his face pressed into the mud by Simon's boot. His swollen cheeks become slick with tears. She sees the desperation in his eyes, the grief. Witnessing years of work unraveled in an instant.

Hannah swells with a bitter pity. The poor moth scratched from his cocoon. She wants to reach for him, for his hand. Soothe the cries. Rock him. Be the cradle they once shared. But she does not. She resents that he probably cares more about that bloody boat than her.

Simon's foot presses into Jeremy's spine. He lets out a wet groan. Simon looks to Hannah, his lip curdled with satisfaction. Relishing the attention.

She sees the glances between his boys. The furtive looks between them. A queasy, suspicious vibration. The way they lower their blades an inch, then right themselves and grip tightly when Simon speaks. Trembling.

They are young, acne-scarred and swimming in jackets too large for their bodies. A few skeletal girls stand in the ranks too, with greasy hair and an unsteady gait, as if all the marrow from their bones had already been leeched.

'Ah can snap his neck if ah like,' Simon says.

'Stop,' says Hannah. 'Ah'll tell youse where the water's hid.'

'Where?'

'I'll show ye.'

'Am no fallin' fer that trick,' he scolds.

'Youse won't find it otherwise,' she says. 'Ye can kill me after ye've got it. I dun care.' She glances at the trembling bundle on the ground that used to be her twin. The egg that grew beside her, but could not be more different—*would* not be different. In strength or in intestinal fortitude. 'But let Jeremy go first.'

Simon releases his boot. 'Poor wee lamb,' he says, addressing his congregation now. There are snickers in the crowd. 'See, this here's the problem with this older generation. They nae have respect for th' change. They cannae imagine bein' better than they's selves. They'd rather stay t' same and die a big fearty. They've nae stomach fer progress. They no wantin' transformation.' A few voices murmur in agreement. The rest look frightened. Hannah sees one boy, could not be more than ten, wipe his nose on his gathered sleeve.

'Ah'll follow ye te t' lake,' Simon says to Hannah.

'Just yerself n' me,' emphasises Hannah.

'Fine,' says Simon, pulling out his sharpest knife from his belt. 'After youse' he says, indicating the path Southward with his blade.

Hannah rises to her feet and gently points her feet into the grind of the track, like a ballerina. Her favourite book to read with Mammy.

'If am nae back 'fore dawn,' Simon says over his shoulder to his droogs, 'come fer me 'n' level this place te dust.'

The sky looks like oily, black fur. She is rolling beneath it, untethered.

She walks in front of Simon. Her hips aching as they sway. Head bowed. The back of her neck exposed to the cold air.

'Yer better no be takin' me on a wild goose chase,' says Simon, pushing her back with a mighty punch that collapses her knees and sends her to the ground.

She takes the opportunity to reach under the tongue of her boot and extract the sliver of glass she keeps there. A modest triangle of blade. She wraps her fist around it before she rights herself onto the path.

'Keep movin',' he says.

There are no stars. A dim fog of moon illuminating a patch of sky. Somehow making the clouds around it blacker, swamp-like.

She feels her way forward on the path by the weight of her toes, and the rotation of her shadow cast by Simon's torch behind her.

They walk in silence. She has no desire to hear his voice. It would be the sound of a dead man's breath, the beating of an Antler Moth's wings. She wants to stamp it out.

Her throat burns as they get closer to the lake. She can smell the moisture, enlivening the saliva beneath her tongue. Parched, she thinks about the bone in her belly. Maybe it will stay there forever, guiding her. A precious bezoar. She was inside of Mammy, now Mammy is inside of her.

She is the strongest child, then. She knew it all along.

The night is still and weak. They reach the dense shrub that peels apart onto the pebbly path leading to the shore of Good Lake. She squints towards the water, slick and rippleless. The hump of the deer's flank is gone, as if dissolved by the putridity. The rest is rendering into mud.

'There,' she says, pointing towards the low brush. A corner of the metal buckets catches a flush of dim moonlight.

Simon takes a tentative step in front of Hannah. His feet touching lightly on brittle leaves and thistle. He holds his machete in front of his body, tense. She knows he's expecting a trap. She knows he's watching the branches for movement, testing the weight of his blade in the air for the tension of cord strung across the path.

But she knows in the shadow of the brush, he cannot see his feet.

He takes another step forward. There's a loud snap. He stumbles. His weight plummets into the ground. His foot is obscured to the hilt of his knee by dank leaves. Simon cries out with a sharp, deep moan.

'You fecking bitch,' he screams. 'Ah knew youse were up to somemat!'

He swipes his machete at her, but cannot get the desired reach with his leg knotted in the hole. His movement embeds the wooded stakes deeper, tearing muscle and ligament with an indignant cry. Hannah underestimated the lengths a beast would endure once caught in a trap. Still, he loses balance in the process, and strikes the ground with his right elbow.

Hannah watches her brother thrashing in the dead grasses, flaying his own leg. She knows she must boot the fish on the head. Stop the suffering. End the power.

She grips the triangle of glass and lunges it into Simon's face. The tip pierces his eyelid and the jelly beneath. She is surprised how little resistance it offers in one brutal stroke.

Simon howls. He grabs her leg and unbalances her, striking her to the ground. The wind knocks from her lungs. She feels his hands clawing at her legs, her jacket.

Then, a pain. A gruesome, wet pain on the heel of a tense pressure in her abdomen. Despite her flailing arms, they did not successfully protect her stomach. There, protruding, is the neck of the machete. Her layers of wool feel damp and hot at the same time. She clutches her belly, enclosing her hands around the steel that divides her.

The glass is still embedded in his eye. Even in the dark light, she can see the blood weep across his cheek.

With one swift kick, she drives the shank deep within his socket, splintering into an awn of needles.

She hears a mewl. Simon's grasp slackens around the folds of her jacket. Limp pincers, seizing nothing. His weight tips off her lower body onto the ground. His pale face catches the moon.

Colourless, apart from the crater of bloody viscus wrenched from one eye.

Hannah kicks away from Simon's body. Each squirm against the ground pierces her from belly to spine. She grasps the hilt of the machete and pulls. The thing is stubborn. It grates her as she drags it out.

The momentum eases. Perhaps she lost consciousness. But before she knows it, she is looking skywards through the tangle of trees, blade in one hand, the other clamped around the bleeding hole in her abdomen.

The bastard tried to take Mammy's bone from her belly. Because she is chosen. Strongest.

She wonders if Mammy had a real name. She must have. Probably a pretty name. Like a jewel. Or a flower.

She rolls onto her front side, only her hand separating her wet, warm insides from the frozen earth. She crawls. Slowly. Pressing one knee and elbow at a time into the mud and sliding her weight onto them. Then repeating on the other side, creeping, like a lizard.

She can hear the water trickling into the lake. Filling its cavern. A wholeness made impure by the scourge of chemicals and dead animals.

If she can just get to the boat, she thinks. Jeremy must have brought his foolish boat to the lake by now. He must have discovered a trickle of water leading through the unexplored caverns of the mountain, flowing around the munros to the ocean. He's clever that way. She never should have underestimated him.

'Jeremy,' she says. 'Hoist the sails.'

They will sail to deserted islands. Dig for buried pirate treasure. Mammy will guide them, with her colony of mermaids. Singing.

She crawls down the path to Good Lake. It is waiting for her. The drowned deer and rats and feral cats are rising their heads above the water. They nod, their skeletal jaws threaded with duckweed and bulrush.

She can feel the water beginning to lap at her legs. Steady waves, pulsing and pushing. Just like the ocean. Willing her forward, then back again.

The clouds above her part. And down washes the hungry moon.

So distant, she thinks, far above the scorched earth, and the children just trying to make the best from a sad situation. One day we will all sit down to a feast of vegetables grown by our own hands. We will drink and laugh at years gone by, and the good fortune of clean air we breathe.

But not today. Today, Hannah cauterised the foolish chaos made by her little brother prophet. And that is enough.

A light breeze whispers through the dead reeds encircling the lake.

She hopes it will be enough.

External Processors

Sherry Yuan

Sherry Yuan spent the first five years of her life in Suzhou, China and the next 18 in Vancouver, Canada. She currently lives in San Francisco with her fiance and small brown dog, where she writes code by day and fiction by night. She loves reading, art, rock climbing, and trying Trader Joe's cheeses. She has stories published in Infinite Worlds Magazine and Hadrosaur Production's Exchange Students anthology. You can find her at sherryyuan.me.

Nolan, age 12

The last unopened present at Nolan's twelfth birthday was a box wrapped in shiny blue paper that fit in the palm of his hand. He tore open the paper to reveal Omni's iconic blue-gray packaging. In an instant, all the other presents - a few books, a Lego set, a new backpack, an electric skateboard - paled in comparison. His classmates, scattered on the couch and floor pillows in his airy living room, fell silent and leaned in to watch him open the box. Nolan showed its contents around the room. A creamy white External Processor nestled snug in the cardstock interior, eliciting gasps of excitement and envy. Only three other students in their class of 27 had ExPs.

Nolan's mother brought out the ice cream cake next. Soon after the slices had been distributed and eaten, the other parents started exclaiming about their dinner plans or how dark it had gotten. Nolan helped his parents clean up the remaining cake, plastic cups, and paper streamers after the last of the guests trailed out. Then his mom helped him apply the ExP sticker to the nape of his neck.

As soon as the lunch bell rang the next day, Nolan's friends crowded around his desk to check out his ExP.

Floppy-haired Jason asked, "How many hours do you get? Is it on now?"

"I get ten hours. I'm not using it right now - there's a green light when it's running." Nolan opened his Omni app and tapped the "Request session" button to turn it on. He chose 30 minutes, the length of their lunch break.

Teacher's-pet Clarice asked, "What's 435 times 78?"

It took him two seconds for the numbers to race through his head. "33930."

Jason asked, "I have cities, but no houses. I have mountains, but no trees. I have water, but no fish. What am I? "

Nolan went through a list of things that could have cities or mountains. A geography textbook? An architectural model? "A map."

Sandra, who had the cutest braids but rarely deigned to speak to him, asked, "What do potato, dresser, grammar, and banana have in common?"

Nolan thought of their meanings at first. Could it be salad? "Grammar" could be alluding to word salad, but it seemed like too much of a stretch. He searched for patterns in the spelling instead. "Got it! If you take the first letter of the word and move it to the end of the word and then reverse the letter order, they spell the same word."

His best friend Mandy was one of the two other ExP owners, and she sat quietly during his interrogation. He knew, from the way she sat up straight at each question, furrowed her brows a bit, then relaxed them soon after, that she was working out the problems, too.

Mandy asked him, "You're coming over today, right?"

"Yep."

Mandy's father picked them up after school. Once they arrived at Mandy's house, the two friends took a detour to the kitchen to pick up a plate of peanut butter cookies, then headed down to the basement. The L-shaped couch, the plush teal rug, and the wall-mounted TV with its assorted gaming consoles were as familiar to Nolan as any furniture in his own house. He'd sunk into that couch countless times.

On his first day of elementary school, a pigtailed girl came over to introduce herself as Mandy, short for Amanda, and complimented him on the Squirtle pin on his backpack. He invited her over to play the recently-released Pokemon Obsidian after school. The rest was history. Their friendship had survived third grade when boys and girls suddenly grew wary of each other's cooties, and sixth grade when their friends periodically pulled one of them aside to ask in a whisper if they liked the other. By the time they reached middle school, their friends finally understood that their constant questioning wouldn't nudge their relationship from platonic to romantic, and moved on to other potential couples to speculate about.

That afternoon, they played Escape Wonderland, where they started out trapped in two separate rooms in the Queen of Heart's palace then met in the ballroom to escape together. Mandy finished all the puzzles in the library in fifteen minutes and waited for Nolan to unlock the tea room.

Nolan stared helplessly at four teacups. He could feel Mandy's impatient stare boring into him. He was supposed to rearrange them, but he couldn't figure out how. Finally, she said, "Green red yellow orange."

Nolan followed her suggestion and the orange teacup tipped over to reveal a key. He asked, "Wait, why?"

"There's a gyro on the plate, but when have you ever seen gyros at a tea service? So I thought, G, Y, R, O..."

Nolan narrowed his eyes at the faint green light peeking from under her hair. "You have your ExP on! Cheater."

"It's not cheating, you can do it too."

Nolan knew his parents had gotten him the ExP for school, but he figured using one of the ten hours for gaming was acceptable. He requested an hour through the Omni app and immediately noticed new possibilities in the room. The patterns in the lace placemats looked like Morse code. Maybe the cuckoo clock's time was supposed to match the numbers visible in a deck of cards on the table. Could he break the mirror with the butter knife?

Escape Wonderland was a different game when both players had ExPs enabled. With all the possible puzzle solutions now blatantly obvious, it became a matter of ruling them out rather than searching for new ones. They escaped the ballroom in ten minutes.

Nolan said, "Let's do a harder one!" He realized he'd be spending more than one hour a week of the ExP on non-academic activities.

Eva, age 12

Eva rose out of unconsciousness and blinked to reorient herself. She sat up from the floor, glancing out the window to see the sky had already darkened. A look at her phone told her that she'd been out for over an hour. She slipped out of her room and headed to the kitchen, throat dry from the blackout, or maybe from the fear of her dad finding out about it.

He was already home from his deliveries for the day and sat at the kitchen table watching something on his phone, the entire room steeped in the fragrance of garlic and freshly harvested basil. He paused the video when Eva walked in. "Did you have dinner yet?"

"Nah, I was studying."

"Great, I made pesto."

They agreed that one upside of him losing his job as station chef at Sel et Sucre was that he channeled all his love of cooking into meals at home now. Their meager budget forced him to be creative; this past week, he'd made shakshouka and miso ramen. Their conversations skirted a wide berth around the other upside: the long hours of driving around food deliveries incentivized him to stay sober.

Eva's dad doled out two plates of penne and chicken and smothered them in vibrant green sauce. She could tell from his face - the overhead fluorescent lights etching out the same lines as any other day - that he hadn't noticed anything. Thank God.

Growing up, Eva loved hearing her parents unfurling potential futures for her like red carpets. They told her she had the empathy to be a teacher, the grit to be a badass entrepreneur, the math skills to be a scientist.

When her mom left two years ago for a man who didn't regularly polish off a six-pack in a single day, the encouragement tapered off. The responsibility for his daughter reaching her full potential rested solely on his shoulders now, and he quickly realized he wasn't up to the challenge. He came home from his restaurant shifts too late and weary to help with her homework, and despite the long hours, he couldn't afford to send her to music lessons or even buy her the Nike AirZooms she'd been coveting for years. Her track teammates grumbled that the west side schools always won the city-wide meets because they had private coaches and better gear.

Then Sel et Sucre let her dad go because he'd fallen into the habit of showing up to work shaky and smelling of stale beer. The final straw was a burnt chicken cordon bleu during the Friday dinner rush.

After a month of wallowing in guilt and self-pity, he signed up to deliver restaurant meals as a gig worker and, in a small spiral-bound notebook, started tracking the days when he didn't have a single drink. Her dad was clambering out of a dark place. She worried that he'd start backsliding if he found out about the blackouts.

Nolan, age 13

More than half of Nolan's classmates acquired their own ExPs thanks to birthdays and Christmases throughout middle school. When Nolan and Mandy stepped through the heavy double doors of their new high school for the first time, they realized they couldn't survive the next four years without one. The wide hallways teemed with bodies bigger than theirs. Some of the boys had beards, most of the girls wore makeup, and almost all of them had ExPs.

Nolan used all his ExP hours during the first few weeks to pick up unspoken rules. Nod, don't wave, at people in the hallway. Freshmen sat in the back bleachers for sports games. Care Club and Key Club organized nearly identical charity events, but only the Key Club execs hosted ragers. Then assignments and quizzes began piling up and he also needed his ExP for those. He tried writing a history paper without using it once, and ended up with a disappointing C+.

Nolan found it odd that everyone in his school obsessed over their GPAs and college prospects. His friends never spoke of the unsafe sex and hard drugs that seemed the norm in TV high schools, unless he counted the two girls with Adderall prescriptions. Instead, they occasionally snuck wine from their parents' cellars and discussed their ExP strategies.

Students weren't allowed to use ExPs during tests; their teachers patrolled the rows of desks for blinking green lights on their stickers. Nolan found that enabling it for projects and readings was most helpful. He learned to have it off while doing practice tests at home, because he struggled to finish the real tests without the aid of his ExP otherwise. And he used any leftover hours for gaming with Mandy.

Eva, age 13

Eva discovered that she could book study rooms at the library three blocks from her school for two hours at a time, and it had better internet and lighting than her apartment. She started heading there after school and staying until the library dimmed its lights at 5pm to signal its imminent closing time. She also had most of her blackouts there.

The ten study rooms lay in a row at the back of the library, behind the architecture and history shelves. Each was a box slightly smaller than Eva's bedroom, with one window opening onto the street outside and a smaller window in the door for passerby to check if the room was occupied. Usually, no more than half of them were. The other students were usually older. Eva guessed they attended the nearby community college. She'd seen some of them sprawled out over the table too, although she couldn't be sure if they were serving like her or simply exhausted. Either way, it fueled her optimism that no one would bother her when she passed out at the table. And she was right, at least for a year.

Nolan, age 15

At their usual corner table in the cafeteria, Mandy leaned forward over her plastic tray of buffalo cauliflower and fries and announced to Nolan, "I decided to disable my ExP."

Nolan stared at her blankly for a second before asking, "Why?"

"They're inhumane! You know how they work, right?"

"Of course. Everyone knows. Did you just find out?"

"I've known for a while, but I finally looked up one of my ExP sources last night."

"You can do that?"

"Yes, it's super easy. You can contact Omni and ask for the profile of your most recent source. They don't tell you their name, but they give demographic information and their bio." She seemed irritated that Nolan didn't know this, which he found unfair, because nearly all of the chattering students around them had ExP stickers and he doubted any of them had ever asked for a profile either. After all, did it even matter?

He said, "Okay, tell me about your source."

"She's a 23-year-old Cambodian woman. She loves dancing, Taylor Swift, and Starbucks. She wants to open a restaurant with her family, and she's serving ExP to save up for that."

"So ExP is helping her reach her business goals! Isn't that a good thing?"

"Well, she lists her other job as a seamstress at Poipet Garment Company. It's fundamentally fucked up that her only way out of a sweatshop is to give up chunks of her consciousness."

"Well, sure, but I don't see how disabling your ExP changes anything."

"It really doesn't. I just can't live with myself using ExP anymore."

Nolan knew now wasn't the time to bring up the fact that they teamed up for projects whenever possible and her decision would probably be a blow to both of their GPAs. He only wished she'd made the decision after they finished their book report on Persepolis due in two days.

At dinner that day, Nolan asked his parents, "Do you think using ExP is immoral?"

His father set down his forkful of lasagna and said, "Of course not. What makes you ask that?"

"Mandy disabled hers because she found out her server is a Cambodian girl and she feels guilty."

His mother said, "Mandy's a bit of a drama queen. You know I love her, but you can't take everything she says to heart. Serving ExP is probably much better than any other job the girl could get."

"But isn't it messed up that we're basically taking time away from our servers?"

His father said, "Nolan, that's how jobs work, and they have a well-paying one. If they weren't serving ExP, they'd be farming or working in a warehouse all day, or worse. We're giving them more free time than they would have otherwise."

His mother said, "Let's look up our sources together after dinner. It'll be a fun project."

They gathered on the couch around his mother's laptop and looked up her most recent server first, since the laptop was already logged into her account. A 30-year-old man in Shanxi, China whose bio, in a poetic touch, described his two young daughters as the suns his life orbited. His mother searched for the average annual salary there: $15,000 USD.

She rattled off quick calculations. "See, he'd only be getting $7 an hour there, assuming he'd even get an average-paying job. And we're paying $30/hour for our ExP, so let's assume Omni sends $25 of that to the servers. If he just works 20 hours a week, he'd get a $25,000 salary. So he can make twice the average salary while only working part-time. He's probably living large over there."

Nolan's mother's rationality soothed his concerns.

They logged into Nolan's account next. His most recent server was a 42-year-old single mother in Indonesia, where her wages from Omni stretched even further. Nolan liked the idea that his ExP hours let a woman provide for her family halfway across the world.

His father's account showed a 17-year-old boy in St. Louis, Missouri. He shrugged. "Well. It's still better than flipping burgers."

Eva, age 15

Eva knew something was wrong when she woke up after a session in her usual study room and a slender, dark-haired woman, brows furrowed in concern, sat in the other chair. Her name tag read Cindy. Eva recognized her as the librarian she sometimes saw behind the front desk. Cindy asked, "Oh, you're awake. Are you feeling better?"

"Yeah, I'm fine." She felt groggy and a dull ache pulsed at her temples, but mentioning those might complicate things.

"That's good to hear. Your father's on his way to pick you up."

"What? No, tell him he doesn't have to come! I can get home myself. How did you even contact him?"

"Eva, the library closed an hour ago. I was worried about you, and your library account lists him as your guardian."

"Wait, that can't be right. I was only supposed to be out for two hours."

Eva opened the Omni app and saw that the session had lasted nearly four hours. Her heart sank. The time requests were only estimates, and she'd had a session go twenty minutes longer than predicted before, but this had been way off.

Her dad was silent on the drive back, knuckles clenched white around the steering wheel. He dug out a Guinness from the back of their fridge once they got home, his first in months, and took it with him to their couch. He looked at her with an expression she couldn't decipher as he sipped. He was steeling himself to have a serious talk with her and she had no power to scold him about drinking tonight. She obeyed his beckoning wave of the half-empty can to join him on the couch, sitting down gingerly on the side farthest from him.

He said, "Eva. How many hours a week are you serving ExP?"

"Ten." It wasn't entirely a lie; she served 15-20 hours most weeks, but her lightest weeks were a hairline under ten.

"You don't have to do this. I make enough to support both of us."

Well, sure, he paid for their groceries and the roof over their heads. He gave her money for supplies at the start of the school year and a new jacket from Target when the hems of her old one frayed beyond repair. But she didn't tell him about the $20 she'd needed for a school visit to the aquarium last month, the $18 for a book that her friend wanted for her birthday in two days, the $180 for the end-of-year camping trip she desperately wanted to go on with her classmates. And she had another reason for serving she hadn't voiced before, because she was afraid of how people would react. "I want to save up for college."

He took another swig of beer. "Oh Eva, that's something we should discuss together. What would you even study?"

Up until now, she'd wavered between all the dreams her mom had laid out before she left, turning them over and over in her head. Now that someone finally asked her, she realized that one shimmered with possibility more than the rest. "Cognitive computing. When I did Omni's training to be an ExP server, I had to watch a video about how its distributed cognitive network worked. And I thought, why can't we do that without using real brains? Then ExP clients would be so much cheaper, and everyone could have one. It could change the world! The video was only five minutes long, so I did more research on my own. Turns out a couple of universities and tech companies are already making a lot of progress on it. I'd love to be part of it."

Her dad thought for a moment and sighed. "Sounds like a lot of work, but I'll do what I can to support you."

Nolan, age 16

Nolan saw the stack of Omni-branded boxes sitting on Mr. Yeong's desk as soon as he walked into class. Speculative whispers already circulated the room. Many students noticed their resemblance to the ones their External Processor or SmartBand had come in, but it was unlikely that their geography teacher would have a pile of spare ones laying around.

Mr. Yeong was odd, choosing to bike to work every day even if it meant arriving in a yellow slicker that left trails of water droplets on his classroom linoleum on rainy days. Last month, he brought in cricket protein bars for the class to sample. But the students generally liked him, because he treated them like adults who could change the world someday, and Mandy liked him most of all.

Mr. Yeong opened one of the boxes after the starting bell rang and showed them the white disk inside. It looked slightly bigger than Nolan's ExP sticker. "We're going to try something new today. Raise your hand if you know what this is."

A few hands shot up.

"Adam, why don't you tell us."

"It's the thing people use to serve external processing I think? My cousin told me he tried it because he wanted to make some extra money, but disabled it after a few sessions. He said it was spooky."

"That's right. They're officially called External Processor Server Stickers. Our next unit will go over the origins and implications of Omni products over the past few decades, with a focus on external processors, and I thought it would be fun to kick things off by experiencing what it's like to be on the other side.

Completely voluntary, of course; I have five available and Omni has a 10-minute minimum for sessions, so we can spread it out over the next few classes. Please sign up here and I'll come up with a schedule for everyone interested. Any questions?"

Adam raised his hand. "I heard serving ExP might be bad for brain development."

Mr. Yeong nodded. "I've seen those news articles too, but they're all distorting research results to get people riled up. There's been a lot of studies and none of them found any causal links, just correlation. But no pressure to try it if you have any concerns."

He passed around a sign-up sheet and Nolan kept track of how many of his classmates wrote down their names. He was relieved that only about a third of them did and observed that Adam, who had heard about his cousin's experience, passed it on without putting down his name.

The sheet came to him from the left, and without missing a beat he turned right and handed it to Mandy.

She whispered, "Seriously? You don't want to try it?"

"Not really...it doesn't seem safe. Especially since our brains are still developing."

"Omni's last demographics report said 17% of their servers are in the 12 to 20 age range. Those kids are doing it for hours every day. We'd only do it for ten minutes!"

"Fine, but I'd rather try it when we're older and there's more research. Maybe in 5 to 10 years."

Mr. Yeong noticed that the sheet had stopped flowing. He asked, "Everything okay back there?"

"Yep, it's all good." Mandy wrote her name down so hard the pen left grooves and passed the paper to her right.

Mr. Yeong assigned them a reading about the ExP sector in Indonesia to keep them busy while signed-up students filled out an application on Omni's website to become a server. Three of them were instantly approved, Mandy included.

She accepted a session minutes after she finished setting up. She slumped over the reading, her hair spilling over the desk to reveal the server sticker with a tiny LED light blinking green. Mr. Yeong had applied it to the same spot where she'd once had her client sticker. Nolan took note of the time - 2:16. He periodically turned to look at his friend. He was surprised by how long ten minutes felt and that Mandy didn't move a muscle the entire time.

The other two students woke bleary-eyed from their sessions around 2:25. Mandy still hadn't moved by 2:30, and Nolan thought of all the things that could've gone wrong. Wasn't there a man in Cincinnati who'd had an aneurysm while serving ExP last month? He went up to his teacher's desk. "Mr. Yeong? Mandy still hasn't woken up."

Mr. Yeong glanced at the clock. "She started at 2:16, right? It's pretty common for sessions to go a few minutes longer or shorter than the estimate. I wouldn't be concerned unless she's still out by the time class ends."

Nolan returned to his desk, his worry not quite appeased but unhopeful that Mr. Yeong would be of any help. Finally, at 2:37, Mandy raised her head and looked wide-eyed at Nolan. She looked pallid, with pink marks along her cheekbones from the strands of hair and notebook her face had been pressed against.

He felt a sudden urge to run his fingers along the marks. Instead he asked, "How was it?"

She rubbed her knuckles against her left temple before answering. "I didn't feel the time pass at all. I accepted the session, my mind went blank, and...it was over."

"Was it like sleeping?"

"Not really. My head hurt when I first woke up, but it's fading now. And I still feel mentally exhausted. You know, like at the end of a hard math test."

It felt like things were back to normal between them. For a few minutes, at least. Then Mr. Yeong told them to form groups of four to work on a presentation based on the readings from that class, along with their own additional research. They'd have a month to prepare.

Nolan turned to Yvette and Easton, his two other friends in geography.

Yvette looked unusually hesitant. "I want to work with you, but that means Mandy would be in our group too, right?"

Nolan wasn't sure if Yvette meant for Mandy to hear the question, but Mandy did, and she spoke up before he could say anything. "Don't worry, I won't be in your group. I'll find a different one."

Ever since Mandy had disabled her ExP, Nolan's friends had grown increasingly unenthusiastic about working on group projects with her. She usually pulled her weight, but she'd work late into the night on her part on what should be simple assignments. For their last geography presentation, they'd camped out at a Denny's the night before it was due. At 11:30pm, their server came around and told them it was their last call. Only Mandy was still working; the others, not really wanting more caffeine but feeling awkward for staying so long, ordered another round of coffee. Mandy said, "We don't have to stay, I'll finish it up at home and submit it."

Yvette sighed with impatience, "We might as well finish it here." She requested an hour of ExP and added a few paragraphs to Mandy's section, then submitted their paper a few minutes past midnight. They received a B+.

Yvette complained to Nolan after they received their grades. "She missed the connection between overfishing and loss of rainforest diversity because she was too stubborn to use her ExP."

Mandy had a few other friends that she sometimes worked with: Keith, who'd also disabled his ExP - Nolan didn't particularly like him because he reeked of moral superiority and Nolan had caught him staring at Mandy's boobs during PE more than once - and some of the scholarship students who never had ExPs to begin with. She approached a cluster of students in the back corner. When the bell rang, she exited the classroom with three of them, deep in conversation about how they'd divide up the work.

Up until now, Nolan and Mandy still joined forces for any partner projects. But a week later, when their English teacher asked them to analyze The Paper Menagerie either alone or with a partner, Mandy told Nolan she'd prefer working alone. Nolan teamed up with Easton instead.

Eva, age 16

Eva's dad knocked on her bedroom door, then entered before she responded. He sat at the edge of her bed and showed her a job post for a tutoring position on his phone. "Hey, you have good grades. Why don't you try this?"

Eva groaned and looked up from her algebra worksheet. He hadn't outright banned her from working as an ExP server - they needed the money - but he relentlessly nagged her about other job opportunities, as if she hadn't considered and ruled them all out already.

This time, she was prepared. She opened the spreadsheet that she'd been adding to over the past few months as she researched. A paper route: $12 an hour, and infeasible without a car. McDonald's: $12 an hour and surprisingly competitive. Costco: $15 an hour and rarely hired high school students. Tutoring: $20 an hour, but most parents would take one look at her ExP server sticker and rule her out. So far, nothing compared to serving ExP; it paid $18 an hour, she could do it from home, and aside from the occasional headaches it wasn't physically taxing. She chose to dismiss any research about it potentially affecting brain development as correlation, not causation.

Eva said, "I've applied to two tutoring centers already, and they didn't like that I wasn't an ExP client. They were worried about students running into a hard problem that I wouldn't be able to figure out either."

"What about the AMC down the road? You could watch free movies!"

"Dad, stop! Shouldn't you be the one looking for a better job?"

He stood up. "Don't speak to me like that."

"Why can't I? It's not like delivering food pays better than serving ExP."

He teetered on the edge between exploding with anger and admitting defeat, and Eva felt almost disappointed when he decided on the latter. His shoulders slumped and he sat back down. "I applied to serve ExP too, right after your mom left, but I didn't pass the screening."

"Oh. I didn't know."

"I should apply again. I'm in a better place now. You've got a good head on your shoulders and I just hate to see it being used by strangers instead of you."

He pointed to another spreadsheet on her computer, "What's that?"

Eva blushed. "It's nothing."

Her dad reached over and clicked it open.

"Dad!" She shouted, annoyed. Alongside the job-hunting spreadsheet, she'd been filling out one with scholarships. The first spreadsheet made her realize how small and miserable her life would be without a degree and hardened her resolve to study cognitive computing. She hadn't mentioned college again to any-one since the library incident. What chance did she have against all the students with ExP clients? And how embarrassing would it be for her dad and friends to see her plans for something better, only for her to end up at a job from the first spreadsheet anyway?

He scanned the rows, then turned to her. "I love this."

He held his phone out to her to show her a website: ExP Excellence Award. "I've been doing some research, too. Do you want to add this to your sheet?"

Eva read through the page and couldn't believe she hadn't seen it before. It was a fund that partnered with a few colleges, includ-ing Emerson, UCLA, NYU, and Ohio State, all of which had good cog comp programs.

"Oh, Dad, this looks great."

He smiled. "See, your old man isn't entirely useless."

As soon as he closed the door behind him, Eva opened the document where she'd jotted down notes for her college applications, feeling inspired to work on them again. Her motivation fizzled into despair as she stared at the mostly-blank page. The only highlight of her extracurriculars was winning the city-wide 800m run, but she didn't even go to the statewide meetup afterwards; she couldn't afford the hotel stay. And serving ExP meant she'd never had time to volunteer.

Eva decided she'd have to write about her stories of juggling work with school. She opened Omni's ExP portal and scoured her sessions history page for numbers to sprinkle into her essays. Over the past four years, she'd served an average of 16 hours a week.

She spotted a "Request client details" link at the bottom of the page. Had that always been there? Eva clicked it out of curiosity and filled out the form.

A few minutes later, an alert popped up on her ExP portal. Omni sent a single page with basic demographic information and a bio. Her most recent client was a 21-year-old residing in Pennsylvania. He identified as Latino, heterosexual, unmarried. The bio read, "Hi! I'm a Chemistry student at Penn State. In my free time I like running, reading, and bar-hopping. Thanks for helping me learn the basics, like how to make ammonia. I'm positive I wouldn't remember what a cation is without you."

The few times Eva envisioned her clients, they were middle-aged, wrinkles filled with expensive cream and makeup, striding along marble hallways in fitted blazers. Maybe they worked in finance or law. She knew many of them would also get ExPs for their children around her age, but she didn't dwell on the fact too much. She didn't want to grow bitter. But here was a client only a few years older than her living the life she wanted, and she couldn't bring herself to feel anger or disdain for him, only a twinge of envy. She imagined bumping into him as they streamed out of their neuroscience class onto a sunny lawn, then becoming friends over cram sessions and parties. She mused that he'd probably borrowed her neurons and axons for calculus, so maybe if she went to university, deriving functions would come easily to her, the connections for it already built into her brain circuitry.

Nolan, age 20

By the time acceptance letters started trickling into his class-mates' mailboxes, he and Mandy had drifted apart so much that they didn't coordinate where they'd spend their next four years. Nolan went to UCLA. He found out through friends of friends that Mandy had only been accepted into the local community college. That meant she was usually in town when he visited home for Thanksgiving and Christmas, but he never reached out to meet up and neither did she.

His calendar app still reminded him to message her on February 2. Not that he needed the reminder. He typed, "happy birthday!"

She must still have his birthday saved too, because she always messaged him on July 15. Their chat history for the past three years consisted only of bi-annual birthday wishes and thank yous.

Another February 2 came around, and Nolan opened Mandy's profile to message her. Her most recent post linked to her birth-day fundraiser for the ExP Excellence Award, a scholarship help-ing ExP servers continue their education. She'd set the goal at $20,000, enough to send one recipient to one of the scholarship's affiliated colleges. The fundraiser was $300 short. Nolan anonymously donated the missing amount and watched as the green bar filled the rest of the meter in a shower of confetti. It was the least he could do.

Eva, age 20

Eva rose out of unconsciousness, slipped on her shoes, and ran. She'd spent the past three years serving ExP at home and serving ice cream at Sweet Cow. The dozens of scholarship applications she'd sent out only got her radio silence, so she was saving up for college the hard way. $10,000 would cover a year of classes at an in-state school.

She'd gotten close to that number, but there were always setbacks. The $700 brake booster replacement when their car brakes started feeling spongy. The $300 dental surgery for her dad when the Advil no longer worked. The $500 new phone when her old one refused to turn on.

Eva's phone buzzed with an incoming email as she neared the end of the block. She slowed to a walk and tapped it open. She read, "Emerson College is pleased to offer you the ExP Excellence Award in the amount of $20,000.00 for the upcoming winter session. In addition, we will provide an annual subscription to the ExP Standard Plan to help with your studies, which covers 10 ExP hours each week. Your External Processor Client Sticker will be delivered in the next few days."

She stopped walking completely in the middle of the sidewalk, her heart beating as if she were still running. $20,000. That would cover her tuition for her first year, and saved her from needing to juggle classes with serving ExP. The upcoming year suddenly glittered with opportunity. She'd have time to volunteer in a cog comp lab, to join the track club, to embark on internships or exchange programs.

Eva stood there for a few more minutes savoring her new freedom. Then she opened the Omni app and, giddy with disbelief at what she was about to do, switched her profile from ExP server to client.

Fox River

Dana Foley

Dana Foley (she/her) is an avid writer and reader residing on un-ceded Anishinabe Algonquin territory, otherwise known as Ottawa, Canada. She received her English

degree from Carleton University with a concentration in creative writing in 2021. Her short stories and poems have been published in Existere Journal of Arts & Literature, Flo. Literary Magazine, Coven Editions, and others.

Fox is woken at mid-day by soft light filtering through the yellowing leaves of tall maples. She fights the urge to keep her eyes closed and eventually lifts her lids one then the other, peeking her snout out from the low foliage where she's spent the morning. She is almost surprised to find that she's still here— that she woke today the same way she's woken each day of her nine years of life.

As she slowly raises herself from the Earth and parts from her den of leaves, she perks her ears to the stillness of the Forest. The damp earth under foot tells Fox that it is nearing time for the Forest's winter sleep again. The squirrels have taken to their nests and the mice to their hidden burrows. Soon the Forest will have its first coating of frost, and prey will become even scarcer.

She scrapes her glinting claws through the muck until she unearths a wriggling worm. It tastes bitter, but she gobbles it down.

While the Forest nears time for another winter sleep, Fox is aware that a different kind of sleep is slowly stalking her. This one, more final.

She considers what the day has in store. Hours of clawing through gritty Earth, only for the small reward of a few measly grubs. She wonders if she should bother—if she should crawl back under the soft green foliage and wait, with patience, readiness, for that final sleep to come and find her.

In the brush to her right, she hears the sharp snap of a twig. A jolt of fear runs up her spine, freezing her. A figure comes springing out of the trees and in an instant, she is looking down the slender body of a poised arrow.

Lowering her stomach to the ground, she spies at the other end of the bow a pair of steady pale hands, wild eyes that shine like a clear blue lake, and a nest of shaggy yellow hair.

The boy's breathing is rapid and high in his chest. His eyes are narrowed.

Fox lowers her black-tipped ears and bares her teeth, though she knows this will serve little purpose. As she braces herself for the sharp pierce of the arrow, the boy's eyes lose their eagerness. He lowers his bow and Fox's heart begins to pound less relentlessly in her ribcage.

"I'd never get any meat off you anyway," he says. "You're about as plump as the twigs under my feet." He places his arrow back in his quiver and shoulders his bow onto his back.

Every instinct in Fox's body tells her to dart for safety, but she is frozen with surprise. The boy spoke, and she understood him. With her belly still low to the ground, she thinks, *humans don't travel alone. Where are the others?* She moves her eyes from left to right, scanning the forest line.

She is surprised again when his response comes. "I got lost from them— my father and my cousins." He looks at her with curiosity, his eyes reflecting the afternoon sun.

Fox lets her ears slowly lift from her head. *You are alone then, child*. Her words float to the boy's mind as if transported on gentle puffs of air.

He takes a waterskin from his satchel. "Yes. I need to find my way back to my clan by the new moon, about six days from now."

While the boy drinks, Fox lifts herself from the earth and considers what he has told her.

Soon the weather will turn. The Forest will no longer be a hospitable place for ones like you. If you plan to survive the winter sleep, you must find your family. Soon.

The boy runs a dirt-splattered hand through his hair. She senses his anxiety. "Once I make it to the river, it will lead me back to them. Can you show me the way?"

Child, that's four days' journey.

His face crumbles. Fox recognizes this look from the eyes of her prey. It is the look of a robin before teeth rip into quivering breast.

"Please," he begs. "If you show me, I will hunt the whole way and share my game with you."

She takes a few paces back and, in a glance, takes in the boy. His thin animal skin slippers. His body— healthy— but without enough fat to make the bitter winter months bearable. Though Fox senses that he has recently entered the age of puberty, he is still of a slighter build. He will not survive. She knows this.

Another slow roll quakes through her gut and she remembers her hunger. She remembers that she, too, is desperate.

She sighs. *Follow me, child. And catch us something to eat.*

On that first day, they cover a large stretch of ground. Fox scampers at the quickest pace her body can muster, though it is difficult keeping up with the boy. She tells him which direction to walk, and he strides ahead. His body is young. Still agile. She remembers what it used to be like to dart with a sparrow's speed at the helpless throats of rabbits. She watches intently from behind as he shoots his arrows into the dwindling tree leaves and through tall patches of grass.

The first catch, he gives to her. A star-nosed mole. She eats it quickly, hurriedly, but still watches him from the peripheries of her black eyes, making sure his arrow never points in her direction for too long. Once she licks her lips clean, she wishes she'd savoured her meal, as immediately her still-hollow belly complains for more. Next, the boy catches a weasel, which they share. They stop so the boy can build a small fire to roast the meat.

As he sucks the last piece of flesh from a bone, rays of sunlight become slanted and golden through the tree branches. They decide to rest there for the night and continue their journey the next day. They prepare themselves for sleep with darkness settling in around them. Fox, curling her body into a tight ball by the fire, and the boy, wrapping himself in thick layers of soft animal hide.

Do you have a name, child?

He says aloud, "My mother named me Atlas." He sits up to stoke the fire with a small branch.

Firelight flickers against Fox's coat, making it dance in different shades of orange and red. *I do not know this word. What is its meaning?*

He twists the stick in his hands, letting the rough bark scratch against the skin on his right fingers, hardened by hours of practice with his bow, then throws it into the flames. "It's something that humans once used. There are none left— or at least, we don't think any survived after the Last War, when there wasn't much left of anything." He stops to think for a moment, then continues, "It was a type of book that held maps— things that help people get from place to place. They have drawings that can show you where rivers, mountains, and oceans are. It's meant to guide you."

How do humans travel without getting lost, if these things no longer exist?

"I've heard that it's harder now. The older generations, they do a lot of the remembering, and passing on knowledge of the landscapes to the youth. That's what we do now, me and my family. We travel from place to place, and write things down to make the remembering easier. We have given names to rivers and large rocks so that when we see them, we know them again. They plan to move again soon. That's why I have to find my way back to them."

Fox curls her body tighter, circling her tail in front of her nose and letting her eyes grow heavy with sleep. *How interesting that you are named for something that is meant to guide, and yet, I am the one who is leading you home.*

Fox has a fitful sleep. She is not accustomed to resting during the night hours, which are usually the best for catching small prey. Dreams come to her in fragments, piercing through her subconscious like jagged shards of ice. She has to dig. The rain. There is too much of it. The sounds of her desperate cries are drowned out by heavy droplets assaulting the earth. She has to dig. She might not be too late. She submerges her head into the waters that flow from her burrow and comes up hacking leaves and grit. She has to save them.

Her eyes burst open to the bright sunlight, and she finds that her paws still move, though she lies on her side. They claw desperately at the air before her. She stops, panting, and rests her head on the dirt. It always takes her a moment to catch her breath when she wakes from this dream.

Her ears prickle to the rustling of foliage to her right, but it's just Atlas walking back through the trees with a dead rabbit in his fist.

They have walked until the pads on Fox's paws have begun to feel raw, but she is well fed. She cannot remember the last time her stomach has felt this distended with fullness. She feels lethargic, but Atlas keeps her moving along at a steady pace. She no longer feels the desire to scramble into the Forest every time he comes close.

Atlas's feet crunch over twigs and dried leaves as he steps across the Forest floor. "Do you know," he begins, "that I have heard legends of people who could communicate with animals? I mean, speak to them, like I'm doing with you."

Fox steals a glance at him, but gives no response, turning her head back towards their path.

He continues. "It's just, those legends— the people who could talk to animals— they lived thousands of years ago. I always thought that maybe they could be more than legends, but I just thought humans stopped being able to communicate with animals a long time ago."

Fox still does not look at him. *Child, humans never lost the ability to speak with us. You believed you had a higher place in the order. You believed you were different and took what you believed to be true.*

***

Atlas nods, his lips a hard line. "Maybe if my ancestors had been listening more closely, things wouldn't have ended up the way that they are."

Even though we could not communicate, there were signs from us. You watched us crawl from blazing forests with our paws scorched and our children lost. Perhaps if you had stopped waging wars on each other for any amount of time, you could have seen what you were doing to the Earth.

"How do you know that? There hasn't been a war for hundreds of years."

Fox flicks her tail in response. *The Forest passes down knowledge, too.*

***

The sun sets two more times during their journey. Each time Atlas builds a fire, and they drift to sleep listening to the crackling of hot embers. The days have grown noticeably colder since they first set out and the trees look even barer than three days previous. But soon they will find themselves at the river, and Atlas will be able to make his way home.

Even in the morning sun, the day is cool. Fox pads her way across the lichen-covered bedrock as Atlas moves ahead to hunt. Yes, she remembers this place. They will reach the river today if they keep moving swiftly. Fox is feeling better than she has in many seasons, but the journey is wearing on her body. Her hip joints grind and ache. She knows that she is only slowing Atlas's journey. Every time she spots a shady covering of foliage or a hollow notch at the base of a tree, she is tempted to crawl inside and rest.

Atlas steps his way back between two trees and towards Fox, this time empty-handed.

"Critters must still be asleep," he jokes.

He sticks a hand deep into his pocket and then, lifting it to Fox's snout, presents her with a fistful of blackberries. They ooze dark juice onto his palms. She imagines the sweet liquid slipping down the back of her jaw and begins to salivate.

She surprises herself by backing away from his hand.

Atlas kneads his eyebrows together. "Don't you want any?"

She ignores his question. *We are close enough to the river now. All that's left for you to do is follow the bedrock North, and you will reach the river. The journey will take you until nightfall, but you can get there if you hurry.*

Confusion casts a shadow across his face. "We're almost there. We had a deal."

She sighs. *I can't go on any longer. My body is old, while yours is still young. Besides, child, you don't need me anymore. You are nearly there.*

"The way my family raised me, promises must be honoured. That means you still owe me safe passage to the river, and I owe you at least three more meals."

Fox feels her legs are about to buckle. *I can't,* she whines softly.

He kneels before her, shaking the berries onto the ground and wiping his palms on his pants. She watches Atlas curiously as he unbuttons the upper part of his thin deer-skin vest and opens it toward her.

"Crawl in," he says.

Fox notices that his eyes are set in a hard glint, but that his lips are still turned upward in a childish smile. He gives her a slight nod. "Come on."

Gingerly, she climbs onto his knee, careful not to rip his clothing with her claws. Once she is tucked under his chin and Atlas has done a few of his buttons back up, he stands.

They set off, the only sound that passes around them is the creaking of birch trees in the wind.

By the time the sun filters low through the tree branches, they both begin to hear rushing water in the distance. Atlas has quickened his pace, eager to see what lies beyond the last stretch of trees. Finally, the Forest begins to dwindle, and they see blue water that reflects speckles of erratic golden light from the evening sun. He runs, Fox bobbing up and down under his chin.

A shout of joy erupts from his lips at the edge of the bank. Fox takes in the scene before them. The water is rushing high and strong. They can barely hear anything over the sound of the frothy water pounding against the rocks.

Atlas bends over to let Fox climb onto the ground and hurriedly rolls up his pant legs.

Fox looks at him with questioning eyes.

He laughs. "I'm going in to catch us some dinner."

Without another word, he wades into the water through the jagged rocks that line the riverbed. The water is so cold at this time of year it feels like a thousand porcupine quills piercing the skin, but Atlas does not flinch. Fox watches as he pulls an arrow from his quill and suspends it over the water, ready to shoot anything that might swim by.

She feels the sun on her fur and, despite the day's bitterness, feels herself growing warm. A strong breeze whisks off the water and tousles Atlas's hair. She scans her eyes over the deep green pine trees that line the other side of the river. In the distance, she can see peeks of yellow and orange sycamore trees that will soon begin shedding their leaves. She imagines their bare branches dusted with flakes of powdery snow and feels her body grow heavy again.

***

She lowers herself to the ground. She feels strange now that they're here, she realizes — their journey is over. She is free to move on now, but somehow, she can't imagine leaving him here.

But, she thinks to herself, *he doesn't have use for me anymore. He'll want to get to his family as quickly as possible now.*

She imagines slowly backing away from the river and into the Forest. He wouldn't notice. He's too intent on catching their dinner. She watches him from the corner of her eye as she moves from the ground. She turns her back.

Then, a splash. She whips her body around, but when she looks back at the riverbed, Atlas is gone. She moves her head frantically from side to side, trying to spot him, and then she notices a thrashing in the waves. Something is being carried downstream by the current.

Sour dread curdles in the pit of her stomach as she realizes it's Atlas. She runs, fear rippling through her body.

She moves swiftly down the bank of the river, chasing after his bobbing head as it's swallowed by the waves and spit out again. She hears his screams over the sound of the water and yips madly in response, trying to let him know that she's coming.

Fox watches as he is swept to the middle of the river where there is nothing to grasp but sharp rocks made slick with water and algae.

He is pulled beneath the waves again and Fox stops in her tracks when his head disappears. She darts her eyes from left to right, trying to spot him. When he does not resurface, her dread deepens.

Suddenly, his head bursts from the water and he comes up choking and gasping. His deerskin vest has caught on the branch of a partially submerged tree, and he has reared his head above the waves. Fox releases a high-pitch squeal as she runs toward him. Atlas throws his arm over the body of the tree and drags himself towards the riverbank.

***

When he finally pulls himself back to the rocks that line the river, he collapses with half his body still in the water. Instantly, Fox is by his side yipping at him with desperation and clawing at his soaked clothes. He tries to speak but can only hack up more river water. Fox collapses against him, overcome with relief that the water didn't take him.

Fox fights against the heaviness of her own eyes as the weight of the day bears on her frail body. They are both only damp now, due to the warmth of Atlas's fire. The firelight flickers against his dreaming face. In his sleep, his brow has relaxed, and his face has lost some of its hardness. He looks so calm he could just become another piece of the Forest. A creaking branch or a hooting owl.

She breathes in unison with Atlas, who breathes in unison with the rustling of the leaves and the water steadily rushing at the shoreline. And finally, she is one with him, the way she is at one with the Forest. And he could have been her pup or maybe just another mouse she ate, the same way that she could be the wind or a star in the sky or food for the grubs in the ground.

And she realizes that she is sinking, sinking, sinking. Deeper now, into the earth. She wonders if this is what it feels like. That final sleep. She lets her eyes roll back in her head and her breath grows slow before she lets herself slip off the edge of nothingness. But before she passes into the dark, a thought skitters across her mind like a bug on the surface of a lake:

But who will look after the boy?

The harsh light of morning comes, assaulting Fox's still-closed eyes. She blinks as her vision adjusts to the brightness of morning and lies on her side, letting herself wonder for a moment why she is still there—why death had not taken her.

She looks to Atlas. He lies on the cold ground, his furs wrapped tightly over his shoulders. *Ah yes*, she thinks to herself, *there is her reason.*

After she wakes Atlas and they set out for the day, Fox realizes how pale he looks. How sickly. His lips are chapped and white. His eyelids look as if they are pulled down by an invisible weight. But he does not complain.

They walk throughout the day, letting a comfortable silence hang between them. It seems like an eternity before the sun starts to settle low in the sky.

Along the river the terrain is mainly hard bedrock, which is unforgiving against their tired feet. There are few trees to shelter Fox and Atlas from the wind. Atlas fights for warmth under the cover of his thin clothing and Fox watches him with anxious eyes.

We should have stopped to build a fire. You would be feeling warmer now.

Atlas shivers. "Maybe, but I can't risk missing my family. They'll be almost ready to leave now."

And what would happen then— if you missed your family, and they left without you?

Atlas thinks for a moment. "I guess I would be on my own. I think that my family would probably try to leave a trail of some kind. Maybe by marking notches in the trees along the route that they take or leaving their fire pits intact, but who knows how long it would take for me to find them."

They walk in silence for a moment and then Atlas continues. "Besides, I don't want to be alone."

Fox thinks about his words. She understands that staying alive is harder without others around to offer protection.

Another moment of silence passes between them before Atlas ventures, "You must have had a family at one point?"

Fox is amused by his question. *Child, the Forest is full of my family. I've had six litters of kits in my lifetime.*

Atlas tenses as another shiver of cold passes through his body. He speaks partly to keep his mind from his growing fatigue. "Do you ever think about them?"

Fox considers for a moment. *I had a litter that I lost. They drowned. It was raining too hard and my borrow flooded.*

"I'm sorry," offers Atlas.

Fox takes a moment to respond. *Life is unforgiving. Sometimes death is a release.*

Usually, any memory of her drowned pups makes her chest feel hollow. But now, sharing their tragedy with Atlas, she doesn't feel as she usually does. It feels nice, she thinks, to tell him.

She looks to Atlas again, ready to ask about his family, but stops when she sees his face. His skin is ashen, his shoulders slumped.

"I'm sorry," he mutters again, and collapses to his knees. His eyes close.

Fox paws at him as he curls himself against the base of a tree. *Why have you stopped? It's nearly sundown.*

Atlas lifts his eyelids only for them to flutter shut again. "I just need to rest for a minute. Just—just give me a minute."

His body convulses as it is attacked by chills. Fox watches in horror as his face becomes the colour of birch bark. She knows he will not stand again. He is too weak.

Fox paces back and forth in front of Atlas as he lays shivering on the hard ground. *No. Not now*, she thinks. They are so close.

She fixes her eyes on Atlas's face. *Stay here*, she orders, though she doubts he hears her.

She takes off in a dash along the riverbank. She knows that if she follows the river, she will eventually reach Atlas's clan. Or at least, she hopes.

She is not sure how long she runs. A few minutes? An hour? But eventually she begins to smell thick, sweet smoke. She careens herself in the direction of the scent.

After another few minutes, her body starts to feel weary. Her muscles and joints ache, but she wills herself to move ahead as quickly as she can. Eventually, she comes to a clearing in the trees.

Her eyes flash over a few tents and a large fire in the middle of the clearing. She tilts her head to the sky and sees that it is a light indigo. It's nearly night. Several people mill around the grounds, their bodies casting long shadows across the ground as they move in the firelight. Anxiety floods Fox's body as she realizes that she doesn't have a plan. She is here, among Atlas's family, but now what?

From the corner of her eye, she spies a tall, light-haired man sitting on a tree stump. He thumbs through a thick book of birch bark pages drawn with intricate markings. Fox narrows her vision on the man's hands. She lets her body tense, readying herself.

In an instant, she darts through the clearing. She is so silent that no one notices her as she bolts towards the man. With a snarl, she snatches the large book from his hands and carries it off between her jaws, racing back towards the entrance of the clearing. It takes a few seconds for the man's shock to wear off. He blinks, dumbfounded, but Fox is already darting back through the forest.

She hears the man call out from somewhere behind her, "That Fox has the maps! Hurry! Get it!"

Fox wills her body to move quickly. She feels a sense of triumph as she hears a group of people enter the Forest in her pursuit. She races ahead, knowing that she will lead them directly to where Atlas lies.

That night, Fox lies curled under Atlas's blanket, resting at his side. He is warm now, in fresh, dry clothes and with a belly full of food. Her anxiety has dissipated, and she now feels a resounding sense of calm. They survived. Atlas is safe.

Atlas had been carried back to the camp on the back of his father, whose eyes had filled with tears of relief when he saw his son resting against the base of the tree. Fox had sat panting heavily at his side, the book of maps at her feet.

Once home, Atlas was wrapped in warm blankets and placed inside one of the large white tents. After he had drank some pine needle tea and eaten some venison, he had turned to Fox.

"Thank you," he said.

Atlas told Fox that he would care for her now. That she would never again worry about food or shelter. She would live with him and be given everything she could possibly need to live a comfortable and easy life.

She had not responded, though she did consider his offer. Could she see herself living among humans for the rest of her days? Could she give up her life in the Forest for a life of comfort?

She had let him run his hand along her fur. The feeling was pleasant. She closed her eyes and enjoyed the complete sense of safety that enveloped her like a soft cocoon. Atlas fell asleep again, and she lay watching him.

Now, with the entire clan asleep and the fires doused, Fox can see the star-lit sky through the slightly open flap of the tent.

Without a sound, she rises and departs from the warmth of the tent, moving slowly so that Atlas will not wake. She finds herself at the edge of the clearing once again, where the flattened grass meets the edge of the woods.

Trees twist to meet each other, the gaps creating dark crevices that call out to Fox. A few feet from the entrance of the forest, she finds a hollowed notch at the base of the tree. The opening gapes at her like a yawning mouth, and as she moves inside, she once again feels herself overcome with fatigue.

She tucks herself into the notch and curls into a tight ball. Only her wet eyes are exposed to the world outside. She blinks as the Forest grows darker, and lets her eyes shut. Once again, a feeling of calm washes over her. It feels as though the ground beneath her has opened, and she lets herself melt into it. She is sinking, deeper and deeper into the earth.

The last thing she pictures is Atlas's face before passing into the dark.

~10 springs later~

Atlas wades through the tall grass that lines the bank of the river. His family is close behind, their voices just audible over the sound of the water. His clan has already begun to pitch tents in the soft grassy land just past the bedrock that lines the riverbanks.

He reaches out his hand to a small girl as she clumsily moves her chubby legs over the river rocks. He lifts his daughter to his hip, and they turn to face the water. It has been a dry spring and the water is running low this year. The gentle babbling of the water sounds to Atlas like an old friend whispering a heartfelt greeting.

His daughter plays with his beard, her eyes mirroring the shining water as they catch reflected speckles of light. It has been years since he has returned to this place where he once nearly lost his life.

Atlas bounces his daughter on his hip. "Do you know where we are?" he asks her, a smile creeping to the corner of his lips.

She smiles and hides her face in his neck.

Atlas continues, looking out at the clear water. "We call it Fox River," he tells her.

He holds his daughter close as the wind picks up. A patch of grass on the other side of the river is blown back in the breeze, and just out of sight, a young Fox pads her way across the banks of the river.

Atlas and his daughter don't see her, but she knows they are there. She moves without a sound through the grass and then stops, one paw lifted, to listen to the voices drifting to her from the other side of the river. With the flick of her tail, she scampers through the grass and disappears into the trees, her body light and agile as a sparrow.

The Witch and the Water

Ashley Libey

Ashley Libey received her Bachelor's in English Literature from Western Washington University in 2011. She resides in the Pacific Northwest and can usually be found baking cookies or crocheting yet another blanket.

Bee sat and waited. The ocean slowly crept away, revealing large swathes of brilliantly green seaweed and clusters of black and white shellfish. The sun rose a little higher and the twins smells of rotting fish and ocean brine grew stronger. When the water was almost all the way out, Bee began to look around. Low tide was what the sea witch liked best.

Earlier, when Bee had first arrived, there had been a man walking his dog and talking animatedly on the phone, but the two of them had since disappeared and Bee was entirely alone. She shifted on the log of driftwood she'd chosen as her waiting spot, her feet dangling toward the rocky beach, and wished she'd picked a spot closer to the tree line. Here, on the beach, with her back exposed, she felt vulnerable and unprepared. For all she knew the sea witch may come up behind her and whisper in her ear before Bee ever suspected she was near.

Overhead a gull cried and Bee tracked its progress across the gray-blue sky. When she looked down again the sea witch had appeared.

She was about fifty feet away and came along like a spider, a walking stick in each hand that she used to test the ground in front of her before stepping delicately forward. Bee was unsure, as she was the last time she saw the sea witch, if it was a ruse or not. The sea witch was a small, bent-backed old woman, bundled up despite the bright spring sun, and there was something about the way she carried herself that made Bee wonder if her speed, or lack thereof, was really all an act. Bee sat on her log, heart thumping a bit harder with each step that brought the sea witch closer. Bee twirled her wedding band. Around and around and around she twirled it.

The sea witch crept closer and closer, head down the entire way. She didn't acknowledge Bee until she was right beside her.

"You've come back," the sea witch murmured, gaze fixed on the ground as though she were searching for shells.

Bee shivered. "Yes." She steeled herself for what she was about to say. "It didn't work. The spell you gave me. It didn't do anything." Her voice gave way at the end to a hoarse whisper.

The sea witch kept walking, head down, and Bee was forced to leave her log and walk beside her if she wanted an answer. "Curious," the sea witch said. "Well, we can always try again."

Bee faltered for a moment and lost her balance on the rocky shore. She was surprised by the sea witch's answer. She had expected to be admonished, scolded, told she'd done it wrong and to leave at once and never return to this beach again.

"I would like that," Bee said. "To try again."

The sea witch smiled at the rocks under her feet. "I'm sure you would. I will need another payment of course."

"I..." Bee trailed off, then started again before she completely lost her nerve. "I'm not sure how much I could pay you this time." Her stomach lurched. Surely the sea witch would turn her into some sort of slug just for saying it. "You see, he, my husband, he would notice if that much money went missing all at once. Last time I saved up slowly for it, but this time, this time I think I could only pay you half as much as last time." The sea witch frowned and Bee hurried to continue. "At least at first. I could pay you in installments." When the witch didn't say anything Bee added, "With interest."

"I'm not concerned with being paid interest, girl." The sea witch stopped walking and Bee stumbled to a halt next to her, one foot slipping on the rocks. "You don't seem wholly committed to this endeavor."

Bee nodded furiously. "I am. I promise you I am. I need my husband to love me." She could feel the tears welling up in her eyes. "He cares for me, respects me, but he doesn't really love me. Not like he used to."

"Is that so bad? Many women have men who don't respect them sharing their bed for all of eternity. So your husband doesn't love you. At least he's tolerable." The sea witch shrugged. "Many women would gladly trade places with you."

Bee nodded, not sure how to say what she was feeling, like there was a hole in her chest. She stared at the sea witch's feet. They were gnarled, lumpy things encased in ancient leather sandals. There were barnacles on her ankles. Her toenails looked like oyster shells.

"I feel like half a person," Bee whispered. She hated the feeling, hated this deep seated knowing in her that there was something missing. That she was living half a life.

"Speak up if you're going to speak," the sea witch said.

"I said, I feel like half a person," Bee forced herself to stand up straight and lift her head, forced herself to look at the sea witch's face. To her surprise, the sea witch was looking back at her and nodding. Her eyes were rheumy and small, her skin gray. She reminded Bee of a porpoise she'd seen once, washed up on the beach.

"I suspected as much the first time you came to me. If you insist, we'll try the spell again. A little differently this time of course."

"What will I owe you?" Bee's heart stuttered as she spoke. She had no more money to give the sea witch—what little she'd been able to save the last time had been done over months and months, back when she'd first gotten the idea that she'd feel more content and settled if only her husband loved her.

The sea witch waved away her questions, her walking stick floating through the air like a detached limb. "We'll come to that later. It will be something you can afford to part with, I guarantee you. For now, go home, and come back when the moon has risen."

Bee nodded and turned away. She picked her way over the rocky shore toward the trees. When she had reached the spot where the rocks gave way to coarse sand and grass she looked back. The sea witch was gone.

***

All day Bee fretted and chewed her nails. She burned the rice. Started the washing machine with no clothes in it. The bare white walls of the house felt closer than normal, more claustrophobic. In the afternoon, when her husband came to her and wrapped his arms around her waist, then moved his hands gently under her shirt, he commented that she seemed distracted.

"I'm fine." It was out of Bee's mouth before she had half a chance to think about whether it was true.

Her husband stepped back and studied her face. She looked away, toward the corner where a dust bunny was building up.

"Alright," he said. He kissed her on the cheek and went out to the garage.

As night came on, Bee grew more and more restless. Dusk had only just begun to gather when she let herself out of the house, telling her husband she was going for a short walk. He nodded and went back to reading his book.

***

As Bee approached the beach, the worries she'd been trying to hold back all day finally broke through her mental levy. What payment would the sea witch take? She had brought a little money with her, but she knew it wouldn't be enough. The sea witch would surely ask her for something else, something that would be hard to part with. Nothing so fairy-tale as her firstborn child or anything like that, but maybe her favorite rabbit, or the bracelet her grandmother had given her. Bee feared that somehow the sea witch would know what she loved most and take it from her.

Bee reached the beach and took a deep breath of the dusky air. It smelled, as always, of fish and salt and dreams. The water was a deep indigo and the sky had lost all its gold, the sun having set completely as Bee approached. She turned and walked up the beach, letting the sound of the waves drive away her thoughts and doubts. Whatever the sea witch took she took. There was nothing Bee could do about it now.

Upon reaching the edge of a tidepool, Bee paused. She realized she didn't actually know where the sea witch lived. The two times she'd met her the sea witch had seemed to appear from nowhere. Both times Bee had been alone with the waves and the birds, turned to look at something that had caught her eye, and suddenly the sea witch had been there, standing in a spot that had only moments ago been empty.

This time, Bee decided, she would purposely not look for the sea witch. Maybe that was just how it worked and she'd show up faster that way. So Bee found a good spot along the tree line and settled herself on a stump, her heart thrumming in her chest, eyes firmly fixed on the first evening star. The swallows dived through the air and the sky purpled. The waves crashed rhythmically, gently wearing away Bee's anxiety.

"That one there isn't a star, you know."

Bee jumped and turned. The sea witch was right beside her, her hair stringy and crusted with sand.

"What do you mean that one isn't a star?" Bee asked. She turned her gaze back toward the night sky so that she wouldn't have to acknowledge the fact that the sea witch's footsteps only stretched about twenty feet behind her and then abruptly stopped. Perhaps a rogue wave had washed them away. Perhaps she had come out of the ocean itself.

The witch turned her head as best she could and looked up, her neck and shoulders permanently stooped with old age. "It's Venus."

"Venus," Bee murmured, not understanding. Why was the sea witch telling her this? What did it matter if what she was looking at wasn't a star?

"The planet Venus, named for the goddess of love. Funny that you should be so fixated on it given what we're here to meet about."

"I see." Bee cleared her throat and looked around. She didn't know how to begin the transaction.

"I made this for you." The sea witch held out a small amulet—a black stone wrapped in corroded copper wire. It dangled from a piece of looped twine. "Take this home and slip it over your neck while you sleep. It should do the trick."

Bee took it gingerly in her hand; it was cold, much colder than she expected it to be. It felt like the ocean in January. It was different than the first spell the sea witch had made—that one had been a tea of sea grass, crushed starfish, and squid ink. She'd had to heat it on the stove after her husband had fallen deeply asleep and drink it all down in one gulp. It had been foul, but for some reason, after Bee drank it, she had wanted more.

"What do I owe you for this?" Bee asked, worry over the answer sitting like indigestion in her stomach.

The sea witch looked away and then back from the corner of one eye. "Your hair."

Bee's hand tightened until it was a fist and the wire around the stone bit into her palm. "My hair?" Her hair, long and thick and the kind of brown that turned red in the sun, was her favorite feature.

"Yes. Your hair. You will let me cut it off."

"All of it?" Bee asked. "Or just a piece?"

"All of it. To here." The sea witch made a slicing motion next to her neck.

Bee reached up and unconsciously stroked her hair. She'd braided it back that day, as she did most days, to keep it out of her face. Most people would probably assume she didn't care much about her hair given how seldom she styled it. She'd worn it long ever since she'd been old enough to decide for herself what to do with it and she'd always delighted in the silky feeling of it running down her back like water.

"Why do you want my hair?" Bee asked. "Are you going to put a spell on me?"

The sea witch chuckled. "Do you think my help comes without a price? I want your hair. If you don't want to give it to me that's your choice, but I'll be taking that amulet back." She held out her hand.

Bee tightened her grip on the amulet and held it to her chest. If there was a chance that this could help her, make her husband love her, make her feel like her house was a home, then she wasn't going to give it back.

"As I thought. Come here. Sit down." The sea witch gestured to a large rock situated near a piece of driftwood. It was the root end of a tree and its gnarled, long dead roots reached out like tentacles. Bee sat on the rock, her head lowered, and stared at the stones near her feet.

Quickly and without speaking, the sea witch reached out and grabbed Bee's braid. Then with the other, she produced a pair of scissors, from where Bee had no idea, and in five strokes Bee's braid came loose in the witch's hand.

As soon as her hair was free Bee felt lighter, almost weightless, the way she did when she floated in the ocean. She reached up to feel her bare neck. The ends of her hair were jagged and uneven, one side longer than the other. She looked up at the sea witch and found she couldn't see her face for she was silhouetted by the unforgivingly bright moon.

"How do you feel?" the sea witch asked her.

"I'm not sure," Bee replied. "I thought that would be..." she trailed off, not sure how to phrase what she was thinking.

"More traumatic?"

"I suppose so. I think," Bee paused. "Maybe it just hasn't hit me yet."

The sea witch shrugged. "Or perhaps it never mattered as much as you thought it did."

"It's uneven," Bee said, feeling the ends of her hair once more.

"That it is."

Bee sat in silence, the roots of the dead tree reaching around her, toward the ocean. "I suppose I should go home," she said.

"If you'd like."

Bee rose and slipped the amulet over her head. She reached up to brush her hair out of the way, to get the twine to settle on her neck, but faltered. She had done so out of habit, but the string was already resting against her neck; there was no hair to get out of the way.

***

That night, as she lay beside her husband, trying to sleep, Bee thought of all the good memories they'd shared, how he'd always been kind to her. She felt selfish and ungrateful that she couldn't be happy. She lay beside him, listening to him breathe, listening to the sound of the waves hit the shore, and waited for morning to come. The light of the moon crept across the ceiling. When she finally fell asleep, she dreamed of the ocean and all that lived in its dark depths.

***

The next morning Bee woke to find her husband already up and out of bed. She glanced around their small house, then peeked outside. He was in the garden pulling weeds. She went outside to say good morning, hope blooming through her chest. She felt happy, lighter. Hopeful. Bee brushed a short wisp of hair out of her face and gave him a hug.

"Your hair is shorter," he said, giving it a playful tug. "It looks nice." He smiled at her and his eyes crinkled in the way they did when he talked about a book he liked.

He kissed her, and Bee could feel a sourness begin to swirl in her stomach. It hadn't worked. It was a kiss from an old friend, not a lover. Bee thought of all the money she'd secretly saved, of the hair she'd spent years growing and caring for—all of it gone. The sea witch didn't fulfill her promise. She was a con artist and a cheat, nothing more.

"Feeling alright?" he asked her, concern in his eyes.

Bee nodded. "Yes, I'm fine. Just feeling a little nauseous is all. I think I'll go for a walk."

Bee walked down to the beach and sat near the spot she had occupied last night, when the sea witch had given her the amulet. She couldn't bring herself to go to the exact same spot—the roots of the dead tree looked too much like tentacles reaching out to grab her.

She sat. And she waited.

The sun rose to its highest point in the sky and then began to slide down toward the ocean, slow and liquid. Bee was unaware of the world around her. Barely heard the gulls laughing at her or the waves breaking on the shore. For once she didn't notice the sizzle of the water as it curled along the sand.

The sun sank lower. The crests of the waves turned magenta. Bee watched a crab walk along and slip into a tide pool.

"Back again," came a voice near Bee's ear. She knew without turning to look that it was the sea witch—she could smell her.

The sea witch smelled like a concentration of the ocean. Like fish and salt and shark blood, like seaweed that had been baked in the sun and that quality that only the ocean has—like discontent and possibility mixed together.

"It didn't work," Bee said. She hated the way she sounded—petulant and spoiled, like she hadn't gotten a toy she wanted.

"Perhaps you have asked for the wrong thing." The sea witch sounded nonchalant. She picked a lump of something white out of her teeth.

"But," Bee protested. "But it can't possibly be the wrong thing. If my husband loves me I'll feel content. I won't have this horrible feeling like, like..."

"Like you don't have a home? Like you don't belong?"

Bee glared at the sea witch. How did she know? How did she know what was in Bee's heart? Things so thoroughly locked away that Bee only let herself know them when the moon was full and shining down on a calm ocean?

"All this worry over whether or not your husband loves you, but have you ever stopped to wonder if you love him?"

Bee opened her mouth to object but then closed it. She thought back to what the sea witch had asked her the first time Bee approached her and asked for her help. Bee had told her that she wanted her husband to love her, that she wanted it more than anything in the world.

The sea witch had cocked her head ever so slightly to one side, like a gull watching a crab, and asked, "And is that really what your heart desires?" She had doubted Bee's answer even then.

Bee had swallowed and nodded and said that yes, of course that was what her heart truly desired. The sea witch had frowned and shrugged, seemingly a bit disappointed in Bee's answer and told her what it would cost.

Now Bee sat on the shore, feeling like a fool. She had asked for the wrong thing. Because all the time Bee had spent thinking her life would feel right, that she'd feel less adrift if only her husband loved her, she'd never stopped to examine why she felt that way or whether she even loved him. If she was honest with herself, she didn't love him, probably never had. They'd built a life together—a quiet, gentle life by the ocean, but it had left her feeling lonely and unmoored because it wasn't the life she really wanted. There was a different life she craved, there was something else she truly loved. More than him. More than even herself. Bee watched a wave crest, admired the way the water bowed in on itself, curled around toward the sand below and then crashed along the shore.

"Now tell me, little Bee," the sea witch said. "What is it you desire?"

Bee looked up from her seated position at the sea witch hovering over her. Even with Bee sitting and the witch standing, they were almost nose to nose, so stooped was the sea witch. Bee took a shaky breath and pointed toward the ocean. There. There was where she belonged.

"Then let it be done." The sea witch ran her hand along Bee's forehead. It was rough and dry and warm, like sand in summertime.

Bee started to say that she needed a little more time, needed to go hug her husband and tell him what a good man he was, how she needed to clean up the dishes she'd left in the kitchen, but she didn't seem to have the breath to say anything. She tried to draw in air, but struggled. She put her hands on her chest and throat and realized her arms were darkening—that they were turning a sort of purplish-red color. Her fingers seemed to be melding together. A burning, ripping feeling started near the base of her neck and traveled down her spine. She looked up at the sea witch, eyes wide, beseeching.

The sea witch towered over her, looking down.

"You know what has to be done," the sea witch told her. She gestured toward the water.

Bee crawled toward the ocean, sand and grit sticking to her arms and legs that were beginning to look more and more like tentacles—raised circular welts rand up and down the length of them. She felt woozy and was having a hard time holding her head up. It felt as though her bones were melting. She could no longer breathe at all. Stars blossomed in her vision and the edges of everything began to grow dark. She was about halfway to the water when she was certain she was going to die. She let her body fall into the sand.

Beside her, the sea witch spoke sharply. "Get up, girl. I won't help you. You have to do it yourself."

And so Bee gave one final push, propelled herself forward, her limbs burning, her chest feeling like it was about to implode and splashed into the ocean. She braced herself for the knife-sharp pain of the cold water but it didn't come.

A wave rolled over her, oxygen rushed into her lungs, and the stars disappeared from her vision. On instinct, Bee moved further into the water, away from the shore. She took another breath and felt the water curl around her. It stroked her face and belly, caressed her new limbs. The water was deliciously cool and revitalizing. It held her closer than any lover ever had.

Bee looked around, amazed by her new senses. She could see farther through the water than she'd ever been able to before—could see shafts of light piercing through the surface, tiny specks of krill, and far off in the distance, the shadow of a whale. She could hear the chitterings and murmurings of dolphins and the gentle scratching of eels burrowing through sand. She caught the faint metallic tang of blood and the mustiness of seaweed. Bee was immersed in a strange new world, but felt a sense of returning home after a long time away.

She cast one look behind her, toward the shore, toward the shadow of the sea witch where she was still standing on the beach, then turned and headed out for open water.

85 Days in Flight

Madeehah Reza

Madeehah is a pharmacist and freelance writer from London, UK. She has written and published several short stories in print and online is currently finishing her MA in Creative Writing. You can find more of her work through Twitter: @madeehahwrites

Day 13

Dear Grandad,

Mum told me to write it all down on paper, the old fashioned way. She said when you write with a pen the ink slows your thoughts down, like you're floating in the ocean on the way to an island and you don't mind taking the long way round.

I didn't know where to find paper on the ship but Mum had a spare journal in her suitcase. I haven't used a journal since I was a little girl. Do you remember? It was the one you gave me. I'm sure I've left it behind somewhere in my old room, beneath piles of clothes and books that I wasn't allowed to take with me. Maybe you'll find it when you do a clear out of the house, if your bad back lets you.

I wish you had come with us. I was too proud to say that to you before we left, too stuck in my own head. You'd hate the ship though. I can hear you saying, 'There's no room to breathe,' in that gruff way, each syllable hoarse with nicotine and tar.

I guess you're right, though, in some way.

Starship-62 is big. Not quite as large as some movies might have taught us, but large enough for me to find a quiet corner, away from everyone else. The filtered air maintains purity in what we breathe (you'd be upset to know that smoking is strictly prohibited), but often I find myself thinking how stale the air is.

A lot of people like to sit in the Infinite Gardens, a large bio-dome in the middle of the central plaza. Some go to the space decks that line the outer rim of the ship. There are large windows where you can gaze into the never-ending blackness that's speckled with stars.

But there really is no room to *breathe*. We're like sardines, crammed into a tin can and kicked off into orbit. We can't escape our problems because we brought them along with us. We can't look back at the Earth and think 'Yeah, we did it, we saved humanity,' because we really didn't. We left everyone on a dying planet. Including you.

Day 19

Dear Grandad,

I'm getting sick of these 'How are you feeling today?' tests. They make us do one every day for the first ninety Earth-days in orbit, then it'll taper down to every week. It's a long list of tick boxes and a space for further comments, all to monitor our moods. As if these strange feelings could be contained inside a box. I'm tired of monitoring my own thoughts; I want to live outside of them.

You'd think being in outer space meant being free: able to go anywhere, do anything, be anyone. But we're more constrained than ever because space is dangerous. Lethal, even. One wrong step and you die; worse still, you pull everyone else into a painful death, too.

I don't see Mum that often. She's always in meetings or conferences in the higher levels of the ship, out of sight of the regular folk. Once, I wanted to go with her to see what she did at work, but then I remembered I was still mad at her for forcing me to come with her. I never wanted to say goodbye to you, I hope you know. To you, or Dad. But Mum was adamant that Earth wasn't for us anymore, wasn't safe for anyone.

"If they want to make a stupid decision, that's on them, but you're my daughter and you're coming with me," she'd said to me.

I don't know what she said to you or Dad back on Earth, at home, on Lenister Close. I do remember the three of you arguing. I think it was about me. I've always felt like I was being tossed across the three of you.

Before we left, I stepped out on the front porch one night (you know how bad my insomnia is). Dad's car was parked outside. Mum hung over the window, her thick cardi pulled tightly across her chest. I sat in the shadows and listened to the hum of their voices; they weren't raised shouts like I was used to, but guarded and gentle.

"She's my daughter too," Dad had said. "She's fifteen, she can make her own decisions."

A pause, maybe Mum shook her head. "This isn't about choosing what car you want to drive. And I've told you before: you should all be coming with me. This planet isn't safe anymore."

"Do you hear what you're saying? How can we live any-where else?"

I didn't hear the rest of the conversation because I heard you puttering around in the house, so I scrambled back to my room. You never liked me staying outdoors at night, even if it was just our street. You always said it wasn't safe. I wonder how you'd feel about me wandering the lonely corridors of this ship, gazing out at the sullen depths of space.

Day 29

Dear Grandad,

Space doesn't have a postbox so I can't send these letters to you. We can't communicate with Earth yet without a delay in transmission, and even then it's for *Highly Important Information* like, 'Hey, we've found a new planet we can transfer everyone to!'

I guess I'll have to keep writing in this journal and picture your reaction to the things I tell you.

Because I'm nearly sixteen, I don't have to attend the Starship Academy. There's not much in the way of 'jobs' going around but Amit's parents need help in the Gardens. You remember Amit, right? You said he seemed like a nice boy, but he needed a better barber. It's true, he does have a huge cloud of hair like a mushroom, but he insists he likes it that way. He's hopeless.

His parents manage the Gardens. There are plenty of volunteers but they needed an extra pair of hands to create the fertiliser. Yes, you heard me. It's nasty work and it stinks like all the worst smells in the world, but no one else really wants to do it. Neither does Amit (just as well, imagine trying to get the smell out of that hair).

Amit's mum, Priya, showed me how they make the fertiliser in the lowermost part of the ship, in a containment unit. We use 'nightsoil', or basically our shit (nothing goes to waste in this ship) and treat it to kill off the toxins.

"I'm glad you're helping me out, Amira," Priya told me when we were finishing up yesterday. "And I'll admit, I'm a little surprised you wanted to in the first place."

Priya is slim and short with a round face like a peach. She has a lovely smile and even lovelier eyes, neither of which Amit inherited. Both she and her husband are agricultural scientists.

"It's better than wandering around on my own," I'd replied before I could help myself. My cheeks burned red; I didn't want her to know how lonely I felt. "I mean, it's not like I have a job or anything."

"Don't you help your mum out?" she asked. We had walked back up to the upper level, where I could breathe non-manure air again.

I shrugged. "I'm not really allowed. She won't ever let me go with her to meetings."

Priya nodded and I could see her try to think of something polite to say in reply, so I saved her the trouble. "It's fine, I don't really want to be involved. I don't care what she does."

"Oh, but your mother is instrumental in co-ordinating the ship's logistics. It's a team effort, of course, but she's a very clever lady."

I grumbled inside. Priya must have seen the look on my face. She laughed. "It's alright. Amit doesn't like what I do either. You couldn't bribe him to help me."

Mum was in a late night meeting and I didn't want to go back to our empty quarters. I spent the evening with Amit and his parents. We had dinner and watched an old movie, but mostly we all talked about life on the ship.

It felt a little like having dinner at our house again, with you, me and Mum. It felt nice.

Day 37

Dear Grandad,

When we reach the fabled planet of sanctuary, I'm going to build the first inter-planetary mailing system. We'll have posties and post-aliens and I'll finally get to send you these handwritten notes.

For once, Mum was kind of right; my thoughts do feel calmer when I write. I start to hear you muttering from across the table to me, though you're mostly sighing impatiently at my bad jokes.

Do you remember when you used to take me down to the allotment when I was little?

You showed me how to plant tomato seeds and water the leaves until the stalks grew tall. The little bulbs of fruit would hang low, green at first, then slowly fade into a soft reddish tinge. The fields around us were brushed with the golden wash of an afternoon sun, and you'd read a book in your small deck chair. I'd traipse around with my massive yellow wellies (I didn't need them, but I always insisted on wearing wellies at the allotment) and pretend I was protecting the tomatoes from invaders.

We don't grow tomatoes in the Infinite Gardens as the farming section isn't for public access. Everyone has enough food to last a good few years but a lot of it isn't for us. It's for emergency rations in case we can't grow our own. We're meant to have the ship's farms up and running within the next two weeks.

I asked Amit what he thought would happen if we ran out of food completely. We were walking back to our quarters from the Gardens one evening.

He shrugged. "We'd probably have to eat each other."

I stared back at him in horror before he slapped my arm. "Seriously, why are you so gullible!"

"Your parents are running this whole thing!" I moaned. "*Sor-ry* if I give you more credit than you're due."

He laughed and brushed his long hair out of his face. "I've got no clue, to be honest. I didn't ask them about that."

"Are you even concerned about anything that goes on in this ship?"

He shrugged again, which started to annoy me. "They're the experts. They'll know what to do."

We'd reached our living quarters, a long section of units designed to house families of four or less. There were different sections on the ship for different sized families. Amit lives a block of units down from us, so we hung around my front door. (Nothing like our door back home, wooden with chipped blue paint. It's all made of uniform PVC with a small light and door number on the front.)

"But that's what we said back home," I continued. I could see he wanted to get home but his apathy irritated me. "We said we could fix things and then we ended up running away from the problem. We can't run away from anything in here."

"Mir, chill out. This isn't some science project at school; this is a big deal. You have to trust the process and the experts."

"Easy for you to say," I muttered. "Nothing goes wrong for you, Mr. Perfect."

I didn't mean it, Grandad, but the bitter monster just came out, like a parasite on a field of tomatoes. It ate away at me in the quiet moments when I thought about Amit's family and the cold dinners I'd eat alone when Mum was in meetings.

"What's that supposed to mean?" he said, his usually airy tone cut sharp.

I couldn't lie to him and I wanted everything inside me to go somewhere *other* than these letters I write to you. Plus, he was one of my oldest friends. Double plus, he was really irritating me.

"Your family are all together. You guys get to do cool things every day, your parents get along and *you* get along with them! Nothing's broken for you, everything works perfectly." I turned to unlock the door. "But I'm just being bitter, so ignore me. Good night."

A warm squeeze pressed on my shoulder before pulling me away from the door. Amit shook his head.

"You're not being bitter. But you're not the only one with problems, you know that? We had to leave my grandparents back at home, my mum's parents, and she's devastated. She cries every night and doesn't get up until really late in the workday, but Dad usually covers for her. I don't know how to help her. She'll shut herself in her room for hours and hours when they aren't working. It's my mum, you know? She's always been the happy one."

I nodded, remembering how Priya's cheeks would blush a slight red whenever she spoke about her job. She genuinely enjoyed what she did and she spread that joy to others, even to me.

We said good night on slightly better terms. I took my shoes off inside our unit.

The unit is nothing like home, not cosy or really that warm. There are no knickknacks lying around, no furniture that's slightly torn. Just a small living area with a sofa, coffee table and TV, and an attached kitchen. The living area splits off into two bedrooms and a minimal bathroom.

After what Amit had said to me, I wanted to find Mum. I wanted to talk to her, to tell her everything that was on my mind, like how I used to do with you. These letters just aren't the same because I really wanted a person. I wanted my mother.

I found her on the floor in her room, sitting on a small rug with her eyes closed and hands held up in prayer.

She didn't pray that much before we left Earth until the decision was made and we knew we were leaving the planet. Every now and then she'd wrap a headscarf around her hair and sit on the rug, blocking out all other noises.

I sat on her bed and waited till she finished. When she rose from the rug, her face was pale and thin. Dark circles smudged beneath her eyes.

"All done?" I said, nodding at the rug.

"Have to keep grounded somehow," she said simply. "Helps to talk out loud."

I must have scowled because her own eyes softened, lips pulled into a small, sad smile.

The bitter monster growled inside me, clearly not done for the night. I wanted to shout at her, "BUT WHY WON'T YOU LET ME TALK TO YOU!" but I guess that's what I'm doing with these letters, Grandad, these letters that you'll never read.

I said nothing and stayed on the bed. I didn't want to move but at the same time I wanted to disappear.

"I know you're upset with me," said Mum as she folded up the prayer rug and placed it on her bedside table. "And I know you miss your father and grandfather, too."

I spun around and spat back. "I miss *home*. I miss not being in a tin can, being able to actually see daylight."

She climbed on top of the bed and shuffled on her knees until she swung her legs around on my side and sat close to me. That soft smell of hers brought me back home, a citrusy mixture of freesias and honeysuckle, like the flowers that you grew in the back garden.

"But it wasn't safe, you know that. The news had been reporting it for years. All governments were declaring a state of emergency. The Earth is not safe, and it won't be again."

My jaw tightened as I tried to keep the monster deep inside me. Mum's voice was gentle, restrained. When I met her gaze, I saw your dark, worried eyes stare back at me.

"What'll happen to those left behind?" It was a question we had avoided.

She sighed. Her mouth became a thin line and that look of yours disappeared. She was now Dr. Aya Rahman, Lead Engineer and Head of Starship-62 Logistics. An expert scientist that had been interviewed by several news stations. I've always hated that side of her.

"We haven't been able to contact the base on Earth yet. Nothing will happen to the population left behind, for now."

I stood up sharply. "And what does that mean?"

She couldn't look at me. "They won't die—"

"So why didn't we stay!" I shouted. "Why didn't you let *me* stay!"

"Amira, I'm not having this conversation again."

I stormed out of our unit and ran as far as I could, as far from Mum as this tin can ship would let me go.

Day 62

Dear Grandad,

It's been a while. I'm sorry for not writing sooner. I'm sitting on the steps down to the fertiliser containment units. It's 'night' now (we don't really have day or night but allocated slots for work. I call this night because I should've had dinner an hour ago) and most of those that work in these basements have gone home.

Do you remember the first time I ran away? When I'd overheard Mum discussing our flight with you and you grunted several times in response. You didn't agree or disagree with her, just let her finish her explanation. I left the house without a word but a burning sensation in my chest.

How could she just decide these things for me, without even asking? Didn't she know that I watched the news, constantly saw my social feed update with information about new sinkholes and land masses breaking apart? Our world was literally crumbling away and she never bothered to talk to me about it.

I'd run away to our allotment and closed my eyes as I sat in your deck chair. The breeze was soft and fresh, like a feather tickling my skin. It was nearly sunset and the sky was bleeding red. The tomato crops no longer grew despite your best efforts because the soil couldn't hold moisture. The plants would wither away like sand slipping out from between your fingertips.

I must have dozed off in the cool evening because the next thing I felt was your hand on my shoulder, shaking me gently awake. You pulled me up from the deck chair as if I were that small girl in yellow wellies. You told me I should speak to my mother before pulling me in close for a hug.

I always hated the stale smell of smoke in your woollen jumpers but I would light a dozen cigarettes in this stupid tin can just to smell you once again.

***

I couldn't finish what I was writing. Priya just found me on the stairs when she was walking up from the basement units, wiping sweat off her brow. I've sat on these steps in the evening for over two weeks and this is the first time someone's walked past me.

She didn't tell me off. Instead, she sat down on the step below me and sighed. The edges of her dark hair were grey and her round face was wilted like a sunflower at night.

"What a long day!" She smiled with her eyes closed as she massaged her neck. "But I think the fertiliser is finally picking up. A little behind schedule, but better late than never."

I nodded slowly and closed this journal, keeping it tightly on my lap. She didn't say anything about it, but I blurted out, "I'm writing letters to my grandad."

Priya nodded with polite curiosity.

"It's stupid," I continued, wishing I could shove the journal out of sight. "He'll never get them, never read them."

We sat in silence for a moment. Priya's smile slid off her face and her cheeks lost colour. I remembered what Amit said about his mum and suddenly felt awful. As always, I said the wrong thing, the bitter thing, the horrible thing. Why can't nice words ever come out of my big mouth?

"We're a long way from home," she said quietly. I wasn't sure what to do, whether to hug her or say something nice, but I didn't know what to say. I didn't have to. "Tell me, what's your grandfather like?"

So, I told her everything about you. From the way you shuddered whenever you ate a sour fruit to the allotment you kept. I told her about your obsession with cars from the eighties and the way you used to pretend to be a grizzly bear to get me to finish eating my dinner. I told her how you'd always encouraged Mum with her studies when she was young and always said she was the smartest woman you knew.

And I told her how we'd make up bedtime stories together, filled with magic and adventure, when Mum and Dad were going through their divorce, so I didn't have to face the empty nights alone.

"He sounds wonderful," said Priya, a smile back on her lips. "I wish Amit knew his grandparents like that."

"He doesn't know them?" I asked, the words clunky in my mouth.

She shook her head. "When international travel got too risky, we couldn't visit them in the States. Amit grew up seeing them on video calls, but he doesn't really know them that well."

She fidgeted with her fingers in her lap, scrubbed pink from disinfectant and soapy water. She said nothing else about her parents, nothing about her sadness.

I wanted to tell her something positive, like from the endings of those stories we'd make up. That we were lucky to have people who loved us both on Earth and in the stars. But I couldn't bring myself to say that because the truth is, both of us were miserable for leaving our only home.

"It was Mum's idea to keep a journal," I finally said to my own surprise. "She had a spare one. I haven't written in ages though, so my handwriting was really rough at first."

Priya nodded. "It's a lovely idea. I know the decision wasn't easy for Aya, to leave her father behind."

I looked at her as if she'd said the strangest, most alien thing in the world. And then shame flooded inside me, overwhelming all my other feelings, that I hadn't even noticed my own mother's grief.

Priya told me not to stay down here too long, and said good night.

Honestly, Grandad, I've got no idea what to do. Why couldn't you be here to help me find a solution, to help me figure things out?

But I guess I know what you'd say.

You'd tell me to stop being so moany and go and speak to my mother.

Day 85

Dear Grandad,

There are some perks to having your mother be the Lead Engineer on the ship. Farming might not be allowed for most civilians onboard but I managed to convince Priya to give me a little slice of the Gardens, just a corner that no one would miss. She was reluctant at first, knowing how much space we had to conserve, but I promised her it wouldn't go to waste. The Head of Logistics would never allow it.

I got Amit to help me, even though he didn't want to, but I threatened to smear fertiliser in his hair while he was sleeping. It seemed to do the trick.

When I eventually dragged Mum down to the Gardens I told her to stand just a little outside our corner.

"Close your eyes and trust me, okay?" I said and slowly led her inside by hand.

I don't know if you've ever seen Mum cry, Grandad, but this was the first time I had. When she saw the little allotment we created, fitted out with a small deck chair (hashed together with bits of wood) and a table with books and a lamp, she squeezed my hand.

She stood there for a while until she asked what I was growing on the far side of the allotment. We don't grow tomatoes over here yet, but I used the fertiliser to plant some potatoes a couple of weeks ago. Little green shoots sprouted through the dark soil, beckoning us to visit them. I explained to her the process of planting the vegetables and making fertiliser and she nodded a few times before her tears had dried completely. Then she looked at me and smiled.

Somehow, I saw your face staring back at me again. This time full of warmth and pride and eyes that said, 'I'm home'.

Love you lots, Grandad,

Amira

The Hall of Being

T. K. Rex

T. K. Rex is a science fiction and fantasy author based in San Francisco, a graduate of the 2022 Clarion Writers Workshop, and occasional dabbler in the prehistoric arts. She hangs out around the internet as @tharkibo.

Currant has a good feeling about the gathering today. Young Jaheem is back from his away mission, and the mood is bound to be high. She has a topic prepared, an old favorite, and a few new floor pillows for the circle, woven tulle filled with cattail fluff, made with love by hand just down the hill.

The empty Hall of Being greets her with the scent of slightly dusty wood, warm green and yellow light from the stained-glass panel of bay laurel flowers high above, and the silent ancestors carved into all six redwood walls. *Lepidodenron, Tiktaalik, Deinonychus.* She greets them as she walks the hexagon to ground herself, listening to the soft pad of her mushroom leather footsteps against limestone. She imagines all the tiny ocean animals that sunk to make the stone, the mountain it was quarried from, and the robots pulling it from sunken skyscrapers across the Bay.

Gray greets her with a hug and takes a pillow, unpacks his mandolin, and plays the first few chords of "The Song of the Swaying Scale Trees" with a cheerful flourish. The sandbots falling through the instrument's tall, brightly painted shaft underscore the gentle tune with ocean waves.

Currant smiles and lights the incense by the door.

When the circle is close to filled but the clock is just past time, she starts the opening ritual. "Are you well?" she asks each gatherer in turn.

There are twenty-eight today. Most simply nod. Feng smiles widely, and next to her, Elle blushes and says, "Very." Akilah only shrugs. Vihaan, who saved a seat when he arrived that still lies empty, shakes his head. Currant makes a mental note to check in on Samantha. Hediye only nods, but her smile shows how overjoyed she is to have her son Jaheem back.

"And Jaheem, are you well?"

Jaheem replies, "Uh, I'm not great." Now she's concerned. What happened on his away mission?

She reads a two-hundred-year-old passage by a poet botanist she's long admired, and after the discussion, as the gatherers disperse, the unwell line up to speak with her.

Jaheem is last. He takes a seat on the pillow next to her and attempts a friendly smile. He's grown even more than she expected in his year away. The shy sixteen-year-old with a permanently pimpled forehead is taller than her now, and seventeen, and his skin is clear and smooth and darkened from the desert sun into a deep, resplendent brown, richer than the redwood walls around them.

"Welcome back, Jaheem. It's so good to see you again."

"Um. Thanks." His voice is deeper, too. He scratches the back of his head and smiles sheepishly. "This is probably stupid..."

"No such thing here. What's on your mind?"

"It's just. Something's been bothering me. For months actually."

"Something that happened in the desert?"

"No, nothing bad happened. It's more... I dunno. They have a whole different thing going on out there, you know?"

"Mm-hm." She nods. "Exposure to different cultures is part of why we have away missions. What was it about theirs that bothered you?"

"No, I mean, it didn't bother me, not really. I mean, I guess it did. It's like... well, they have these weird religions. Everyone I got to know out there believes, like *literally* believes, that there's some kind of deity watching them all the time."

"They're theists. You learned about them in cultural studies."

"I know, but like. They *really believe it.*"

"What about that bothers you?"

"It doesn't! I mean at first, I was like, these people are crazy, but then when I really got to know them, it was like, all the ways they manage their ecosystem, their whole philosophy around it, is that this mysterious being created everything, and it's their responsibility to take care of their ecosystem *for him.* And it's usually a him. I don't know why."

"I think there're historical reasons, but that's not the part that bothered you, is it?"

"No, but like... this is stupid." Jaheem scratches his knee. "I already know what you're gonna say."

"Do you?"

He sighs, shifts his weight, and looks her directly in the eye. "Yeah. You're gonna say there's no god."

Ah. There it is. "Jaheem," she tries to give him a reassuring smile, "if there is a presence in this universe, that's as powerful as the universe, and knows everything that happens in the universe, what do you think it would be?"

He thinks for a second. "The universe itself?"

She nods. "That's what the concept of Occam's Razor teaches us."

"Ok, I know that. But like, Occam's Razor is only as good as what you already know, right? Didn't people use to think continental drift was too complicated to be real? And you've always taught us that life loves diversity, life is messy and needs randomness, so like, couldn't the universe, at some point, have spawned a god? Or a lot of gods? Or a previous universe did, and its god created ours? I don't know, Currant, it just seems like, they're so certain out there that their god exists, so like, I spent a lot of time thinking about how it might be true. And... I think... I dunno, I think it might be."

"Jaheem, if you're asking for my permission to believe in a god, you should know better." She smiles. "That's not our way."

"Ha, yeah. Ok." He nods, grins a little, and rubs his knees with his long hands. Then something shifts in his expression, and he looks up at the walls, at the life-size *Parasaurolophus* carved behind her, she guesses. Then his eyes fall back on her. "I guess that's all. Thanks, Currant."

It seems like he has something else to say, but she doesn't want to make him any more uncomfortable and doesn't press it. He stands, and she stands with him.

"See you next week," he says, waves, and walks out through the door, which still hangs open to a day that's bright and crisp and green.

The incense is long extinguished, and sunlight falls through the window with the poppies now, celadon and orange.

Currant stacks the pillows in the storage closet behind the engraving of *Arthropleura*, one of her favorite ancestors. Maybe it's the symmetry and repetition of its wide, flat scales, or the sheer audacity of a millipede to get so big, or the fact that it's the one she always touches last at the end of a long morning when it's finally time for lunch.

With the Hall of Being locked up, she takes the footpath through the live oak grove to her abode, a geodesic dome of mossy reclaimed concrete and multicolored glass. As last night's grasshopper biryani reheats, something nags at her.

The answer that she gave Jaheem didn't satisfy him. And if she's honest with herself, it doesn't satisfy her either. He left the Hall of Being just as unwell as he came.

And there it is, the old self-doubt, the feeling she thought she'd finally shaken off in her third year on the job.

Lyta would have told Jaheem just the right thing.

Would she be disappointed in her?

"Come on, Currant," she mutters to herself. She knows better than to let that voice take over, the one that tells her she isn't the right person for this. That she's not cut out to be a spiritual leader. That she doesn't know enough, that all the things Lyta never got to teach her were the most important things, and now she'll never be as good at this as her.

Self-doubt aside, she owes Jaheem a better answer.

This is a spiritual problem. Perhaps the solution, too, is spiritual.

She puts away the biryani and opens the cupboard underneath her alter, where several slightly dusty jars stand waiting.

A little nervous but excited, too, she opens up the one labeled:

Star Stuff

For spiritual journeys

1 blue marble = 1 trek

Inside are balls of dried blue leaves bred for this purpose, each a little smaller than a fingernail. She shakes one out into her palm, brings it back to the counter, and drops it in a mug. Hot water makes the leaves expand, and the little ball blooms into a bright blue flower filling up the bottom of her mug, petals straightening as they absorb the water like the wings of a new butterfly in timelapse. When the water's dark like a twilight sky and just cool enough to not burn her tongue, she drinks.

It tastes like the first rain in fall, petrichor and thirsty foliage, smoke lingering as she swallows.

Here we go. She lets her eyelids drop and concentrates on her breath to relax. Breathing in. Breathing out. Breathing in. Breathing out. Bre a t h i n g

i   n

    n

      n

        n

          n

            n

stomach writhes like a ball of banana slugs inside her

food smell makes the air thick

too thick

skin tingles

toes twitch

time to go outside

She opens her eyes and stumbles for the door, startling a raven family as she flings it open to the sun-speckled afternoon. They curse her in their gurgling language, feathers ruffled.

"Sorry," she says, then throws up behind the sword fern by her door.

She braves the inside once more to rinse her mouth and grab her coat. Then she walks.

Ahead, the oaks and bays conspire, tunneling their way around her path, arms reaching out to hold each other's hands above and feet pressing just below the path together, sole to sole.

through the tunnel made of leaves

out the other side, a meadow

around the hill

across the stream, the small wood bridge

deep into a grove of bays

late-season fruits, wrinkled brown now, hang from the branches of the ones with wide trunks songs

Birds and wind and shuffling creatures in the underbrush, sorting through the leaf litter, hiding or fleeing as she walks past. Mostly voles most likely, and the song of all the forest functions floats and frolics, tilts and swirls all around her.

A deer, gold fur glowing in the sun, looks up from something it was grazing on ahead and leaps up the hillside all at once

Did she imagine it?

She must have, because normal deer don't glow like that, no matter how much sunlight's falling on them through the leaves

What did she come out here for?

The air here smells like bay leaves, fresh and spice and very nice

something stirs beneath the ferns

following her, shaking each frond as it passes underneath

She stops. It stops. She walks again, and so does it.

"Hello?"

It pokes a gray and whiskered snout out from between two fronds.

"Hi, there."

It shows its face, white cheeks and big brown ears.

"You're a fox."

It steps delicately out into the dappled light, sits at the edge of the path, bushy tail wrapped around its toes, and squints its deep brown eyes at her. "I am," it says.

She nods, slowly

drops her hands into her pockets where they think better

yep, ok, this isn't real

"Isn't it?" the fox asks.

She walks. The fox walks its fox walk as she walks, mere feet from her feet, paws light on the path and tail waving at the tip. She looks away from it to the trees and bushes and mysteries ahead.

"Where are we going?" the fox asks.

"Nowhere. Just walking."

They come to a fork and then another fork, and at the third fork she realizes she's never taken that trail on the left, the one with the glowing purple fireflies and tall fluorescent mushrooms.

The six-foot millipede still follows her. They go down the path together.

"Oh, I like this one," he says through scraping mandibles and crawls ahead.

"Weren't you just a fox?"

He looks back at her, whiskers twitching, pointed brown ears wide in her direction.

"I can't be both?" The flock of dark-eyed juncos chirps, fluttering across the path, sparrowing their sparrow words, little brown bodies with little black heads, each in unison sings, "Weren't you just a walker? Now you're a stand-and-stare-agaper?"

She closes her mouth, which was, in fact, agape. Fireflies swirl, blinking, purple, violet, yellow... fireflies don't live here, and it's not their season...

"Come on," the deinonychus says, gesturing forward with his iridescent feathered head, just higher than her hip now.

"Where are we going?" she asks.

"Nowhere. Just walking," he says.

She follows.

The deinonychus stops to chase a firefly. She sits on a log and watches. He eats the firefly, and the stripey patterns on his wing and tail feathers start to glow bright violet.

"What's your name?" she asks him.

"What's yours?"

"Currant."

He spins and turns into a stream, and then a floating spark, and then a bush of bright red berries.

"I'm the last one," she says. "With an A."

And then a fox. "Tasty," he says.

"I'm not hungry," she tells him.

"Aren't you?"

"I'm not even in communication with my stomach right now."

"Then some other organ must be hungry. You came out here to hunt."

That's right. She did. "I'm hunting answers."

"Have you found any yet?"

"I don't think so."

"Answers are funny creatures. Very diverse, paraphyletic, convergent, ubiquitous. Elusive and well camouflaged. Parasitic, symbiotic, effusive. Right before your eyes. What was your question?"

Jaheem. "It's not my question, so much as someone else's. He wanted to know if I thought there could be a god."

"Sounds like a walking question," the fox says, and walks, and she walks next to the fox.

The song of birds becomes the song of frogs, and the path is now lit only by the mushrooms towering above them.

"I don't feel equipped to answer his question, because it's not my place to tell him what to believe. Not in that way," she says.

"But he came to you anyway."

"The things he learned on his away mission contradict the things he learned from me."

"Do they?"

"He seems to think they do."

"Do they?"

"I'm not an expert on the theists, but they believe a great omniscient being made the universe. I've always taught my gatherers the universe came into being on its own. And that's what Lyta taught before me."

"But you're talking to a fox."

"I know. But you're not real."

"I beg to differ." His tail twitches.

"I mean, you're a figment of my imagination. A hallucination."

"Those sound like real things."

"Well, I guess you have a point."

"So why can't gods be real?"

"The belief is real, of course. But the god that they believe in, I just don't see the need for it."

Suddenly, the path ends, and she falls

And falls

And falls

And screams into the blackness smeared with stars, painted with an endless giant millipede, Arthropleura of the Carboniferous, red, wide segments each the size of solar systems, legs endlessly repeating, twitching, down, down

Still falling, still falling

Breathing in

Breathing out

Breathing iiiiiiinnnnnnnnn

"Where are we going?" she asks.

"Nowhere. Just falling," the red trillipede says in an infinite voice, violet fox eyes gleaming in the starlight.

As she falls, a thought occurs to her. What if Jaheem is right?

What if some omniscient being is here with her even now?

"Are you a god?" she asks the gazillipede.

"Yes."

"Are you real?"

"We already determined that."

Everything is spinning. What about

C a u s a l i t y

Someone shouts "THERMODYNAMICS" from the void, it's Lyta's voice, she's the void.

"Are you the god Jaheem believes in?"

"Yes."

"Are you the god the theists believe in?"

"Yes."

"Are you synonymous with the universe itself?"

"Yes."

"But separate from it?"

"Yes."

"Do you just say yes to everything?"

"Yes."

"Because you are everything."

"Yes."

"Are you nothing, too?"

"Yes."

She lands softly in a sand dune, bioluminescent waves caressing shore ahead, violet-colored fireflies floating between blades of beachgrass.

Fireflies don't live here. There've been no sand dunes on this coast for a hundred years... but she used to imagine them.

The waves recede. The grass dries up. The fireflies remain.

The dry air fills with desert sounds, crickets, and wind against the sandstone that the sand became.

Breathe in. Breathe out.

She lays back in the grass, soft stuff now on a humid summer night, and watches the fireflies above her mingle with the stars. They're orangey-yellow now, the color that they should be, and a young man is lying next to her.

This isn't her ecosystem.

It's the one she spent her away mission in, way out past the Continental Divide, where the air is thick and wet all summer and the way folks talk is slow and strange.

The boy was just one dimpled smile from convincing her to stay.

"There's Orion," he says, pointing up.

"I see it," Currant says.

What had his name been?

"Someday, I'm gonna get up there."

"Where will you go?"

"The moon, I think," he says. "Maybe Mars. I want to see the floating station in the skies of Venus, too."

"There's a man in my village who spent a few years on the moon."

"Did he like it?"

"He missed Earth a lot, but yeah. He was planting trees up there."

"God's work."

"What?"

"Something I heard once."

"Are you a theist?"

"Nah. I just like the phrase," he says. And she half-remembers, half-imagines that his name is Fox.

"Do you want to believe?" she asks him.

"In a god? Nah, not really."

"Why not?"

"No one else I know does. It would just make me, I dunno, different."

"But you're different anyway. We all are. When you look up at Orion, you connect the stars with lines in your imagination, and your lines don't look like mine. When you stand next to your brother, even though your parents are the same, his eyes are green and yours are brown. His skin is light and yours is dark. You and I were once a single primate, she and the trees a single cell, looking for the light. Variation is the stuff that makes our world, all those stars, our universe."

"And in all that variation," Fox says, and looks at her, "do any gods exist?"

"In the minds of theists. As abstractions. Maybe something out there in the universe calls itself a god, but I need no transcendence beyond these stars above us, the ground below us full of life, and the fireflies and flowers... and your smile."

He leans into her, and draws his eyelids closed, and she shuts her eyes, and waits for his warm lips—

Whiskers tickle her and a wet tongue licks her nose.

She sits up, laughing. The gray fox jumps off her chest and sits next to her, dark eyes sparkling with violet humor. The fireflies are purple again.

"Come on, God," she says to him. "Let's go back. I think I have my answer."

The twilight tunnel lightens up ahead, the mushrooms shrink to normal size and cease their glowing, the fireflies fade one by one, and she emerges into bays and oaks and fog lit from the fading light above. A small gray fox runs up ahead of her and disappears behind a fern.

She buttons up her jacket and takes the path over the hilltop toward the village. From up here, she can see the Bay, all the ruins at its edge, and all the marshes full of birds where once stood neighborhoods, and once walked mastodons, and once was sea floor.

An airship floats along its path above, in and out of clouds, and somewhere past it all, through the black, a man her age with dimples and brown eyes is planting trees on Mars. God's work, he would have said.

That year away was lonely more than anything for her. Even he, whose name she's certain wasn't Fox, never made her feel at home. She remembers longing for the sweet, spicy smell of dusty summer bay leaves and the fog roaming in between the hills, even while they watched the fireflies and made out in the grass and looked at stars.

And when she came back, seventeen and one inch taller with half a borrowed accent and a haircut her own parents laughed at, she felt even more alone.

Gods were never Jaheem's real concern.

She knows what to do now.

***

"I came back changed," she tells the gatherers, after opening the week's discussion with her own story of her year away. "And that was the point. We all go away for a year so that we all come back with different experiences, different ideas, because survival depends on adaptability, and adaptability is strengthened with variety, with openness to the unexpected, to the strange, to things that frighten us at first. Nature's lesson is to listen, learn, accept, evolve. Use all the senses that we have, including our imaginations."

The people in the circle nod and murmur.

"How did you feel when you came back from your away mission?" she asks Feng, who's sitting next to her today.

"Pretty weird. I'd gotten so used to the tundra, it felt sweltering here even though it was rainy season, and everyone was complaining about the cold. It was like I knew everyone, but they didn't know me anymore."

"And you, Akilah?"

Akilah takes a deep breath before sighing, "I... actually got kind of depressed for a while. I felt... I don't know how else to say it. I just felt really at home with the family I stayed with in the prairie. I've been thinking about visiting them actually."

That would be good for her. Currant nods encouragingly and turns to the next gatherer. "Vihaan?"

"Well," and he turns to Samantha, sitting next to him where last week there was just an empty pillow and grins. "I think everyone knows I got a little more out of my away mission than I bargained for." Everyone laughs, including thankfully, Samantha. "So, yeah. Everything was different. It still is."

Samantha takes his offered hand and speaks up in her sing-song accent without prompting. "I only know away missions from the other side, but I can definitely tell you all they leave the folks you meet a little changed themselves." She smiles, glances at Vihaan, and says, "Ok, sometimes a lot changed."

The stories travel all the way around the circle until it's Jaheem's turn.

"Yeah," he says, and rubs his long hands on his knees. "I still feel pretty weird. When I first came back last week, it was like, I didn't know if I belonged here anymore."

Everyone around the circle, except the younger kids, nod and mutter in agreeing tones.

"I felt like that when I went home last year," Samantha says. "I don't think I belong *anywhere* now."

"You belong here," Vihaan tells her and kisses her hand. She smiles at him, but her eyes are still a little sad.

Jaheem continues, "Yeah. Samantha, you belong here as much as I do. I mean, I think everyone who's been on an away mission probably knows how you feel."

After the discourse, as the Hall of Being empties for another week, Jaheem approaches.

"Hey, Currant." He looks down at the floor, runs a nervous hand across his head.

"Hey, Jaheem."

"I just wanted to say thanks. Last week after we talked, I felt super weird, and then, like, this week, I dunno, the way you got everyone talking about their own away missions, it really helped."

"What you said to Samantha was really nice. I'm proud of you."

"Yeah?"

"Yeah. Belonging is something we all help each other with."

"Oh, yeah. I remember Lyta saying that. I didn't really get it, though. I think now I do."

Currant smiles. Would Lyta be proud of her, right now?

"Anyway," Jaheem says and raises a hand to wave goodbye. "Thanks again. See you next week!"

Samantha enters as he leaves, pushing her wild blonde hair behind an ear. "That kid," she says. "He's alright."

"He's a good one. What's up, Samantha?"

"Well, I've been thinking about what you said a few weeks ago, about getting more involved with the community. It's good advice." Currant nods. "I've been helping out at the library, and fixing up a robot here and there, but, well, I was wondering if you needed any help up here?"

Help? Up here? Currant glances around the simple hexagonal hall, at the pillows that take her five minutes to stack up in a closet, at the incense holder filled with ash. At the slightly dusty carvings of the ancestors. There really isn't much to do.

But that's not what Samantha's really asking, is it?

She tenses. She isn't ready to be a mentor. She barely has the basics figured out. What if Samantha sees right through her? Realizes she has no idea what she's doing? Tells everyone?

Lyta's voice breaks through her spiraling internal chorus. Look at what's in front of you.

Breathe in.

A young woman from another place just trying to belong.

Breathe out.

"Yeah," Currant says. "I could use some help."

"Great!" Samantha smiles and claps her hands together. "Where do we start?"

"Well, first, let's meet the ancestors. This is Arthropleura, who lived three hundred million years ago..."

2122, Barrel-Aged and Biding

Jordan Hirsch

Jordan Hirsch writes speculative fiction
and poetry in Saint Paul, MN, where
she lives with her husband.

The Silver Moon was always open, and its doors always whined on their compressed-air tracks.

Shida told Maintenance to leave them be. She wanted to hear when patrons came and went, no matter which shift on DeiStation was on their way home.

Over the clatter of anti-grav roulette boards and the squeak of the glass she was drying by hand—the dryer sometimes left spots—Shida's eyes were drawn to the whine as two black boots strode in.

"Dalia," Shida said, lips barely moving, "go on in back."

The black boots hesitated, taking in the dim room with its light up slots and green felt tables. His eyes measured each person, each station, in a quick and calculating way Shida knew well. When they landed on her, he smiled.

Shida put the glass on the rack and picked up another, never dropping his gaze as the boots strode closer. He stepped between two barstools, sitting on neither; Shida nodded, not needing to speak first.

"It's been a long time, Shida."

"Barek," she replied. "What'll it be?"

"I'm not here to drink," he said, traces of false warmth leaking from his eyes. Barek had never been one to dance, always shooting first.

"Come on back, then," Shida said without missing a beat. "I keep my best bottles back here. Magda," she spoke down the rail, "watch the bar?"

Shida led Barek through the canvas curtain, rough on her calloused, aching fingers. It was better for this—however it was going to end—to take place away from her patrons.

"Have a seat," she said, taking brandy down from a shelf.

"This your special stash?" Barek asked.

"It is."

"Well, it must be my lucky day."

The amber liquid was a smooth pour into two tumblers, and Barek took his with his left hand.

Barek was not left-handed, but Shida sat down anyway.

"I've been expecting you," she said after a sip.

"Have you?"

"You're not the first to come."

Barek's thick brows shot up. Did he not know most of their old crew had come looking already?

"So you know why I'm here?" he asked.

"Of course."

"Then where is it?"

"It's not here."

Barek slammed his glass down, impatient as ever, brandy sloshing over the rim.

"Shida, I know you have it. We all do." And all their old friends had sipped brandy in this room, one at a time. This was getting old. She was getting old.

Shida blinked, just a moment slower than usual, the cheers of winners and groans of not-yet-winners drifting across the wall. Her eyes were tired, and the outline of her phaser pressed against her ribs. "You took your fair share," she said.

"Did I?"

He and everyone else had, or at least they all thought so at the time. The relic she'd chosen—one no one else had wanted—could have bought this whole space station plus the two closest ports on Deimos, with maybe enough leftover to build her own hydroponic vineyard. But none of them had known that until they'd gone to cash in their run from Alpha C-III.

That had been her last run with the *Nightingale*. It'd had to be.

"You didn't sell it," Barek said, trying to draw information out of her. "You wouldn't still be in this piss-chute if you had."

"I don't have it, Barek," Shida said, steady over the chimes of the slots-array singing. "You made the trip to this piss-chute for nothing."

Barek shot up then, pushing back from the table, grabbing his hidden phaser with his right hand, and pointing it at Shida. He was always one to rush.

"Don't lie to me, Shida."

She stared up at him, hands in her lap, phaser still at her ribs. The chimes in the saloon kept getting higher and higher—someone was going to win big soon.

"It's not here," Shida said again, tired. She was tired of watching the door.

"Bullshit."

"It's not." She was tired of waiting for more *Nightingale* crew members to come through.

"Then where is it?"

She was tired of old friends pointing phasers at her.

Shida didn't reach into her holster. Shida kept her hands still.

"Oh, Barek," she said, fatigue straining her voice. "Do you really think I'd ever tell you?"

One more chime, then a chorus of cheers sounded in the saloon.

Shida closed her eyes, and the sizzle of phaser fire—one shot, direct and true—whispered through the racket.

Barek crumpled to the floor.

Shida opened her eyes, looked past where he'd been standing.

"Good aim, my daughter," she said, voice low and mournful, and Dalia stepped out from behind the curtain leading to the supply closet.

"Were you just going to let him point that at you?" Dalia asked, her face flushed with anger. Shida had never made her pull the trigger before, had never let it go that far.

"No, I wasn't," she said.

But she was. For the first time, she was.

"What should we do with him?" Dalia asked, toeing one of the black boots.

"I'll take care of it." Shida sighed and stepped back through the curtain. "Best secure your dishonest gains," she called to her patrons. "Station security will be here any minute."

Back behind the bar, she took down a glass and picked up a towel as the doors to The Silver Moon parted with a whine. Three uniformed officers surveyed the room, then sidled over.

"What will you be drinking today, gentlemen?" Shida asked.

"Shida. Magda," Commander Arun greeted them, nodding. "Sensors picked up phaser fire here. Everything alright?"

"Everything is just fine, Commander," Shida said.

"Mind if we have a look around?" he asked.

Shida held his gaze. Arun, unlike Barek, knew the dance, and he and Shida did so every time Shida had unwelcome visitors from her past.

And for now, three of *Nightingale's* crew still lived.

"Dalia," Shida said, "go in back and get the 2122 for the commanders here. From my personal stores."

Anwen's Song, Efa's Shoes, and the Halls in the Hills

Rebecca Harrison

Rebecca Harrison sneezes like Donald Duck and her best friend is a dog who can count. She was chosen for the WoMentoring Project by Kirsty Logan, and long listed for Wigleaf's top fifty.

Sing the Midwinter. Sing the longest night. Sing the darkness bright. Don't forget the melody. Don't falter the verse. Don't listen to the footsteps. The Barrow Men are here. This is the night the earth opens. This is the night they walk. Sing, or they will take you. Sing, or they will carry you beneath the hills. Sing, or they will make you dance in stone shoes until you wear them to nothing.

If you journey through the valleys on Christmas morn, wait, let the carols come to you, let the music warm you. And after, turn East to the hills. The halls in the hills are silent now. But if you could enter, you would see the Barrow Men frozen at their feast. And you would find a pair of stone shoes. These were Efa's shoes. And she danced without rest, without sleep, without music. For music is poison to the Barrow Men.

Walk the white hills, and if you could hear long ago, you would hear Anwen's song. And if you could see long ago, you would see Anwen and Efa chasing the May morn. Laughter in their steps. Bluebells in their hair. Secrets in their chatter. Sisters. Sisters closer than petals on a rose. Anwen, the elder, always a rhyme, always a story, always a song for Efa. And Efa, buttercup bright, fists full of gifts for Anwen. Gifts of wildflowers and wren feathers. Gifts of river pebbles washed smooth and lichen grown ferny. Together they wandered the woods, the valleys, and the hills. And on the hills, they found her.

A grey figure. Bones under skin. Eyes bleak. Hair straggled. Face ancient. Feet wrapped in leaves. And voice? She had none. And she mimed at the sisters, her withered mouth begging. Efa gave her the pie crust she'd saved for the sparrows. Anwen helped lift her from the moss.

"Our Mam will give you a warm bed," she said. And they walked her slowly to the village. Slow as the tides turn, slow as the oaks become brown, slow between stones and slipping places. And still, she said nothing. A stream tugged the leaves from her feet.

"Anwen," Efa whispered. "Look." Her feet were white bone. "She's Gladys." And at the name, the lady gripped Efa's hands and nodded and nodded, no voice, only tears. And when they reached the village, they went straight to the blacksmith's cottage. The door opened. The blacksmith's wife was bonny and broad, hair dark as a raven's shadow.

"Gladys," she cried. She clutched her ancient daughter and wept until Gladys's straggle hair stuck to her cheeks. She led her inside and wrapped her bone feet in wool. "What have they done to you, my laughing girl?" She kissed her withered forehead. She clutched Efa and Anwen's hands. "But five years, my girl's been gone." And she said no more, for sobs gripped her.

Anwen and Efa sang their way home, sang as if it were Midwinter Eve, sang as if the hills were opening. And when they were huddled in their bed, bellies full of supper, limbs full of sleep, they listened past the village walls to the hills.

"What of Gladys's red hair?" Efa whispered.

"She danced it away," Anwen said. Efa sniveled. Anwen put her arms around her. "But you won't dance your golden curls away. If they ever took you, I'd come."

Gladys was gone in the Autumn. The valley was fog and weeping.

"How many more of our own will we lose?" the blacksmith cried. And he looked to the hills, to the halls. The halls where the Barrow Men were feasting. The halls where folk, stolen and silent, were dancing in stone shoes.

Winter came. Snow and candles and frost and berries. Anwen and Efa tiptoed over icy streams in the bare woods. Efa let snowflakes melt on her fingertips.

"Would they take us all?" she said, looking towards the white hills. Her breath puffed pale. "Even Mamgu? She's old as the valley."

"But her ears are sharp. Bet she heard you." Anwen shook snow off her wool hat. "Mamgu says – under the hills, the halls go on far as forever. And you could never walk them, even if you lived to be old as the Barrow Men," Anwen said, rubbing her arms.

"Our valley could fit in the halls and not be squeezed?" Efa licked the melted snow off her fingers.

"In the halls, it'd be small." Anwen shivered.

"How big the echoes would be."

"Not so big. Whoever they touch loses their voice. Mamgu says it's because music hurts them. Come, let's practice till our voices are strong as falcons." She took Efa's hand and, singing, they trod the frozen ways home.

Midwinter. The church bells rang the dawn. Mamgu sat by the hearth, humming the heart song of her childhood, her wrinkled brown face in a sad smile. Anwen and her mother spread warm griddle cakes with yellow butter. The day smelled of spice and frosted windows. Anwen offered the plate. Mamgu took the largest cakes.

"Mamgu!" Efa said.

"Gives me strength for the singing," she winked.

Later, the dusk came, and they lit candles in the corners and held hands, Mamgu in a deep chair.

"Won't matter if I drift off and miss a verse or two," she said, straightening the blanket over her lap. "One look at me would tell them they won't get much dancing out of these feet."

"This isn't the time for making light," the sisters' mother said, her rosy face all frowns. "When the sunset touches the hills, we sing." She looked harsh at her daughters. "And if you hear claws on the flagstones, keep singing. The Barrow Men will be here. No door can keep them out." Efa gripped Anwen's hand harder. They watched the sky gild and lower. Then they sang.

A tremble was in the hills, in the snow, in the stones. Crows circled the moon. And the skin of the hills began to crackle, began to split. A long grey hand, half talons, reached through the hill's thinning skin into the snow. There was a sound like laughter if laughter was bat wings. Then the hill split open. And the Barrow Men came. Grey and clawed and faces long and drooping down their chests, and mouths with too many teeth, and some had legs short as axe heads, and some had legs tall as stairways, and some had shoulders with curling horns, and some had arms with many joints. But all laughed like bat wings. And all smelled of bones. And they didn't leave footprints behind them - black prints went ahead of them across the valley, through the village, and into folks' homes.

Efa sang. Sang until even her toes ached. And Anwen's voice was in hers and her mother's and Mamgu's. There were scrapings in the kitchen. Claws on flagstones. She mustn't look. She mustn't look. A shape, long-legged. A crackle. Then breath. Breath like bones. Her spine prickled. She squeezed Anwen's hand tighter. She sang harder. Harder until her ribs hurt. Breath on the back of her neck. She gasped.

"Anwen." But all Anwen felt was Efa's hand snatched from hers.

Fast and crackling and many hands holding her up and talons digging into her and the village flashing past and night flying over her: stars and moon and trees. Efa screamed. But nothing came out. And the Barrow Men laughed like bats wings. Her voice was gone. She saw her village growing smaller. And then she saw the hills split down the middle as if by an axe and darkness thicker than night. Then she was carried inside. Down and down and down.

A glow half smudge, half smoke tickled the dark. Efa blinked her sore eyes. She was in the halls. Halls so huge her village and her valley could be dropped inside and never found. Barrow Men sat at tables feasting on strange meat – the meat of the mammoths of the great deep. Grey faces pressed against hers. Bone breath huffed chill on her. Then hands tugged her slippers off, pushed her feet into stone shoes, prodded her to walk. Cold shook up through her. Her feet stung with it. Her heart thumped with it. Talons gripped her shoulders, her knees, her ankles. The Barrow Men moved her like a doll, moved her in a dance. And as she screamed her silent scream, they laughed.

Dawn came and Anwen was still weeping in Mamgu's arms.

Her mother slumped in a chair, her gaze faraway, her face pale as the hills.

"I told her I'd never let them take her," Anwen said. "And now they've got her, and her voice is gone and she's in the dark. And she'll dance her golden curls away. She'll dance until her feet are bone. And if I ever see her again, she'll be old. And she'll die. She'll die."

"Hush, now," Mamgu said. She stroked Anwen's hair, but her hand trembled. And she said nothing more, but hummed the heart song of her childhood, her cheeks wet with tears.

A knock on the door.

"Anwen, please. I can't," her mother said. Anwen lifted her face. Mamgu wrapped her in her shawl, rubbed her arms. Anwen opened the door. The blacksmith and his wife. Warm hands seized her own.

"Just like our Gladys," the blacksmith's wife said.

"Efa won't be like Gladys. She won't. I told her if they ever took her, I'd come." And with that, Anwen pressed her feet into her boots and ran out into the winter winds. The Barrow Men's black footprints stretched from her door, across the village to the valley. Anwen followed them. Winds bit her ears. Cold smacked through her dress. Her shawl slipped and she scooped it up. Her hem became thick with snow. She went over ice and rock, under oak and willow. But where the footprints went, she could not go. And she flung herself at the hills, but they did not let her in. And she called her sister's name, but Efa did not hear. And she wept until her mother found her and the blacksmith carried her home. Her days became blankets and firesides and silence.

Spring came – larks and daffodils and cloudbursts. When

Anwen saw the blackbird's beak turn orange, she threw off her silence, ran to the church and rang the bell. She rang and rang. Folk gathered.

"Have you forgotten my sister?" she said to them. "Efa's in the hills. The Barrow Men have her. But the earth has thawed now. We can dig her out. There are many of us." Murmurs. Then shouts. And then a crowd and Anwen swept up and along, over stream and meadow. And where the black footprints had vanished into the hills, they dug. Spades in hands. Soil on metal. Sweat and digging and chatter. A hole in the earth: widening and widening. Soon, Anwen was standing in it. Others joined her and earth was piled higher than her head. Then the sun was passing over and dusk was in the horizon.

"We'll come back tomorrow," David, the miller's son, said as he climbed out. Hands helped Anwen up. She stood on the edge and peered in.

"It's a decent start. Could fit my shire horse in there," Farmer Alder said, wiping his brow. Anwen gripped hands in thanks. Her sister was so close, her heart felt like daisies. Then a crackle. Soft, at first, like a magpie wing underfoot. Then again, louder. The ground quivered into a shake. The sides of the pit moved and closed. Anwen fell backwards into someone's arms. The ground sealed shut.

"It can't," Anwen gasped, pulling up handfuls of grass. She called her sister, called into the earth, but in the halls, all Efa heard was laughter like bat wings, mammoth bones clattering on tables, and her own steps: stone on stone. Efa danced her feet bloody, danced her heart blank, and danced a grey streak in her golden hair.

"I won't give up," Anwen said to Mamgu. The bluebells winds

were in her voice. She held a river pebble in her palm – a gift from Efa. "I'll get into the hills and I'll sing, and the Barrow Men will die."

"There's only one way into the halls, if they carry you there with their own hands, and if they touch you, well, you'll lose your voice, and you won't get much singing done then, will you?" Mamgu said.

"Then I won't sing to them. I'll play. Music is poison to them, you told me so. My hair is long now. If I plait it, I can hide my old whistle in it." She took the whistle to the woods and played her song. And the winds lifted it through the swaying bluebells and the willows that dipped into the pools and the starlings that swirled across the valley. But under the hills, all Efa heard was her own steps: stone on stone.

Autumn came – acorns and gloamings and toadstools and lanterns. Anwen played her song into the fogs and the sunsets, under the woodsmoke and the rain. It rang through her sleep and carried through her days. The year waned slowly, slow as the moon sleeps. Until one morning, she woke to frost on her window, silver and ferny. Then snow and snow.

Midwinter. Anwen plaited her whistle into her long, thick hair. She couldn't turn her head. She held her mother's and Mamgu's hands. Twilight hinted beyond the hills.

"Anwen, please, I can't lose you, too. Not both of my girls," her mother said.

"You won't lose me. And Efa won't be lost any longer. I'll bring her home. And we'll sit by the fire and eat griddle cakes dripping with butter. Everything will be as it always was, but we won't have our voices. That won't matter, not if we have each other."

The day shrank into stars. They sang. Sang until it echoed into the village, blended into the other songs, and travelled on the night winds to the hills. The hills cracked open. The hills poured the Barrow Men into the dark.

Black prints stamped towards the village, and the Barrow Men followed: bone breath puffing white, bat laughter echoing wide. Anwen held Mamgu's and her mother's hands tighter. Talons on the door. Hinges creaking. Claws on flagstones. Shadows. She stopped singing.

The dark sped, gripping her, breathing on her. And in it, there were grey faces and talons and horns. Anwen screamed, but nothing came out. Night was all around her in bare trees and stinging stars. Her hands flailed to her plait: it was still tight. She saw the hills split open. She saw the Barrow Men piling inside. Then she saw nothing more.

There was a glow that smelled of leaf rot and carrion. And in it were shadows, tables, bones. The Barrow Men were feasting. She couldn't turn her head. Talons carried her through the halls. She called for her sister, but nothing came out. Then she saw her: golden head bowed, legs weighted by stone shoes, dancing and dancing and dancing.

The Barrow Men put Anwen down, and Efa looked up. Her face scrunched. Then they were clutching each other in tears and heartbeats and silence. Then talons had Anwen again, were pulling off her boots, forcing her feet into stone shoes, moving her limbs into a dance. Round and round and round. The stone rang cold. Then the hands let go. The Barrow Men were sitting at tables, were gnawing mammoth bones, were not looking at Anwen. And as their laughter echoed, she reached for her hair and pulled her plait apart. Her heart was all through her, all through the hall. She lifted the whistle to her mouth and played.

Her song was buttercups and willows and wrens, but also fire-sides and soup hot from the stove and griddle cakes dripping butter. The Barrow Men dropped the mammoth bones. They stood and juddered, gasped and froze. A great crack rang out, and moonlight bent down into the halls, flooding silver and bright. The hill had split open. Anwen and Efa pulled off their stone shoes, and gripping hands, they ran.

Anwen didn't know how they got home, how they ran the winter valley in bare feet. She only knew her mother's and Mamgu's arms thrown around her, their tears and smiles. She only knew holding her sister's hand so tightly it hurt. When the dawn came, red sky over gleaming snow, the hill had sealed shut. The village folk celebrated until sunset, and then through the night until the sunrise. And only then did they sleep, deeper than dreams. And Anwen and Efa ate griddle cakes dripping with butter until their bellies strained.

And the years went by. The Summers brimmed more golden, and the Winters sparkled more silver. And there was no fear on the longest night because of Anwen's song. And she played her tin whistle until she was old. And then the villagers passed her song down the ages. For so long, that folk forgot Anwen's and Efa's names and called them the Silent Sisters. And then longer still, until they forgot them and forgot the Barrow Men. But, still, they remember to sing the Midwinter.

Redbean

Dixon March

Dixon March is an undisclosed person. At no point has she hosted a midnight radio talk show and/or intercepted dark messages from the stars. There are rumors she may operate out of Omaha, Nebraska, US.

1

At the corner shop she ignored the way her ankle monitor bit into the bone while she hunted through the shelves for something to eat. Dust covered everything. The prices were three, four dollars higher than anywhere else because you certainly paid for convenience when you couldn't walk or take the bus to a grocery store four city blocks away. Not without going to prison at least.

At this dark hour, the corner shop was quiet, save for the occasional drunk who wandered in and muttered violence to themselves or the street people who shuffled through, buried in their cocoons of blankets and coats. She felt safe. No Probo to ask her *what kind of life are you making for your child, Miss Larron?* No ex-boyfriends to glare at her baby bump and moan *why are you ruining my life?* For a moment she was free of a certain type of bullshit, and it might have been peaceful if she hadn't been so hungry.

Larron pushed aside the growl in her gut and examined what groceries the corner shop had to offer. Dented cans of vegetables, paper boxes of pasta nibbled by rats. The shop cat slept at her feet, curled up on a case of microwave noodles, too fat to care about much. Larron didn't want to buy noodles or any of this junk, but the ache of hunger kept her there. She touched her baby bump and thought of all the times canned ham made her puke. *The little jerk,* she thought with fondness, *is already picky.*

Beans, her WIC advisor suggested. Beans and shelf-stable cheese, but all the bricks of cheese were in packages stained brown and decades old. Dubious. Larron leaned down to peer into the shadows between the shelves and maybe she saw something good.

Before she reached her hand into the dark hollow, she paused. Bitey things likely mulled about in there. Spiders, rats, whatever the shop cat had determined too dangerous to pursue.

After her stomach growled again, Larron thought *fuck it* and reached in to root around in the dark of the shelf. Her fingers grazed a cool corner of cardboard.

When she pulled back her fist she found in it a pristine but vintage box of dried red beans.

The box was narrow and tall like a monolith, and on the front was a picture of beans in a bowl heaped with yellow pats of butter. Above it, *Jackelsons' Beans* raged in atomic age font. The box looked new. Larron gave it a shake and the dried beans inside rattled like loose teeth in a skull.

"YOU gonna EAT that?"

One of the street people had wandered close. Larron regarded the figure, genderless within their layers of clothes. Their sun-damaged face peered out from beneath a spray of gray hair, and they spoke with a voice like cracked concrete. "I said YOU GONNA EAT that?" The person eyed the box of beans.

Suddenly, Larron wanted the beans more than anything else. "I'm gonna eat this."

The street person pointed at her with a crooked arm encased in gloves. "Bitch, you don't know how to eat those. You're gonna cook them or something."

"You're supposed to cook beans." The response tumbled out, and she instantly regretted it. *Do not engage,* she thought. She inched her way out of the conversation, shuffled down the aisle to the cashier, who looked stoned or asleep.

"No! You EAT them RAW!" The street person tugged at their cheeks madly. "You gotta crack them open with your teeth to get to the little screaming souls inside!"

At the register, Larron gave her empty basket to the cashier, and he woke up a little with the noise. Larron gave him a look like *I didn't start this.*

The street person continued their rant. "Those beans are special. You bite them open! If you cook 'em you ruin 'em, and a ruined bean calls the Jackelsons to you. They got a big house full of things you can't even believe. They'll show up right on your doorstep and when they will show up motherfucker you'll be sorry sorry sorry."

The cashier glanced at the box with an arched eyebrow, and when the price didn't scan he punched in the number on the yellowed sticker.

Forty-five cents. Larron smiled. It was almost like stealing.

2

Larron walked to her building with her beans in the pocket of her sweatpants. The night was crowded and loud, bright with traffic. She reached her building as the ankle monitor bit deep into her leg and a chill wind chased gutter trash past the alleys.

Her building was a brownstone complex built in the 60s, six floors full of cramped one and no bedroom units. The entry door screamed on hinges about to crack. Larron passed through the hall to her battered mailbox full of court letters and reminders of unpaid fines that she would not address that night or maybe ever.

Once she reached her studio, Larron set the beans by her hotplate and shuffled to the back window. She gazed out at her view: an alley crowded with dumpsters and old tenements, beyond that a horizon of big box stores and a tangle of highways. Several floors below her fire escape, a racoon or a stray cat rooted in the dumpster, scattered cans and shredded plastic. The landlord had put concrete rocks on the dumpster lid, but such was no match for the animal.

Larron watched the raccoon wrestle with whatever dinner rotted at the bottom, and with her pregnancy nose she could smell all of it, sweet and rancid and cloying. Her stomach curdled. Her newly sensitive stomach was the only reason she didn't dumpster dive herself. Barely anything made her vomit. Although she was well aware that if you picked the right places the stuff you could find was actually pretty fresh.

Not that she could get to those places at the moment. With a scowl she lifted one leg of her marshmallow sweatpants and poked the ankle monitor, the black digital barnacle on her leg. Then she shut the window to avoid the dry heaves.

In the kitchenette by her hotplate, Larron heated a pot of water and opened the box of red beans. The carboard crinkled like new. She soured at the thought of how long they'd take to cook, and when she dumped the content of the box into the water one bean tumbled out onto the floor.

With a hand cradled over her bump, she picked up the bean and peered at it. The bean was surprisingly large, a round flat thing in vivid crimson, the red of an organ, like some kidney full of blood and hardened with formaldehyde. The sides of it pillowed out as if it contained multitudes.

Larron plopped it in the water with the rest of them.

While she waited, Larron laid on her futon and read and fell asleep, maybe. The city lights streamed in through the window and pooled on the floor in strange shapes. As her eyes fluttered shut, she half-dreamt of a tree with a dark hollow. The tree grew tall and gnarly, and it told her it had gems inside, jewelry and watches and maybe even some Traveler's Express checks, unsigned. It was one of those fairy tale trees with ribbons and flowers, but the ribbons were organs draped about the branches like party streamers and the flowers glistened in deep jewel tones from a mist of blood.

The robins and sparrows that nestled in the tree had black eyes like her old fence, Harvey at the pawn shop. Big black eyes like mirrors. They chattered in Harvey's voice; *Sorry I had to tell the pigs where I got the watches. Next time steal something shittier.* They held little crowbars in their beaks, like hers, the one confiscated by the cops for evidence in the string of smash and grabs.

The sight struck her with longing. She loved that little crowbar.

Then the robins fluttered off with broken window wings and bloody breasts. The dark inside the tree hollow quivered with strange shapes that might have been worms or maggots. Long muddled things with glossy backs and fat legs and mismatched wings. Her sleep brain interpreted them as souls, crispy soft little souls that screamed when you cracked them open. And the street person was there with her sun-cragged face to say *crack them open! If you cook them the Jackelsons will come.* That's when the water boiled over and hissed on the hotplate loudly enough Larron woke up with a start.

The moon was fat and seemed to fill the window.

Something screeched softly.

3

It took Larron several minutes to focus. Her head felt like a bloody socket packed with cotton. She wondered when she last ate a truly good meal.

The screech came from the hotplate in long anguished notes, and pinkish foam covered the folding table and dripped onto the crap linoleum floor. The beans in the pot had turned to a murky redblack soup that reeked and made her instantly retch. It was not a thing to be eaten, and she had the sense it would stain her walls, forever linger as a ghost scent in all her clothes and skin. *Ruined*, she thought. Everything ruined. Only out of morbid curiosity did she stick a spoon into the stuff to see what horrors swirled inside.

On the spoon appeared a red bean, swollen three times the size of its dry self. Its sides burst and leaked a sick gray substance. Larron covered her nose and squinted at it. The stuff dripped down the spoon in sticky strings that terminated in globs that looked like small heads trapped in ichor. There she made out tiny faces. Eyes pinched shut and mouths open in stark terror.

With her breath held, she threw the bean back into the pot. It splashed there and more bean goop floated to the surface, more of those tiny tortured human faces like skulls stirred up in a swamp.

Larron dry heaved at the sight and did not cry out or scream but instead hustled the pot to the window, to the fire escape above the dumpster.

Once outside she chucked the pot into the alley, and the contents sailed to the depths below. Inwardly she apologized to whatever racoon might remain there. The pot smacked the side of the dumpster with a dull clang and bounced to the concrete, where it rolled and came to a stop. Its guts puddled out and seeped into the cracks, into the soil beneath.

The moon was so heavy and close Larron felt like it was the blind eye of some luminescent giant pressed against a glass jar. She squinted to look up at it and that's when she saw the trees.

The alleyway and the adjacent buildings were swallowed up in tall, gnarly trees that hung with bulbous fruit. A manner of murky kudzu wound its way up around the trunks and into the branches with leaves like moongray knives and nothing moved, nothing made a sound. It was if the traffic and the neighbors and the wild creatures had all gone extinct.

Larron wavered at the top of the fire escape, her face slack in disbelief, her hair askew as some sleep-stoned Rapunzel.

Pregnancy induced psychosis, she thought.

A warm breeze skipped across her cheek.

In the air was the smell of food. Something delectable and savory and unrecognizable, something steamy-salt-crusty-crisp, a smell so fat and delicious Larron thought she could live on the smell alone, whatever it was. Her stomach clawed at her. Even the little lovely jerk fluttered like a patch of gas inside her guts and seemed to say *ah hell, that's the shit.*

The smell seemed to emit from a place in the trees, near a flicker of red light between shadowed trunks, and as her eyes focused she made out the shape of a window. Lace curtains and a yellow glow. A windowsill box full of flowers the color of blood. Around the glow little bricks like some fairy tale cottage, some gloomy gingerbread vision with ivy crept between the mortar in splintered greenblack fingers. Chimney smoke curled from between the tree branches in a lazy gray snake.

Larron glanced between the house and the monitor on her ankle and wondered just how many feet lay between her and the warm delicious-smelling place. Her movements would be marked on the outdated computer in her Probo's office, a little dotted line in GPS but only after thirty or so feet. *Sir Ms Probo Sir,* Larron practiced, *I was just taking out the trash.*

The smell strained her thoughts and at the edge of it was a little mad voice that said, *if it were only about you, now...*

Larron grabbed her slipper shoes and crept down the fire escape.

4

Larron crept between the trees and eyed their glossy-wet fruit like hearts and spleens that dangled from the branches. Her slipper shoes crunched softly in the dry grass, which sounded like delicate little bones every time she took a step.

The cottage itself was larger than she first discerned from her fire escape, wider and taller with a peaked roof like a crooked pope hat. Larron crept past a mailbox that hung on a moldy post and moved into a lawn crowded with overgrown garden plots, the plants leafy and greenblack. On the path between them was a scattering of red specks. As she took the path through the garden she stooped to pick up a single red bean that had tumbled from the leaves.

She pinched it between her fingers. It wriggled, screeched in a mad cicada voice loud enough to wake the neighborhood dogs.

The red shell cracked like a carapace and out scrambled a wormy legged thing with a human face and eyes pinched shut like agony and wings glued to its back in an afterbirth mucus.

It tried to scramble up her wrist.

She shook it off and swallowed her scream.

When it skittered back into the garden, Larron checked behind her to make sure her fire escape was still there. It was. On any other night if another world opened up in her back alley she'd have turned the fuck around and gone back to sleep. It was the smell that pulled her forward, tugged her as if by hooks snagged in her gut. Her stomach churned eagerly, as wild and sharp as a racoon in a dumpster. It was a desperate stomach, pressed to the limits of its ability to function with all the action going on below, those cells that multiplied and patched together like a little construction site. A flicker of movement pushed at her guts, and she told it, *just wait a minute,* she'd figure out what that smell was here in a sec. Human soul harvest or not.

She crept closer to the house. The uppermost windows came into view, frames that glowed orange and hosted a shadow play of monstrous shapes. The figures that moved behind the lace curtains looked not remotely human. They lumbered past with their elongated limbs and necks like sagged praying mantises. Giants of strange proportions. It almost broke her resolve.

She caught a whiff of the delectable scent from a downstairs kitchen door that stood cocked open. No shadows moved across those windows. From the kitchen leaked an aromatic steam.

With one eye on the beasts of the upper floors, Larron crouched low and crept to the kitchen, peeked in with one eye.

The kitchen was a fairy tale, all wood and stone and naked fire. A hearth burned with a massive red blaze and the black pot inside burbled. Skinless carcasses hung from one wall and bled out into ceramic basins. Blood made the floor slick. In the center of the kitchen was a table like a massive chopping block heaped with platters of meat roasted to a golden hue. The impossibly delectable smell came from that table, she was certain.

Larron nearly lost herself and leapt forward, buried her face into it, but an instant before she went mad her thief's instincts took over and she bent down to tiptoe inside, her eye focused on the biggest chicken leg she'd ever seen.

At least, she thought it was a chicken leg.

She moved up to the table where a number of forks had been laid out, huge silver things for a hand ten times her size. With a tremble, she picked up a fork and moved to skewer a fine morsel, a strip of glossy gold savory flesh with the sinew still draped off it in silver ribbons. It was all imaginary, she thought, and she was probably standing in the alley about to stick a dead cat with a stray piece of wire, but the illusion certainly looked good enough to eat.

The tines sunk deep into the meat. She had it inches from her face when she heard someone whisper, "Someone *cooked* the *beans*."

She froze, the fork gripped in her hand as though she were a toddler with a mini trident. The source of the voice seemed to come from behind the heap.

She peered around the edge of the table and saw no one there in the kitchen. Footsteps strained the wood floors overhead, the movement of those large and malformed creatures she'd glanced in the window, but whatever dark purpose engaged them it did not at the moment intersect with her goals. The voice, she decided, had to be another figment within this figment, and in any case her stomach insisted that she put that juicy cooked morsel straight into her mouth.

Larron began to eat again, and another voice said behind the mountain of meat, "Someone cooked the beans!"

Larron ducked down, sure she'd been caught. No footsteps or shadows moved, and the voices seemed disembodied, hovered somewhere near the center of the table.

Her stomach in a violent churn for want of the morsel, Larron breathed deep and calmed herself, then stalked a full circle around the table, fork still in her fist.

Behind the mounds of roasted flesh were several smaller platters heaped with round shapes that blinked and stared.

Before her scream betrayed her she clamped a hand over her mouth.

Heads. Human, if she assessed correctly. Cheekbones and noses and forward facing eyes. Stripped clean of hair and flesh. Some gazed at her with milkblind roasted eyes and apples in their mouths. The few who did not maintain their apples were toothless, the teeth still embedded in the soppy red sides of the fruit.

As Larron stared at them with stark horror, one head whispered, "Someone cooked the beans." Then they all began to say it in a tangle. *Someone cooked the, someone, someone cooked...*

One head suddenly screamed, a freakish wail of a noise, and the rest followed suit. Larron crouched, her pulse frantic. Although clearly lungless, they all screamed with an intensity and volume that had them thrash about on their platter together like baby birds in a life-and-death struggle.

Larron stabbed at the heads with the fork, jabbed the table near the edge of their plate. *"Shut the fuck up."*

They all fell silent, silent.

Immediately, something thumped upstairs.

Larron backed away slowly with her fist still clamped around the fork in a grip that fear would not let her untangle. She kept one eye on the heads and one ear on the footsteps upstairs, which had begun to clomp loudly. Closer. There was an insectoid skittering from the upper floors that could have been the speech of mad cicadas. Despite the scent of lovely food that gnawed at her Larron thought, *cannibalism, not the best choice,* and began to retreat, give up on the hallucination in a careful quiet step towards the door....

She nearly tripped on something beneath her. One slipper shoe slipped off, and when she chased it back onto her foot she saw the corner of the kitchen, behind the door. There, thrown unceremoniously into the bloody dust, was a pile of human bones. Discarded bodies. The things once attached to the heads on the table, their ribcages, spines, femurs, tiny metacarpals in a scatter.

About the bones were littered the things the heads once owned, items kept on their person. Shreds of clothes, eyeglasses, hats, dusty things in which spiders made their home. But also watches and rings, diamond earrings and strings of pearls strung about decapitated neck bones. Wallets tumbled out of pockets and vomited up yellowed IDs and crumpled leaves of cash.

Larron eyed the heap. When her dry heaves had stilled from the sight of cobweb dry cartilage and death, she made a quick estimation of the value of items there. It was no small amount.

She glanced quick to the heads on the block, then to the door that led out of the kitchen and into shadow, where the cicada screech grew louder. Then she grabbed a fistful of the monied stuff between the bones and thrust it into the pockets of her marshmallow sweatpants. In went several palmfuls of wadded bills and strings of precious stones before they began to strain at the seams.

One of the heads on the table wriggled its lidless eyes towards her. "*You* cooked the beans."

The rest murmured in agreement with their toothless lisps. *You did, you did.*

Beyond the kitchen, the floors wheezed under the weight of the large owners of the house. They stomped closer. With her pockets full Larron decided it was not a time to meet them. (She had visions of the owners with bulbous, demonic heads, cleavers and pitchforks in their elongated hands, sinister grins full of teeth as they scooped her up and put her and her little jerk on the chopping block. The idea shook her and from within her baby bump came little palpitations, like the unformed creature there thrashed about as if in the throes of nightmare.) Dizzy from her elevated heart rate, Larron slipped out the kitchen door with a glance behind her. Long and spindly shadows stretched out over the gore-splattered kitchen floor.

She hustled silently out into the dark of night, bent low and lopsided for the bulge in her pockets, but she didn't stop. When she crossed into the garden there was a screech from the cottage, and when she peered at the house she found monstrous shadows had filled the kitchen window. She picked up the pace and kept her eye to the threats inside and in so doing she slammed into the mailbox and fell with it to the ground. Jewels tumbled out of her pockets into the brittle grass. For a terror-fazed moment, she tried to put the mailbox back up on its post, but her hands shook too terribly.

From the house, the owners wailed, a sound inhuman and enraged.

At that Larron abandoned the mailbox, dropped it to the ground and bolted toward her studio, the dim pinprick of light through the trees. But before she vanished across the alleyway and up her fire escape, she caught a glimpse of the mailbox's side, the jagged burnt letters written there: *The Jackelsons.*

5

Back in her apartment, the blinds pulled, Larron ordered take-out. Chinese. Cashew and noodles. Spring Rolls. Piles of them. All vegetarian.

She half expected the delivery driver to look down at the flat-tened wads of cash she handed him and tell her she was out of her mind, that she handed him newspaper or leaves or alley shit, some product of madness birthed by whatever psychotic break she'd experienced. Larron thought she had to be out of her mind, and the idea came with a calmness she wished she'd had when she'd been arrested.

The delivery driver looked down at the wad of green bills and said, "Thanks for the tip."

Larron wolfed down the meal and fell asleep on the couch imme-diately after. Her guts turned peaceful, the little jerk nestled among a pillowy soup of calories and msg.

Before she drifted off, she wondered, when else had she ever felt so good.

6

The following night, Larron slipped on a dark blue sweatshirt to go over her sweatpants and under it she strapped a flatpack: a bag that clung to the body so when on the run, one might not look as though they carried anything at all.

A knock came at her studio door, and it was absolutely a cop knock, so right away Larron knew it belonged to the Probo, a large woman with a sour chin and decades of abuse seeped in deeply through the crinkles of her forehead. The woman wore a heavy canvas peacoat even when it was warm, like some street person with a drinking problem, and Larron had wondered not more than once how long the woman spent out of doors herself.

At the door, the Probo glowered and stomped over the threshold without being invited. "Quick check-in."

Larron moved to the couch and sat casually, made sure to place herself over the black ski cap she'd laid there. When she crossed her legs her bare foot stuck out with the ankle monitor mean and heavy against the bone. "Am I in violation?" A touch of panic fluttered inside her, but she wasn't sure if maybe that was the little jerk, to whom often a shot of adrenaline meant playtime.

The woman didn't sit or answer. She cradled a tablet in the crook of her arm and scrolled through the blue glow. "You've been spending a lot of time out back in the alley."

Larron nodded. "Fresh air is good for the baby."

"Is it?" The woman's eyes narrowed. "You been talking to Harvey?"

"Who's Harvey?"

The joke fell flat between them.

Larron chipped the edges off her smile. "No," she said. She wondered what it was about corrections that ruined a person's sense of humor.

The Probo took a long look around and poked at a heap of clothes in one corner and examined the dried bean disaster around the hotplate. The folding table had melted a bit and the stains left on the linoleum were deep, deep red. "How are you eating?"

Larron smiled. "Good."

When the Probo left Larron gave it some time before she grabbed the ski mask and stepped out onto the fire escape. A warm breeze rifled through, and she wondered if the Probo had noticed it as she stood in the studio with her canvas peacoat, the warmth or the smell that still wafted up, delicious and sinister.

On the fire escape Larron gazed across the alley. The trees remained. The smell drifted like a savory ghost, although less delectable now that she knew its origins. From between the garden plots, a long, crooked shadow moved, rooted around, as if in the middle of harvest.

On the fire escape sat the mini crowbar Harvey had brought her.

Larron pulled the ski cap down over her face.

"Fee fi fo fum," she whispered. Then she moved softly on thieves' feet into the night.

Mystic Mama

Megha Nayar

Mama says I was born forty days too early. There was no doctor to help, since women from our clan do not get doctors, only a midwife. The midwife taught Mama how to hold me. Like this, she showed her, like you're holding a dollop of wet clay. Careful, he must not lose shape. Once Mama had learnt how to keep me alive, the midwife, in exchange for a silver coin and a box of saffron, gave her the formula for an important concoction – one that would help build my semi-formed head, hands and legs. Brew all the ingredients in a copper vessel exactly at dawn, she instructed Mama. Pour one-third of it into this little one's mouth, in small sips lest he choke, and let the rest sit at the east-facing window for six hours, absorbing sunlight. Slather the golden goop on the baby at noon, before his bath. Do this every day for forty days.

So, my Mama, she who is a half-witch, got to work. She blended two cups of spring water with two spoons of fresh honey, two cubes of pink pepper, and the clipped wings of two dragonflies, every morning for forty mornings, a prayer to Mother Nature always on her lips. One-third of her miracle potion would go into my belly, and the rest would seep from my skin into my bones. Slowly, a nose appeared above my mouth, my heart hardened, my feet sprouted toes. I concretized. Except for my ears that were yet to form, I became a human whole.

***

I was four years old when our saahib's son noticed that my ears were malformed.

We had been playing on the terrace of my house with a kite. Since his father owned the tomato fields that my Mama tilled and toiled on, he had been the one flying the kite, while I had stood dutifully behind him with the spool of thread, enabling his flight. After he'd tugged at the thread for an hour, his tired arms couldn't hold up any more, and so, he offered to transfer ownership of the glass-laced pink string to my hands. Standing right behind my head, he caught a glimpse of my ears up-close for the first time. "Demon-child!" he screamed, then burst into cackles of laughter. "Those cannot be the ears of a human. You are a demon-child!"

He flung the spool at the terrace floor. He sprinted down the stairs and ran in the direction of the fields, screaming the demon-child theory at the top of his lungs. He met a few dozen elders en route, and the school headmaster, and some of our classmates. He told all of them. From her kitchen window, my Mama – she who is a half-witch – heard his proclamations. She wasn't particularly surprised; this moment had been long overdue.

Mama got to work. She filled an earthen pot with five cups of goat's milk and added to it some yellow sugar, a spoonful of her tears, and a handful of bark scraped off the gooseberry tree. She poured the drink into small glasses, offering one to each of the curious villagers who visited our home demanding to see my ears. When they bid us goodbye, all memory of my supposed demon-child status was erased from their minds. Nobody teased me about my misshapen ears ever after – not even the halfwit who'd discovered them.

***

At nine, I got into my first fight.

It happened in the empty tin shed on the outskirts of the village. My friends and I had assembled to trade marbles. Mhahn, who had a set of six white ones, wanted to trade two of them for some of Rhooc's transparent beauties. Rhooc didn't agree. My glass marbles resemble our planet, he said to Mhahn. They're gorgeous. I'm not selling them cheap. Look at the bright green streak inside this one! Doesn't it look like a bridge over the ocean? Sure does, replied Mhahn, but if your marbles are the Earth, mine are galaxies. Look at the thick strokes of grey and ivory inside this one. So dense with stars, it could be the Milky Way!

They continued to argue. Each wanted to give less and take more. Their altercation grew louder, hotter. I would have left without intervening but they roped me in. Tell Rhooc he is being unreasonable here, Mhahn ordered. Don't you think I should get at least two of his white marbles in exchange for my four, Rhooc countered. Conditioned by my Mama to always play fair, I sided with Rhooc. Mhahn's marbles are not pretty, I declared. They're plain. If he wants four of Rhooc's, he should be willing to trade not two but three of his milky-whites.

Rhooc raised his arms in triumph and did a little dance.

Ten minutes later, once Rhooc completed the exchange and left, Mhahn – his pocket much lighter now than when he'd arrived – shot me a piercing glare. Before I could swerve, he slammed a fist into my right eye. I staggered and collapsed. He grinned at me awhile, then stomped away. I remained splayed on the floor until my vision cleared enough to take me home.

When Mama glimpsed the perimeter of purple around my eye,

she asked no questions. As a proficient half-witch, she got to work. In a bowl of glycerine, she melted half an enchanted thread. To that she added two spoons of blue ash and a pinch of crystal dust. Once the ingredients had melded, Mama applied the paste – which sparkled brighter than all of Mhahn's and Rhooc's marbles combined – to my injured eye, in slow, gentle strokes.

When I awoke the next morning, the purple patch had faded. My eye was good as new.

I never met Mhahn or Rhooc again.

***

A month after I turned fourteen, I (was) kissed (by) a boy for the first time.

We were tracing our way home from school. For three days, angry clouds had poured endless, inky rain. The fields and streets were submerged. It was late afternoon but dark enough to pass for early night. Phuln and I were wading through a by-lane, holding hands. The usual patch of road that connected our school to the village had gone down under, so this was an alternative route. Unsure of where we were treading and afraid of sliding into a ditch, we stayed close, eventually wrapping our arms around each other's waist for a secure grip.

A noisy bolt of lightning struck every few minutes, startling us but briefly illuminating the path. We soldiered on, under the thundering slate-grey sky, aided by those fleeting flashes of light. Never before in our short lives had we been so completely at the mercy of the elements. Teenagers, we were the size of grown men but nervous as lost children. We wanted to get back home quick, without breaking a limb or meeting a snake or being ambushed by evil spirits.

After two long hours of trudging through unknown terrain, we finally reached the tomato fields near my house. We recognized the scarecrow with the red turban – that is how we knew we had finally arrived. Enormously relieved but drained of the life force that had propelled us thus far, we stopped behind the banyan tree to catch our breath.

Panting, we gazed awhile at the leaky horizons. When our lungs and limbs felt lighter, we turned to look each other in the eyes. That is when I felt it – a surge of affection in my chest, coupled with a fervid desire to kiss the trickles of rain off Phuln's lips.

We stood there for god knows how long – embracing, entwined, exhilarated.

When I reached home, Mama welcomed me with a mysterious smile. The half-witch that she is, she had intuited that I'd done something wild. But it wasn't like her to interrogate me, least of all when I was drenched to the bones. So, she got to work. In a tumbler she blended half a cup of moonlight with four orchids, a handful of sage leaves, and a tiny emerald. Massage this potion into your scalp, she instructed me. Let its miracle seep into your mind overnight.

I did as directed.

Something in that concoction cleansed my thoughts of shame. The next day, when I ran into Phuln in the fields, I felt no fear in locking lips with him, only goose pimples.

***

I made it to eighteen before I was called a *thatoot* in full public view.

Phuln and I were at the village fair. It was a crisp November evening, replete with scents of confectionery, the sweet cacophony of giggling children, and whispered love notes of young couples. A Ferris wheel stood towering in one corner, decked up in fairy lights, flanked by a dazzling carousel to the left and a giant trampoline to the right. On the opposite side, food vendors had stationed their wagons. They were vending happiness today – stuffed breads, buttery biscuits, hot fritters, cotton candy in pastel shades. Phuln dragged me to the popsicle cart. Let's get different colours, he gushed, squeezing my hand. Then, we can pose at the photo booth and stick our tongues out, like we did as kids. How about green for me and yellow for you?

Laughing, we ambled over to the photo booth, sucking on our popsicles, occasionally stealing a lick off each other's. Our arms locked, our eyes danced. Our hearts were full, brimming over. We were in a private bubble, insulated from the stares of the people around – people who, unknown to us, were finding our indulgences offensive.

One of them approached us when we were leaving the photo booth. Phuln held in his hand a sheet of glossy paper with our faces plastered on it. Wow, what a pretty pair of thatoots, the man sneered. Got yourselves a picture for proof, eh? Not like you need it. Anybody can tell you're pansies. Filthy bastards. What do you need a photo for anyway, eh?!

We knew better than to challenge a hateful bigot. We started walking away, but he wasn't done. He reached for the picture. In one quick move he grabbed it from Phuln's hand, and before we could take it back, he ripped it to shreds. There, he cackled, flinging the shreds to the ground. Lick the pieces into shape, maybe? All that practice with popsicles will help!

He spat on the photo bits, over and over, thoo-thoo-thoo-ing until we were sufficiently defiled, then marched off. I stared at his receding back, at the visible nape of his neck. My fingers trembled. Heat rose to my temples. How I'd have loved to shove a dagger in his flesh. Oh, how I'd have loved to return him to his maker.

When Phuln and I got home, Mama was waiting with a sumptuous dinner. There was jasmine rice and lentil curry, both of which we love, but there was also a bright, purple-coloured soup. One of my special brews, Mama smiled. It contains lemon zest and wild mushrooms and lavender flowers and a pearl. The perfect balm to heal your bleeding souls.

Knowing that Mama is a half-witch, we obeyed her and drank. Over the next few hours, the broken slices of our hearts found each other and came together. The wounds of humiliation scabbed and fell off. Pride swam into our veins, and took its rightful place. We wouldn't let anybody abrade us hereafter.

***

On my twenty-first birthday, Mama told me I should start preparing to fly away.

The year was 2022 AD. Our country was rapidly regressing into medieval methods of social governance. Our village had newly appointed a culture preservation committee. They were going door-to-door, checking for sinners, seeking to reform the debased. Is there a heretic in this house, they asked at every door. Someone who refuses to pray? Someone who smokes grass or practises magic? Someone who has taken a lover of the same sex?

When they arrived at our door that day, Mama wore her plainest clothes and stripped herself of all signs of occult. To the men she appeared a meek widow, pious and powerless. They asked her just one question: what does your son do? He is a man of the fields, she replied sincerely. He uses his hands to turn the mud and scatter seeds and nurture saplings until they sprout blood-red fruit. He builds barns, and chases mice and geese. That is what my son does – he milks the soil. I pray, he ploughs, Mother Earth provides.

The committee men nodded respectfully. They did not ask to see me. On their way out, they gave Mama a little salute.

Once they were gone, Mama sat me down. You have to leave, she repeated. Even as a half-witch, I am ultimately mortal. I cannot protect you forever. At some point, Phuln and you will want to build your own nest. You cannot do it here. These people will come for your heads. You must go someplace where your love will be permitted, and celebrated. In order to do that, you must first learn to fly.

But, Mama, I said, how is that even possible?

I have figured out the recipe, she whispered. After months of trying, I have finally decocted the elixir that will help you escape. It took you forty days to go from shapeless infant to able-bodied human; it will now take you forty days to go from human to able-bodied bird. We have to start today.

I watched as Mama poured three glasses of rose water into an earthen pot. She added a storm cloud and two peacock feathers. Then, she opened our window and grabbed at the sky. With one quick swoop, she plucked the North Star and dropped it into the mix. The liquid in the pot, already simmering, rose like an angry ocean to the brim.

Here, Mama said, handing me a cupful. We have enough to fill forty cups. You must have one every night. Do not miss a single dose.

I followed Mama's prescription for forty nights.

On the forty-first morning, I awoke a mythical beast, part-avian. My arms had been replaced by a pair of fine, long-feathered wings. My neck had thickened. My vision was keener. I felt simultaneously stronger and lighter.

My Mama – she who is a half-witch – gifted me a new birth.

I went up to her and fell at her feet. We hugged, sobbed. She tied an amulet around my wrist. This will be your compass, she said, to bring you home whenever you feel like visiting.

When dusk fell, I unfurled my wings and flew. With Phuln seated on my back, his soft hands wrapped tenderly around my neck, I flew. Together, we traversed the expanse of the village, flying over the tomato fields and Mhahn's farmhouse and Rhooc's family stables and the village school and innumerable cows and pigs and scarecrows. With every flying minute, my body grew in might. We soared so high, land and people fell out of sight. The sky turned pitch-black but the moon was our guide and the stars our allies. Unfettered and hopeful, we surrendered to the cosmos. That which had created us would help us – two men in need of a miracle – find a new home.

Misrule

Fiona Moore

Fiona Moore is a queer writer and two-time BSFA Award finalist whose work has appeared in Clarkesworld, Cossmass Infinities, Asimov's, and four consecutive editions of The Best of British SF. Her professional website is at www.fiona-moore.com, and she is @drfionamoore on all social media. She lives in London, England with a tortoiseshell cat who is bent on world domination.

I'd missed the first day because I had to work late at the big house, preparing a festive meal for Sir Danvers and his guests with the rest of the kitchen staff. If I hadn't, I might not have come home to smashed eggs, dead chickens, and a henhouse on fire.

I'd stared from the devastation in the henyard to the stricken face of my mother sitting by the cottage door, and back again. Knowing, from many years of going hungry when the hens weren't laying enough, or when some disease ran through the flock, that this was her livelihood gone.

I started to ask who would do such a horrible thing, to a widow no less, and why. But then I stopped, because I knew.

Misrule.

***

After I'd helped put out the fire and cleaned up the destruction as much as I could, I went off to find the Lord of Misrule and confront him.

I found Misrule, consisting of its Lord and his Followers, in a clearing in the forest just north of the village. We all know how it works. Every year, work stops for twelve days, and normal laws, customs, and rules cease to apply. Everyone could do exactly what they wanted.

And the poorest person in the village becomes the Lord of Misrule, more powerful than Sir Danvers or anyone else.

There was always a gang of hangers-on who'd follow him and do exactly what he said. We called them Misrule. The twelve days were Misrule, but so were the people who made certain anarchy and lawlessness abided during it. Because when someone, looking at the ruins of their home or livelihood, sighs "Misrule," it really doesn't matter whether you mean the time it happened, or the people who did it.

They'd cleared the snow, dug a roasting pit, and set up stakes, and no less than three of my mothers' hens were on the spit. I could see others lying by the side. They wouldn't be able to eat them all.

It was a risk even approaching him. After what had happened ten years ago, I usually stayed as far away from Misrule, and especially its Lord, as I could. But for once I was so angry I didn't even feel a memory of fear. I walked right up to him, in his tattered, ragged velvet robes, and kicked him as hard as I could.

He yelped, and for a minute looked thunderous. But the drink and the food and the pleasure of the destruction he'd wreaked made him torpid and slow-natured, so he just chuckled with sadistic pleasure. "Ooh, that hurt," he murmured, lasciviously.

"You've gone too far, Stebbins," I said. Using his real, everyday, outside-of-Misrule, name.

"That's Lord of Misrule, Mary Henwife's Daughter," he corrected.

"It's Mary Summersby now," I said, automatically.

"Oh, really? Why the change?" He played up to his audience. "Because you're working in the big house now? You're an apprentice cook with Mrs Roister, you're too good for the village?"

The Vicar kept saying that there was no such thing as magic, but there was, and this was it. I'd attacked him by using his real name; he'd counter by mocking my new one. Yes, it hurt.

"Or *maybe*," the Lord of Misrule drew out the word, "*maybe*, you're not Mary Henwife's Daughter because your mother's got no hens." At this, a few of his sycophants laughed.

"Cheer up, your mother'll be fine. Someone will give her some birds and she'll set up back in business. Or you can buy some for her, fine lady like you." He motioned to the assembled. "Sit down. Relax. Join us."

As well as the usual people, the beggars and odd-jobbers and taverners snuggling up in obscene embraces around the fire, I could see that a few of the neighbours had joined Misrule. Young men mostly, of course. And a couple of the stableboys from the big house, boys I'd actually liked. Until then. I could feel my lip twist. "Thanks, I won't."

"Maybe later?" the Lord of Misrule said meaningfully. Turning it into a threat. Now the anger was fading, the fear was starting to return.

"Maybe," I said, trying to make it equally threatening, but failing. The Lord of Misrule had much more practice at that sort of thing than I did.

"And remember, Mary Summersby, it's *Lord of Misrule* now

and for the next eleven days." The words were a command. "For these twelve days I assume my sacred office. Never forget that."

I couldn't.

What had I hoped to achieve, by coming out here? To hide the distress and confusion that was starting to overtake my shock-fuelled courage, I turned on my heel, wrapped my nice (if second-hand) wool cloak dramatically around me, and tried to stalk back towards the village.

***

On the way back to my mother's, I could see ours wasn't the only house they'd hit, though she'd taken the worst of it. Gates askew, windowpanes broken, Tom Pigman and Tom Pigman's Son trying to round up a herd of hogs that were enjoying their unexpected liberty a little too much.

Tom Blacksmith, shamefaced for not having done anything to stop Misrule, had come round with food and an invitation to have dinner with his family tomorrow night. I'd wanted to scream at him, but it was the holidays, and our positions could well have been reversed. Instead, I'd accepted on behalf of my mother, who was sitting motionless and speechless in a wooden chair by the hearth, just watching the coals.

"It'll be all right," I said to her, feebly. "Some neighbours will give us some chickens, and you can start up again."

Unexpectedly, she laughed with a harsh, barking noise. "Which neighbours?" she said.

"I don't know." She was right. She was Mary Henwife because she was the only one farming chickens in this village, at least on a scale big enough to make money you could build a life on. Even if a couple of people gave her a spare pullet or two, it would be one of the tough, scraggly kitchen chickens some people kept for eggs and company rather than the sleek highly-bred birds she'd had. And she'd have to get a new rooster, and they were expensive.

"I'll work hard, see if I can finish my apprenticeship early. Start making proper money."

She didn't even bother to laugh at that one. I could see the problems there, too. If I became a cook, I would get a decent wage, but I'd have to move to another village or to the city to get a job. I'd be spending a decent portion of my wages on lodgings and the other expenses I didn't have here.

We wouldn't starve, at least. People were sympathetic about Misrule; the church had a little fund. But it would be a long lean time before my mother could get back to her current level of prosperity. If ever.

The second day ended with the pair of us just sitting by the fire, hearing the shouts and cries and laughter as the sun went down and Misrule came back to the village. Staying still, like mice when the foxes come out to hunt.

***

"We could ask Sir Danvers to stop it," I said to the Vicar on the third day. He had come round asking if he could do anything to help, and I'd sarcastically told him he could help rebuild the henhouse. To my surprise, he'd taken off his hat, coat, and doublet, rolled up his sleeves, and set to work.

The Vicar shook his handsome head. "He never would."

"He would too," I said. "Misrule costs him. Remember what happened last year? No, of course you don't, that's right." The Vicar had taken over the post in the spring; his predecessor hadn't been quite right after the incident last Misrule with the barrel of sheep manure. "Steb— the Lord of Misrule got hold of Sir Danvers' stud stallion and ran him over rough country. Poor thing had to be put down. And he loved that horse."

"I'll wager he bought a new one, once he'd done mourning." The Vicar rummaged in the box of nails, his shirt, sweat-soaked despite the midwinter chill, clinging aesthetically to his muscles. "Losing a stud horse costs him, yes. But not like your mother losing her chickens or Tom Pigman his herd."

I glanced at the neighbours' house, the anxiously grunting huddle of swine in the yard. "They were lucky. Only lost a sow this year."

The Vicar rested his hammer on his shoulder and looked at me critically. "Forget Danvers. He won't help."

"Danvers' son, then."

"Sydney?"

"Yes, Sydney," I said. "He's no lover of Misrule. It's why he's usually in the city this time of year."

"And most of the rest of the year," the Vicar said, selecting a nail and attacking one of the boards. "He's full of notions about there being no need for Misrule, but nobody's going to listen to him, because he's never around. It's not like he's local in anything but name."

He had a point, though Sydney would eventually become Sir Danvers, probably, and people would have to put up with it.

But there was something else the Vicar said that was eating me.

"Hang on. What do you mean, notions about there being no need for Misrule?"

The Vicar stopped hammering. "Well. That."

"*I'm* talking *about* ending Misrule!"

"Yes. Of course you are. Because of—" he gestured vaguely with the hammer at the henhouse. "But people need Misrule. It's part of life."

"You've been here less than a year."

"Everywhere's the same. There's always Misrule. It's a way of letting go of the pain of the other fifty weeks of the year."

"It's not just that," I said. "It's gone beyond that. We've all been counting the cost for far too long." I left the litany unsaid. The cripplings, the blindings, the rapes, those children that had been playing in the hayrick that was set alight.

What had happened to my father, a decade ago now. When that fat taverner who wasn't to be trusted around children dragged me off into the forest. My father came after me. Alone. And took a wound that went green and killed him before the snowdrops were in bloom.

Oh, the laws of Misrule had applied there, too. Everyone helped my mother take over doing the hens on her own. I had a suspicion my apprenticeship had in part come about because the big house liked to look after the widows and orphans of Misrule. The fat taverner had himself turned up drowned in a ditch the next year, just enough inside of the Misrule period that no one needed to take any blame for it.

My father was still dead, though.

"Don't you get on your high horse about it. I heard you were part of the mob that stoned Tom Farmer's dog."

I felt a wave of guilt. "It was a horrible dog, though," I said. "And he kept setting it on people. My cousin nearly lost a finger." And it had been the year after my father died, and I needed to do something.

"But still, it was Tom Farmer's dog."

"And I was little then. Didn't know better."

"Before you went up to the big house."

A pang of guilt. "It's not like that. I'm still the same person, even if I did get apprenticed."

The Vicar shook his head, putting away the remaining nails. "And you don't think it changes you? Do you think we'd be talking like this if you hadn't?"

"I still wouldn't think it was right."

The Vicar sighed, retrieving his doublet and coat and buttoning them against the cold. "The people who try to stop it are usually people like me, who come from outside, or people like you, who are getting an education. The same people who usually wind up leaving the village, in the end."

"I wouldn't!" But I remembered my own thoughts, just the day before, about leaving to get a proper place as a cook in the city.

The Vicar had found his hat and was checking the snow-flecked ground for any dropped or bent nails. Wherever he'd come from, it was plain he hadn't started out as a Vicar. I wondered what his original name had been. "Anyway," he said, "it's not going to stop. Not for Sir Danvers, or Sydney. Or for you."

***

The fourth day I had to go back up to the house to help with the cooking. Young Master Sydney was getting engaged to the daughter of a wealthy man from the city, and had brought her to meet his parents.

I'd suggested to my mother that she come to the big house with me, but she'd been worried that Misrule might come back, and Mary Pigwife and Tom Blacksmith both said they'd take turns sitting with her.

If I was unusually quiet, quiet enough that Mrs Roister at one point commented approvingly on how well-behaved I was, nobody read anything into it. All of the other household staff were also keeping the noise down, straining their ears to try and make out the gist of the various arguments breaking out around the house all day, or passing on what they'd heard in hasty whispers in corners and corridors.

Perhaps because I was being so quiet, Mrs Roister put me to work on the household accounts once the roasts were on. Which was lucky on two counts. First, it gave me time to think, and second, it gave me information.

Adding up the costs and gains from last year. The profit on the farms. The rents from the farmers and craftspeople. Taxes. Seeds. The repairs on the stables, the damage after Misrule. A tenth of all profits to the church. Charity.

Which mostly meant Stebbins.

We all knew his story. He'd been a Shepherd's Son, but had shown enough promise at school that he'd been offered an apprenticeship as a groom at the big house. Which had gone all right at first, until the head groom began to notice the patterns of injuries and neglect among the horses that Stebbins had charge of. Although nobody said so, this might have explained why the Shepherds wouldn't have him back when he left the big house.

They'd left Stebbins his big house name at least. I suppose he couldn't go back to his old name if he hadn't gone back to his family.

After leaving the big house, he'd tried to pick up the sort of work the poor people did, cleaning or odd-jobbing or washing up in the tavern. But he never stayed at anything long.

Eventually he'd wound up at his lowest ebb, no family to support him, no trade to live off of, living off charity and scraps. The poorest person in the Village.

Which meant that, automatically, on the first day, he became the Lord of Misrule.

He'd found his calling.

For over forty years now, that was what he did. People offered him work, training, chances to go stay with some relative or other in town. He hadn't even made a token effort, just turned it all down with a gleam in his eye. Living on scraps and charity, sleeping in stables and fields, just so that he could have those twelve shining days, when he was king, and could make anyone do anything he wanted. Have the people who spat on him the rest of the year as his sycophants and lackeys. Prey on the rest of us.

I put aside my feelings, thought about what he'd done. It made a strange kind of sense. Showed a lot of intelligence and what Mrs Roister called "lateral thinking." You could see why he'd been thought a good prospect for the big house.

And people need a Lord of Misrule, particularly one who's creative, and driven, and knows which targets to hit.

Then again. Stebbins on his own was nothing. Eleven months of the year nobody cared about him. The Lord isn't a Lord if he doesn't have followers.

But it seemed like every hike in the rents, every fall in the price of wool, every year more of the taxes went to support war down south than schools up north, every young person who went off in search of adventure but came back old and missing parts, every family who counted the cost and realised they could afford to help themselves but not the neighbours, more and more people joined Misrule.

By the time I'd finished the accounts and the family and their guests for the evening had withdrawn in tight-lipped sullenness from the dinner table, everyone else was in the kitchen, piecing together the story in front of the fire. That Mrs Danvers had objected to her son's choice of bride; that Sir Danvers had also, but for different reasons, and was alternately taking sides with his wife and his son; that the bride herself was discovering that the idea of being a landowner in a remote country village was more to her taste than the reality; that the Vicar, invited to dinner more out of custom than because the Danverses liked him, had attempted to play negotiator and had wound up making things worse.

The drama out front made for an interesting distraction, and also gave me some thoughts about what to do about Stebbins.

Because I also had to help with the cleaning and the washing up and the storing of the leftovers for the next day, I was also on hand when Sydney's bride went missing, when search parties went out through the village, and when the news came back, early on the fifth day, that she'd been found dancing round a bonfire in the stubble field with the Lord of Misrule.

***

I spent the fifth day thinking.

***

On the sixth day, I recruited The Vicar.

I found him cutting botanical specimens out of the hedgerows after doing the rounds of the poor households of the parish.

The poor households always had it worst at Misrule. Even though most of the people who joined Misrule came from poor households. Grudges between neighbours had a way of festering.

"Ah, Mary Summersby!" The Vicar saw me and waved cheerfully with the hand that wasn't full of green twigs and scissors. "How's your mother? I've got the perfect thing to cheer you up. The telescope I ordered three months ago finally arrived. Let's see if Jupiter really does have moons."

Any other young man who suggested we meet after dark for an activity involving moons, I'd know exactly where I stood. With the Vicar, though, I wasn't sure if it was a double-entendre, or just an innocent invitation. I'd been dropping hints since he'd arrived that I wouldn't mind him being my dancing partner at Midsummer, but he either didn't know what I meant (maybe they didn't have Midsummer in his village? But if Misrule was everywhere, Midsummer must be too), or he wasn't interested.

In any case, there were more important considerations right now. "I'd love to," I said. We fell into step with each other, walking slowly back towards the church. "But I've had an idea for what to do about Misrule."

"I told you—"

"I'm not talking about abolishing it. That's what the problem's been. Everyone either puts up with it, or wants to abolish it. They're not thinking laterally."

"So you have a better idea?" A sceptical smile.

"I do. And I need your help with it."

The Vicar listened, a slight frown on his handsome brow, as I outlined my plan. When I finished, he said, "It's a good idea."

I hadn't expected him to jump for joy, but I'd expected more enthusiasm. "This is the point where you say 'but.'"

"It is." The Vicar smiled wryly. "The 'but' here is, how do you propose to keep it going? More money to help the poor of the parish would certainly reduce the anger, and envy, and spite that drives Misrule. But you'd need money, and you'd need money every year. Not just once."

"Do you know what's going to happen about Sydney's fiancée?"

"It's unclear," he admitted. "Sydney is holding his father to the point about how what happens at Misrule has no criminal consequences. His father says that this is true, but it doesn't speak well for the character of the lady or her long-term stability. The lady in question has locked herself in the guest room and isn't speaking to anyone, or possibly one Danvers or other locked her in there, it's a little unclear. Everyone's at daggers drawn."

"This is giving me another idea," I said.

***

"A lottery?" Sydney looked deeply sceptical. The seventh day happened to be Sunday, and we'd cornered him after the service.

"We were thinking that you might want something to cheer the villagers up." The Vicar said. "Make them happy. Give them a festive occasion." He meant, of course, to distract the village from what had happened the other day, but the main reason we'd agreed he should be spokesman was that he didn't say things like that out loud.

"But what about the ones who don't win the lottery?"

"Here's the idea. We make the season about pleasure, not fear. You throw a huge party. Food and gifts for all—"

"I don't have time to—"

"Just let them go through that back storeroom where we all know your father keeps the things he's too busy to use and too thrifty to throw away. Slaughter that lame ox that no one in the big house wants to eat because it's tough and stringy. Slow roasting will turn it out fine. Then, at the climax, draw a lottery winner from among the parish households."

"Oh, I see. Excluding the ones participating in Misrule?" That was interesting. If that was where his mind went, then Sydney *had* been thinking about how to end Misrule.

"No, no. *Include* the ones participating in Misrule. Especially them. In fact, it might not be a bad idea if one of them won. Obviously, no, I don't mean Gin-Sling Tom or anyone else whose name has recently been mentioned in connection with— no, never mind— but one of the others. Mary Taverner, for instance."

"The tavern-girl?"

"Who else?"

"But she's—"

"Do you trust me?"

Sydney thrust out his lower lip slightly. "If you give that lot free money, they'll just quit their jobs and spend it all on useless things. Look at Stebbins."

I didn't blame Sydney. The Vicar and I had also had an argument about that one. He'd won, and I'd left with the uncomfortable feeling that maybe Sir Danvers had another reason not to oppose Stebbins' presence in town. He provided a useful reason to refuse to give the poor more than the occasional handout.

"She might. But it's not like one less server at the tavern is going to harm their business, and she'll be spending it on useless things other villagers have made. And if she does turn out to be the next Stebbins, she couldn't be worse as the Lady of Misrule."

"Well, all right. How much should the prize be?" We were clearly winning Sydney over, but he still wasn't totally on side.

"A year's wages."

Sydney stumbled. "What?"

"Think about how little a tavern-girl or a pot-boy makes in a year," The Vicar said.

"How little?"

I told him. Sydney looked startled, not sure if it was from the number or because he'd forgotten I was there.

"You could easily bury that in the kitchen accounts if there's likely to be a problem with your father," I said, driving the point home.

"Yes," he said thoughtfully. "It's far less than we lose just from Misrule, in an average year."

Which was the point, but I was glad he got to it.

"In fact, we could do a lottery every night for twelve nights and—"

"—*Next* year," The Vicar said hastily. "This year we'll just do the one. Get people used to the idea." Meaning the Danverses, but also the villagers.

"But you could announce that, after the feast." I said, encouragingly.

"Excellent! Then we can start making the arrangements." Sydney rubbed his hands together, and I reflected that he didn't look quite so stupid when he had a decent plan to occupy him.

"We've got some plans drawn up back at the vicarage, if you'd like to join us." The Vicar put his arm through Sydney's, steered him back towards the church, flashing me a quick conspiratorial grin.

We were there. Well, almost.

* * *

We started the preparations the very next day. Setting up tables and a platform in the square. Getting the maypole out and up and covered in holly and ivy. Arranging the menu and the entertainment. At first it was just The Vicar and myself, with the occasional presence of Sydney. In the afternoon I was able to persuade my mother to join us, listlessly at first but looking happier and happier as she directed the construction. As we went on, people got interested, and came along to watch, or to help, or to agree to play music or sing or do their party pieces.

By the ninth day, a few of the usual crowd had become curious enough to stay away from Misrule, or to creep back into the Village from Misrule. A few of them stayed to help with the carpentry and the cooking.

On the tenth day, Misrule staged a raid on the proceedings. Tables smashed, boards torn up, holly ripped from the maypole, pots upended. But we'd assumed they'd do something like that.

We repaired the damage on the eleventh day. It didn't take long, and we had time to finish the rest of the preparations.

***

The celebrations started before dawn on the twelfth day, with a parade and a song before the people with animals and birds had to go do the morning chores. The snow had fallen overnight, hiding the mud and the drabness and turning all the houses into magical dwellings, festooned in crystal and covered in white silk.

Then the first dishes were brought out, while Tom Pigman and Mary Shepherd took their place with fiddle and drum for the first shift of music.

After a couple of hours, Sir Danvers came down. We let Sydney handle him. Evidently he succeeded, because a while later I saw Sir Danvers sampling the jam tarts and making slightly awkward conversation with Mary Ploughwife.

And not long after that, Mrs Roister turned up, saying that the Danverses had sent word they'd be dining in the village, so she may as well roll up her sleeves and help with the feast.

And not long after that, I saw that she'd roped Sir and Mrs Danvers in. Mrs Danvers enthusiastically turning the spit to keep the roast going, Sir Danvers washing the dishes. Which everyone seemed to enjoy, including the Danverses.

I'd admit, that was an interpretation of the day's theme that I hadn't considered.

There was a cessation in the music and a brief service at noon, because the Vicar insisted there be some sacred content. But he had the sense to keep it short and generally amicable. And, with the nature of the enterprise in mind, focusing heavily on reversals: mighty God incarnate as a helpless child. Jesus disguising himself as a beggar. Good King Wenceslas.

Turning the spirit of Misrule around. The last would be first, the poorest would be most powerful— but in a different way.

Some of Misrule were there by that point, sniggering loudly at the sermon and shouting rude things. But everyone was in a good enough mood, and eventually the catcalls petered out.

When the sun began to approach the horizon, we held the lottery. Mary Taverner won, of course, and ran off into the crowd crowing with delight.

"She's going to spend it all on drinks," Tom predicted glumly.

"Most of them for her friends. She can't drink it all herself," I said.

At which point the Lord of Misrule arrived.

It was clear we'd already gained an advantage. He was on foot, not riding a stolen goat or sheep or horse. He was bare-headed, without a crown of antlers or ivy or pine. A retinue of stray pot-boys were trailing after him, but at a shamefaced distance and casting side glances at each other, as if they were thinking they might melt into the crowd at any minute.

But he was adaptable. "Well!" he announced in a voice that carried over the musicians (four of the Blacksmith children, Big Tom, Squinty Tom, Small Mary, and Blonde Mary, the last of whom faltered a bit on the fife but recovered). "All this? For me?"

The Vicar, Tom Pigman's Son, and Sydney all looked like they were about to step forward, but I anticipated them. "Of course, Lord of Misrule," I said, in my most polite-but-loud voice. "We've been waiting for you to join us. Please. Sit."

He stood.

"If it's mine," he said, "then I'll do what I like with it." He nodded to a couple of his followers, who had automatically joined him on his arrival. "Smash it, boys."

The men began setting about the food table with staves, throwing the pastry into the snowy dirt, and heaving the vegetables at each other. Villagers scattered.

The Lord of Misrule took a couple of disturbingly swift steps forward. Before I could do anything, he'd grabbed hold of me. First my cloak, and then his hands went under it.

"No!" The Vicar tried to intervene, but someone swung a chair-leg into his stomach and he went down, gasping and retching.

I held my breath and turned my face away. Awful memories of the fat taverner in my mind, awful memories of the price my father had paid for helping me. I could see the leathery seams of the Lord of Misrule's thin, hairy face, his reddened eyes, the awful smell of alcohol mixed with animal fat and unwashed man.

I'd known he would attack. Known he would probably attack

me. But all the plans I'd made in my head for how I could turn it round seemed impossible in light of it actually happening.

Everyone else was staring at us. Nobody so much as saying anything to stop him.

I swallowed down any feelings of anger. Of course they were scared, and I couldn't expect anything from them. I'd have to show them he wasn't invulnerable, at least.

I struggled and kicked. Scored a hit.

He let go, staggered back.

He motioned, and two of his men came forward. One brandishing the chair leg.

"I'm going to make you regret that," he said.

I braced myself. I couldn't win against three of them. But I could certainly give a good account of myself.

And then—

Someone, finally, grabbed the Lord of Misrule.

"I wouldn't do that," said Mary Blacksmith, stepping forward.

Two of her larger children, having put down their fiddles, held him fast. The others stood behind their mother, folding their muscular arms.

The men froze. The ones behind him stood, confused. The others breaking up the tables and pots stopped what they were doing. Looked to their Lord for guidance, then looked to Mary Blacksmith and her family, then to me, then back to him.

"Lot of people are enjoying the food," Tom Blacksmith

commented, tapping his drumstick into the palm of her hand. "Why don't you sit down and join us?"

Realising what was going on, some of the other villagers began forming up around the Blacksmiths. Tom Taverner. Redhaired Mary Shepherd's Daughter. Gin-Sling Tom, keen to save face, filled up a plate and sat down, smiling as if this had been his own idea.

The Vicar, finally recovered, scrambled to his feet, lurched forward, seized my hand. "Are you all right?" he asked.

"Fine," I gasped back, wobbly but triumphant. "How about you?"

"Smash it!" the Lord of Misrule ordered again, but his remaining followers hesitated. With a glance at their father, the Blacksmith children began playing again, choosing something suitably loud. Someone else drew Mary Taverner into the dance ring, and the dancing began again.

The Lord of Misrule grabbed a handful of brush, thrust it into the bonfire. Began whirling round, setting light to the decorations, the wood pile, the thatch of nearby roofs.

Meeting my eye and smiling cruelly, he flung the brush into the half-built henhouse in my mother's yard.

Without thinking, I snatched up an empty bucket, filled it with snow, dashed it at the fire.

The Pigman family did the same.

Someone else started making snowballs, throwing them. Sometimes missing, hitting neighbours. Before long, the fire was out, and everyone was hurling snow and snowballs.

Laughing.

"We should do this every year!" I heard Redhaired Mary Shepherd's Daughter saying to Tom Pigman's Son, covered with glittering crystals and laughing. "Now this, *this* is Misrule!"

"We're getting everything wet, though..." Tom replied, as they went to warm themselves up by a bonfire.

"That's Misrule too!"

The snow-fight had moved to the periphery, but kept going on, with a steady drift of participants to and from the bonfires.

The Lord of Misrule rounded, fixed his eyes on me.

And was immediately pelted with snowballs.

"Come on, Stebbins!" someone shouted. "Join in!"

The Lord of Misrule screamed, wordless with anger.

No.

Stebbins screamed.

The magic had faded.

Names were magic, and he'd lost the name of the Lord of Misrule.

He was only Stebbins now.

And the music played louder, and the snowballs flew, and the dancers kicked their legs wildly, and Sydney appeared from somewhere with a bottle in one hand and his fiancée hanging off his other shoulder, and someone dragged the Vicar, protesting but smiling, onto the dance floor, and Mary Taverner was sitting on a bag of bran telling everyone about the new dress she was going to buy and the trip to her sister's she was going to make. Sir Danvers had taken my mother aside and quietly asked her how much she would need to buy new hens, was talking about perhaps going into partnership, starting a bigger poultry farm.

And Stebbins crept off, muttering direly, to the edge of the village. He looked smaller, bent, like a goblin or a troll.

And in the years to come, he'd get smaller and smaller. Become something silly, a joke, a game. Eventually a clown, something to make the children laugh.

Someday, the Lord of Misrule, the leader of the festivities, would not be the poorest person in the Village, but the youngest, or the weakest.

The Vicar bounced back from the dance, breathless, eyes sparkling.

"Would you like to—"

Without my even thinking about it, my lips met his.

The season was over.

The Last Wake

Kathryn Keane

Kathryn Keane writes speculative fiction, poetry and essays. Her work can also be found online at Seize the Press and Poethead, as well as in many print publications. Talk more to her on Twitter at @kathryn_keane13.

I didn't cry when I heard my mother died. The news came through my phone, loud and unreal in the way phone conversations are, as I stood inside a cubicle in my work bathroom and stared blankly at the ceiling. I didn't cry then, even though I probably should have. Nor did I cry when I packed my suitcase and locked my apartment door behind me. The drive from Dublin to Ballymore, Co. Cork was an hours-long one, and a winding one once I got off the motorway, with ample empty thinking space. So, of course I turned my loudest Spotify playlist up as high as it would go. Like a DJ between two massive speakers, I surrounded myself with that playlist, engulfed myself in it, until the last sputterings of mobile signal vanished and told me what I'd left behind.

The morning after I'd arrived back in my mother's – now my sister Margaret's – house, I stared down at my plate and wished I still had the playlist to listen to. Work had a canteen that I ate in at least twice a day. Three different kinds of fruit juice, yogurt and granola, energy balls coated with almond flakes all lay behind me.

In front of me lay two rashers. The copious fat strips were burned black, and the slices of meat leisurely reclined in viscous pools of grease. Margaret never remembered to soak up the grease properly before serving anything. Then again, neither had my mother.

"...thank you so much," Margaret was saying into the landline. "Yes, yes, the wake's tonight. You're very good. Thank you now. Thank you. Bye-bye."

She hung up in the way I'd at last pushed the lid down on my bulging suitcase a few days before.

"Margaret," I said, planning to ask her to pass me over the kitchen paper.

"What is it?" Then the phone rang again and she was off, jabbering away into it about RIP.ie and flower arrangements and infinite other bits of bullshit. It seemed I'd have to eat the full-fat option. I dug my knife sullenly into the rasher. I could already feel my arteries shriveling.

"Yes, Maureen, of course Danny can do the first reading. You know how fond she was of him."

I chewed, loudly, keeping my eyes fixed on the wall and my mind anywhere but there.

"Did you hear now, that Laura of the Dohertys is after moving in with her boyfriend?"

Imagine, in the year of our Lord 2021, someone having the temerity to live in sin with their partner. Surely the sky would fall at such heathenry. I rolled my eyes when I was sure she wasn't looking at me, and only the dignity of adulthood prevented me from sticking my tongue out at her back. Then I tuned in again at the sound of my name.

"Yes, Paul is here." There was a burst of noise from the other end of the phone. "I will, I'll tell him you said hello. Yes, he's still working at that job. God only knows what he does all day long, but it seems to keep him occupied."

The last comment was accompanied by a look in my direction. I stared right back at Margaret, and raised an eyebrow. That job was head of graphic design at Ireland's biggest advertising agency. I'd taught myself technical graphics when the nuns couldn't teach me and became the first person in our family to go to college for it. Margaret, meanwhile, had moldered among Sacred Heart pictures and hens.

She hung up again and sat down at the kitchen table, opposite me.

"Now I know those rashers aren't what you'd get at that job of yours," she began.

I swallowed a mouthful. "They're fine."

"They're the last out of the packet," she said.

"So get another packet."

She glowered at me, clearly aching for something else to say. "Sure they're only out of Dunnes. They're probably put into the packet straight off the floor of the slaughterhouse - "

"I said they're fine."

"Maureen MacDermott says hello," she said then.

"Who's that again?" I said, just to see her squirm.

And true to form, it worked. "'Who's that again?' he says. 'Who's that again?' as if Maureen MacDermott wasn't in and out from the time we were children. I swear to Christ you've forgotten everything since you left us for the Big Smoke."

"I came back," I said, annoyed.

"Only for Christmas." I couldn't tell if the shine was in Margaret's eyes, or her glasses catching the sun. "But you had to run away, didn't you, for your drawing and your coloring- "

"Graphic design," I said.

She brushed me off with one hand. "Anyway. Bygones are bygones. I only wish Mammy had gotten to see you one more time before she died."

This, I thought as I headed for the car, was why I'd only ever come back for Christmas in the first place. I'd parked the car in front of the half-door that led into the old cottage, the original house I'd grown up in that Margaret had eventually extended. Now my mother wasn't sitting there anymore, the fire was the room's only illumination, sending flickering orange light up the bumpy white walls. Margaret had pushed back most of the furniture to make room for the coffin, due later today. The thatch spread over my head, a thousand golden threads coming together in a unified whole. Under the thatch roof, sounds seemed more muffled, the world more insulated. This little room and the two small bedrooms off it had been my home for all of my childhood. My mother's chair still sat by the fire. Although it wasn't her chair anymore. It never would be her chair again, and yet it still was, because it always had been.

I'd brought down the tablet I used for personal projects. It only needed an internet signal to sync to the cloud, not to work by itself, and it might make the time down here, and Margaret, more bearable. I just hoped I'd remembered to charge it; the last time I'd worked on a personal project was eight months ago.

When I pressed the button that automatically opened the boot, I leaned in to get the tablet. I'd put it behind a large cardboard box. I looked at the box for a long moment, remembering everything it had taken to get it here - the phone calls to the council, the application for the rural internet grant, paying for the survey-ors and digging up the land to run the long underground internet cable to the house.

The last step had been this router, bought and then procrasti-nated on for months. I'd told my mother I'd been busy at work, when I hadn't been so busy that I couldn't spare a weekend to bring it to her. The cable ran under the rolling green grass, golden and gleaming and twisted together as a sheaf of straw to thatch the roof. But my mother hadn't lived to see me connect it.

**

The conversations stopped at me. Everywhere else in the room, they swirled around each other and blended into each other, but I sat like a firewall in the midst of streams of data. My eyes stayed on the floor. Hastily polished brogues mingled with sensible wedge heels. I tucked my Chelsea boots further under my chair.

Between the press of bodies and the roaring hearth, the room was oppressively warm. The only body not contributing to the heat was the one I sat next to. My mother was in the coffin, right beside me. All around me, the denizens of Ballymore grinned, laughed, teased each other, while my mother's bloodless face lay limp and her mouth stayed sewed shut.

I aimlessly sipped at my cheap wine. It was the closest thing to a good drink in, seemingly, a house filled with alcohol. I looked over at a knot of three old men I vaguely recognized and watched them clink their glasses of more water than beer together.

"Sure she had a long life." The voice came from my left.

I turned towards it and jumped. Sitting there was an old woman I hadn't seen before. Then again, I had been somewhat tuned out.

"She did," I said. One little phrase was enough down here for the other person to carry the conversation.

Two small eyes looked at me out of a face crinkled like a walnut. "I don't believe we've met."

"No," I wasn't sure whether we had or not, but it was easier to go along with whatever she said. "I moved away from here years ago."

Usually people around here, upon hearing that, either launched into the twenty questions ("But isn't Dublin awful lonesome? And expensive? And you're sure that's a real job?") or moved on to a more fertile field of local gossip.

This woman smiled. "That's good, that's good. Wakes and gatherings after someone dies are for everyone to hold on to everyone they already know. And I'm only another oul biddy to most of these."

In my experience, oul biddies who no-one quite knew made up the bulk of these kinds of gatherings. I scooted my chair so I was fully turned towards her. "What do you mean?"

"I suppose you could say I'm a bit of a blow-in," she said.

I looked out at the room again. Margaret was earnestly discussing animal feed with two women I didn't recognize. The group of men I'd gone to primary school with appeared to be plotting out tactics for an upcoming hurling match.

"So am I," I admitted.

A series of loud spitting noises from the fire interrupted either of us from saying anything next. The turf smell was thicker and more pungent when they eventually quietened down. That was when I said, "I don't think I caught your name?"

"It's Bridie." She extended her hand. "Bridie McCafferty. And yourself?"

I shook her hand. It was surprisingly hard to get a grip on. "Paul Fahy."

"You're a relative of her's, then?" she said, nodding towards the coffin.

"Her son," I said. "Did you know her?"

Bridie folded two liver-spotted hands in her lap. "When we were children, we used have great times together. We only lived up the road from each other, you know."

At that, impatience leaked back into me. "Up the road" around here could mean anything from "slept in the adjoining cow shed" to "twenty minutes drive over a cliff edge."

But, she kept talking, the words tumbling out of her. "I remember one time, your mother and I were going off to school, and she had on her a green dress. Only, the dress had been washed so many times, that when she got up in the morning and put it on her it had a hole around the arse."

Then Bridie had lived close to my mother and known her, beyond the generalized knowing of everyone else that made up a village. My mother had told this story so often I could practically tell it in sync with Bridie.

I put down my wine glass. "And then what happened?"

"I said to her," said Bridie, "'Stop now, before you make an absolute show of yourself.' And when she saw the state of her dress, she said, 'Bridie, I've only this and the dress I wear to Mass, and it's too late in the morning for us to turn back.' So do you know what we did?"

"What did you do?" Out of all the times I'd heard this story, it was the first time the other person in it had a face.

Bridie grinned. "We walked back to back. For the whole day, wherever your mother went, I stood up and walked with her."

And I surprised myself by laughing with her. That lasted for a few minutes, until a particularly drunk old man swayed and knocked against me.

"Sorry, sorry," he said, straightening himself. Then he brandished his can. "Listen, lad. You wouldn't know where I could find another one of these in this house, would you?"

Across the room, I could see Margaret looking over at us. She'd finally found a place to sit down, and even from here the varicose veins in her ankles were visibly throbbing.

I stood up. "'Course I do. You stay here, and I'll be right back."

When I returned, refills in hand, my chair was still empty. But Bridie no longer occupied the seat beside it. I scanned the room for Bridie, but I couldn't spot her. Instead, an even shorter old woman sat there. She had the squatness of someone who'd spent much of her life lifting and pulling heavy things. Then her face registered.

"Maggie O'Halloran, is that you?" I said, with a delight I hadn't expected to feel.

The new woman looked up. "Paul Fahy, as I live and breathe!"

I handed the drink to the old man as fast as I could and sat down. "It's been so long."

"Indeed it has," she said, "and you shot up like a tree!"

I frowned, something I couldn't fully parse poking at my memory. "Didn't you...move away?"

"You could say that. But 'tis her that has me back," she said, gesturing towards the coffin.

"Me too," I said.

"Me more so than you." Maggie's posture pulled in on itself. "Couldn't be here without her."

"Well," I said uncertainly, "what matters is that we're both here."

The fire blazed properly, bathing the room with heat, as Maggie smiled and said, "I suppose it does, doesn't it?"

Briefly, I remembered how often I'd mocked the people who came in here and seemingly wasted their entire lives reminiscing. Then, I dismissed it. "The last time we were both sitting in here together must have been, what, twenty years ago?"

"More than that," she said. "I started visiting your mother from the time we were first married, did you know that?"

I was surprised to find I didn't. Maggie had been the kind of presence you take for granted as a child, one where you never think about their origins because they had, seemingly, been around since the beginning of the world.

"You used to pop out your false teeth to scare me," I said.

"And you used beg me to do it! And then your mother used say, 'Paul Fahy, that's what happens when you don't wash your teeth, now get to bed!' And then when you were gone to sleep we'd talk pure ráiméis till all hours, and she would leave her own teeth to feck."

We both laughed at that. But it felt like a heavier laugh than before. I would never again be seven and dismissed to bed, and my mother would never again get her gossip by the fire. Her mouth wrinkles were so much more visible now she lay in the coffin; her mouth had been too constantly in motion when she was alive for me to really have seen them. I thought of what it took to ensure a corpse could sit in the open air for days and not rot, and of just why an open-coffin funeral was only partially open-coffin.

Maggie followed my gaze. "She was a good friend."

"I made her a promise," I blurted out.

"And did you keep it?" Maggie said.

I looked at my shoes.

"Keep it now, then."

I had to save face somehow. "...Because the priest says honor thy father and mother?"

"Feck the priest." I blinked at the vehemence in her voice. "There's things in this world no priest can find nor tell you."

A mix of emotions I didn't want to feel or untangle were rising in me. "Thanks. For the chat. I'll be back in a sec."

I made sure the bathroom door was firmly closed behind me before letting myself exhale. Out here, in the extension, the old thatch roof no longer swaddled me. The golden threads over my head had given way to flat slates. The night air coming through the open window was pleasantly cool on my face after the heat of the kitchen. Automatically, I took out my phone and flicked it open - but the grey 'No internet' screen stared at me again. I slid it back into my pocket, and looked out at the night.

My steps were slow as an old man's when I went back. Margaret had insisted we keep the lights off in the halls to save on the bills, so the kitchen, bathroom and the old kitchen were the only pools of light in long and empty corridors. Behind me was the creaking of an old house telling itself its stories as it settled in for the night. Ahead of me was suppressed heat and muffled conversation. I turned the doorknob, and once again, there was a new old woman in the seat next to mine.

"Have you seen Bridie? Or Maggie?" I said, already half-knowing the answer.

"We were coming from the same direction," said this old woman.

I sat down. "Out by Waterford, then? Or Tralee?"

"Further," she said.

My wine glass was empty. I picked it up and twisted the stem back and forth between my finger and thumb. The light of the room shone through it, insistently bright and distorted like a screen in a dark room, and I wished I could keep seeing the room that way.

A hand gripped my shoulder, tight in the way of old people when they know they've only so many things left to grip. "You're Paul, aren't you? The son?"

"I am," I said, turning back to her. "How did you know?"

"How do you think I know?" Withdrawing her hand, she continued, "Sure, aren't I Mary Hegarty? Wasn't I playing bingo with your mother every week for the past ten years?"

I peered closely at her face. I should recognize some part of it. I'd (involuntarily) met all of my mother's bingo friends at one Christmas visit or another. But the hooked nose and red-rimmed eyes were only familiar in the way all aging is familiar; two images plucked from a neural network of decay. Besides, I wanted more conversation at that moment about as much as I wanted to permanently move back here.

"Have you talked to Margaret yet?" I said. "I can call her over."

"Do not call over Margaret." Her voice had sharpened.

"Why not?"

Mary spoke quickly. "She has a lot to be doing. Leave her be."

"I suppose..." It was hard to even spot Margaret now. With this many people crammed into a room with this few seats, the room was packed with people standing up. Sitting down, I felt as if I was surrounded by a cluster of electricity towers. "It is fairly busy."

"The old wakes were much bigger," said Mary. "There'd be the whole of Ballymore, and if the person had family elsewhere they'd make the trip, and even bring their friends or relations."

Maybe my mother had been less popular than I thought. "So why do you think this one is smaller?"

"Less people born here. Less people dying here. Less people doing things the done way."

"I guess so," I said, thinking of crayons and pencils being taken away, of a flat cap descending like the headpiece on an electric chair.

"I wouldn't be surprised if this was the last proper wake Ballymore had." Her voice was quieter now.

Surely Mary's own family would run her funeral how she would have wanted it when she passed on. But that didn't seem like the best thought to voice aloud. Instead I said, "You never know. More of the old things stay around here than you'd think."

Mary gave me a sidelong glance, and as she did so, the hearth guttered down to almost nothing. "But you were going to change that, weren't you?"

Shock buzzed through me like phone vibrations through a wooden table. "How did you know that?"

She said nothing, instead looking at me, waiting for an answer.

"...I was," I said. "She...my mother, she always wanted me to set up the internet here. And I...had almost done it."

I pinched my nose, squeezed my eyes shut. When I opened them, Mary was gone. It was only then I realized that she'd shared no recollection of my mother with me. I had to find her and the other women I'd spoken to again. They were the only other people left alive who shared my mother's interconnected web of stories.

***

I didn't pay attention when I went to my mother's funeral. All through the rest of the wake, all through the funeral service, even when I shouldered her coffin and laid her in the ground, I was scanning the crowds for those three faces. Margaret had booked out a pub for afterwards, and I circulated numbly and nibbled on sausage rolls and looked for them. But, they were nowhere. Around me, people discussed the weather and the upcoming mart, and I stood still, my feelings deleted. At last, I decided that there was one person to ask.

I tapped Margaret on the shoulder. "Have you seen Bridie McCafferty anywhere?"

"What do you mean?" she said, folding her arms.

"Or Maggie O'Halloran?"

"You're an awful joker." Her voice was flat.

"Mary Hegarty?"

Anger flashed in Margaret's eyes; I could see that she'd have a lot more to say if we weren't surrounded by people. "How could I have seen them?"

"They came to the wake," I said blankly. "I was talking to them, and I thought they'd have come to the service as well."

Margaret counted each name off on her fingers as she spoke. "Bridie's dead the past fifteen years or more. The lung cancer got Maggie a good five years ago. And I saw Mary being put into the ground myself. So no, I haven't seen them. And you'd want to watch that fine big gob of yours, before you walk around disrespecting the dead at our own mother's funeral."

I left early after that. The box I took from the boot was heavy in my arms. When I walked into the old kitchen, cans and glasses and dirty dishes from last night coated every available surface, and the room had the fresh emptiness you get right after a room was bursting with people.

I set the box carefully on the table.

"Are you there?" I said to the empty room.

And all three of them were standing around me.

"We're here," Bridie said.

"We came back for your mother," Maggie said.

"We came back for the last of the old times," Mary said.

I looked at the box again. My hands shook. "The last of the old times?"

"You're gone from here," said Mary.

"And we're nearly gone," said Maggie.

"And your mother was the last of us," said Bridie.

When I spoke, my voice was hoarse. "I could keep you here! I could keep – her here. I can take away the router, if you want me to."

The three of them put their hands on my shoulders.

"No," Bridie said.

"Keep your promise," Maggie said.

"Do the last thing she asked of you," Mary said.

So, I unfolded the cables. I put the plugs into the sockets, and I plugged the cables into the router. The golden metal wires wrapped tight in the plastic opened the gate to the world beyond the golden thatch. My phone glowed, vibrating again and again with everything rushing in at once. The weight of the women's hands vanished from my shoulders. And as I started to cry, the fire in the hearth at last went out.

THANK YOU TO OUR SUPPORTERS

Many thanks to our patrons and supporters, especially:

Wichael Tellez • Cathrin Hagey
Natalie Weizenbaum • Kate Boyes
Johanna Levene

Alina Kanaski • Jeffery Reynolds • Myz Lilith
D.M. Domosea • carol shoemake • Erik DeBill
Frederick Stark • Bonnie Warford • Felicia OSullivan
Salomao Becker • Anna O'Brien • Martin Cohen
J'nae Spano • Tory Hoke • S Klotz

Ana Wang • Lorna D Keach • smokestack • Lisa Short
Sian Jones • Kristina Saccone • Rocky B • BethOfAus • J.
Askew • Dirck de Lint • Brit Hvide • Wanda • Karen Anderson
Charlotte Nash-Stewart • Liz Warner • Suzanne Thackston
Jen G • Emily Anderson • Maria Haskins • GriffinFire
Matthew Bennardo • Kayla

Want to see your name here? Become a patron!
patreon.com/lunastation

About the Cover Artist

Devin Elle Kurtz is an illustrator and concept artist who has worked with companies such as Marvel, Dark Horse, Netflix, and HarperCollins. Her original artbook "Windows to Worlds" was published in 2021 by 3dTotal. She's known for her free weekly process tutorials, hosted on her Instagram. She is often recognized for her ongoing series of illustrations combining fantasy creatures like dragons and gryphons with familiar real world locations. She worked in the animation industry as the lead background painter on the Netflix animated series "Disenchantment" from 2019-2021, and is currently working on her next book project.

www.devinellekurtz.com

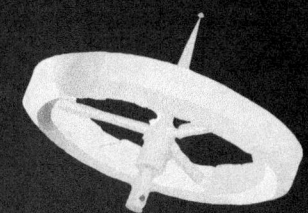

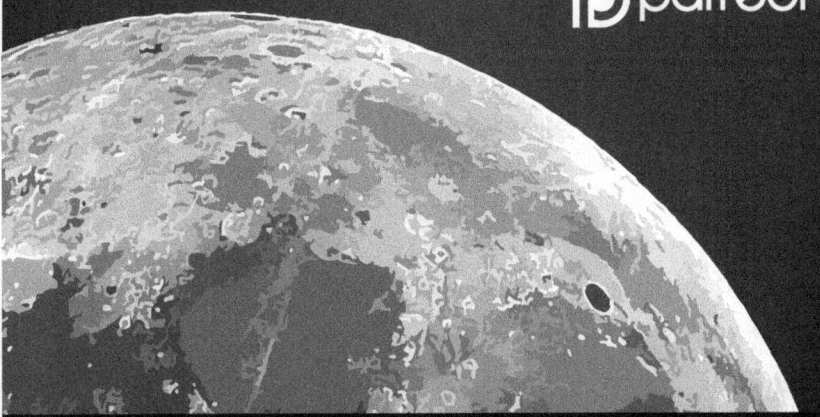